Tempest Rising

Tempest Rising

Tracy Deebs

BLOOMSBURY

LONDON BERLIN NEW YORK SYDNEY

2011000773

Bloomsbury Publishing, London, Berlin, New York and Sydney

First published in Great Britain in July 2011 by Bloomsbury Publishing Plc
36 Soho Square, London, W1D 3QY

First published in the USA in 2011 by Walker Publishing Company
a division of Bloomsbury Publishing Inc
175 Fifth Avenue, New York, NY 10010

A CIP catalogue record for this book is available from the British Library

ISBN 978 1 4088 2018 6

MIX
Paper from
responsible sources
FSC® C018072

Printed in Great Britain by Clays Ltd, St Ives plc, Bungay, Suffolk

1 3 5 7 9 10 8 6 4 2
www.bloomsbury.com

For Adam

My darling Tempest,

I was just in your room, making your bed, looking at all your little-girl things, breathing in the soft, sweet scent of you, and wondering how I am ever going to live the next part of my life without you. I know that you know my secret, but I don't think you truly understand what it means. Every day that I stay on land, I look at the sea and pine for the life I used to have. But when I am in the water, I look at land and pine for you. For you, and my sons and my husband.

I thought, when I married your father, when I had you and your brothers, when I chose land, that this longing would go away. That if it didn't recede completely, it would at least be bearable.

But there is nothing bearable about the pain I feel, as if I've been wrenched into so many pieces I can never be put together again—at least not here, on the shore. I tell you this not because I want your understanding, as I know that will be hard to come by, but because soon you too will have to make such a choice.

Already you have special gifts—your affinity for the water and your ability, even now, to stay strong where others would give in—and there will come a time when you will be graced with so many more. Things are complicated now, more complicated than I had ever imagined they would be. There is so much I want to tell you, and so much that I can't. So I must settle for this.

When that time comes, when the totality of your gifts

makes itself known—sometime after your seventeenth birthday—you will begin to change. And you will have three months to make a choice: to stay with what you know or to become like me, for you cannot be both. When that time comes, when you begin the change, you will crave the ocean unconditionally, and I'm sure you will be frightened and confused. Though things are complicated in relationships between mermaids and humans, if it is at all possible, I will come back to you. I will help you, though I know that you can handle whatever you are faced with.

Please know that whether you choose my way or your father's, I will love you forever. This is not good-bye, only farewell for now.

I love you,
Mom

PART ONE

Caught Inside

Eternity begins and ends with the ocean's tides.
ANONYMOUS

PROLOGUE

I was ten the first time I saw her. I remember this clearly, because my mother left exactly two weeks later—on my eleventh birthday.

We were in Hawaii at a surfing competition—this was back when my father still competed professionally—and it was late, late enough that the moon hung over the sky like a huge, tempting scoop of French vanilla ice cream. Its glow was more than my preadolescent heart could resist, and I slipped into my bathing suit and out the door the second the babysitter got distracted with my younger brothers.

I suppose any reasonable explanation of that night would have to begin with the fact that I'm a water baby. I was born into water, literally, back when that was the hip new thing to do. A bunch of doctors said it reduced trauma for the baby—being born into warm water, so like the womb—and it must have worked. Because, while I obviously don't remember it, my dad says I didn't even cry. I just slid into the water like it was home. In many ways, it still is—despite what happened to me all those years ago.

After sneaking out of the house my parents had rented on a fairly obscure stretch of Kauai, I went down to the ocean. They were at a big party celebrating yet another of my father's wins, and the three of us kids were too much of a handful for the fairly incompetent babysitter the service had sent over. She didn't even know I was missing until my parents got home and asked about me. But I don't blame her—in the end, it was no more her fault than it was mine.

Though I had spent my life in and out of the water—our house back home was less than a hundred yards from the ocean—my parents had one ironclad rule: under no circumstances was I to go in alone. Under no circumstances was I to even *think* about going in alone. The Pacific was brutal in its beauty, my dad told me again and again. Brutal and completely narcissistic.

I had always listened before that October evening, had never considered disobeying him. But that night, something called to me. Staying inside was an agony, staying dry even more so. I *needed* to be surrounded by the power and the passion of the water that was so much a part of me, even then.

I hadn't planned on going deep, had hoped that wading out to my knees would silence the insidious whisper, the crazy voice in my head. But it didn't, and soon I was up to my shoulder blades. The water was relatively warm despite the fact that it was fall, but I remember being cold.

So cold that my teeth chattered.

So cold that I shivered until my bones rattled against one another.

I remember this because it was so odd. Before that night, the water had always warmed me.

6

But I didn't leave, didn't go back inside as a normal person would have. I couldn't. At the time I didn't know what I was waiting for. I knew only that there was a compulsion inside of me that wouldn't let me move. A compulsion that kept me standing there, a gift-wrapped human sacrifice, as the water lapped and swirled around me.

Strangely, I wasn't afraid or excited or any of the other emotions a ten-year-old girl might be expected to feel in those moments. It was odd, but I felt . . . numb. Like there was something I knew I should be doing, but the thought of it—the safety of it—was just out of reach.

Finally, when the whisper had become a shout inside my head, when my body trembled with a surge of energy so powerful it lit me up from the inside and made me feel like I was glowing, I saw her. She was dark and oddly beautiful and swam like a mermaid—like my *mother*—her body cutting through the sea as a scalpel does through flesh.

She circled me like a predator would, her body sliding closer and closer to mine with each lap she took. I tried to look away, to back myself up to shallower water, but I couldn't move. Though I could not describe the specific details of her to you now, in that moment, everything about her was hypnotic and I was spellbound.

Around me, the ocean thrashed and rolled. A wall of water built straight up in front of me—higher than the two-story house we were renting, higher even than the cliffs that surrounded our secluded little inlet. Higher than any wave I had ever seen before.

The wind picked up and the wave began to circle around me as she did, a cyclone of wind and water, power and pressure, with me directly in its eye. And then she was there with me, her

7

voice a sibilant hiss in my ear, her fingers long, translucent talons that clutched at my suit and my soul.

"Give yourself to the water." The words echoed inside of me. "Give yourself to me. Embrace the power."

A part of me was still aware enough to understand that this was dangerous—that *she* was dangerous. But I couldn't listen to that part, could barely acknowledge it when my entire body yearned toward what she promised me.

In those moments I could feel the power inside of me, feel it welling up until its immensity was all that I knew. All that I wanted.

The shudders subsided and in their place was a heat, a purpose so strong that it overshadowed everything else.

I was meant for this. Meant for her. Together we could accomplish unimaginable feats. I reached a hand out toward her—

"Tempest! Tempest, no!" My mother's voice came from outside the hurricane of water, so faint that I never would have heard it if it hadn't burrowed deep inside me.

"Tempest!" My father's crazed shout.

"Come with me!" the water witch commanded, her long red hair flowing behind her like trails of lacy seaweed. "Come now."

"Hold on, Tempest. I'm almost there!" My father again. The cold came back, alleviating the strange numbness she'd brought to me, and I knew that he was getting closer.

I tried to back away but instead of meeting the wall of water, I felt a sharp tug on my ankles—an inescapable force pulling me under. "You are mine!" the voice demanded as she pulled me deeper, and for the first time since I had wandered down the beach, fear overtook my curiosity.

"Dad!" I called.

"Tempest!" Strong hands grabbed my arms, yanked me toward shore, and for a moment I felt like the rope in a game of tug-of-war. But then the hold on my ankles gave way, sharp talons raking themselves down my calves as she tried—unsuccessfully—to hang on.

Finally I was free and on land, the storm vanishing as if it had never been, my father holding me tightly to his chest. My mother tried to tell me that the witch was my imagination, that my terror of the brewing storm had made getting trapped by seaweed seem so much worse, but even then I think I knew she was lying.

Fourteen days later my mother was gone, before I'd even begun to grasp what had happened to me. It would be years before I finally understood—even longer before I accepted that some things really were beyond mortal control.

Chapter 1

❦

"Hey, Tempest, you need to book it!" Mark, my on-again, off-again, presently on-again boyfriend dug into the waves, hard. "We're going to miss the party."

"Don't get your panties in a wad," I yelled back, even as I paddled faster. "We're almost there."

My built-in wave radar was telling me we still had a couple of minutes before the wave crested, but, like Mark, I wanted to make sure I was in the best position to catch it. It was probably going to be the last one we had time for this morning. Already the sky had lightened, the pink and lavender streaks that had ushered in the dawn changing to the usual blues and ice grays of a February morning over the Southern California Pacific.

The waves kicked up spray—ice cold and salty sweet—as we crashed through them. A snapper hit in front of me but I ducked through it. I was angling for the bigger wave behind it, focusing on it like a shark on a blood trail. As I did, the simmering resentment I often felt toward the Pacific and its siren song drained away.

I was vaguely aware of Mark and some of my other friends

laughing and joking as we worked our way around to catch the party wave, but then even that was gone and it was just me and my board and the vast and endless ocean.

The wave started to crest and I pushed up quickly, smiling as my board responded like it was just one more part of my body. But then, it had always been like that—from the first day my dad paddled me out to sea on his board when I was no more than four—the ocean, the board, and I were one.

"Looking good," Mark called to me, and I threw my head back, laughing the way I never dared to on land. But out here it was hard to hold back, even harder to resist the pull of the water and the sheer joy of the roller-coaster ride.

The wave we were jumping in on wasn't particularly big or particularly complicated—but surfing it was enough to send exhilaration rushing through me. More than enough to make me feel powerful and capable and, for a few short minutes, in control of a life that was rapidly spinning beyond my command.

The water surged beneath my feet and I shifted a little, searching for the sweet spot I knew was just a knee bend away. Laughed, again, as I found it. Braced for the downside—

I never caught it.

Instead, my legs turned to jelly beneath me.

Throwing my arms wide, I struggled to regain my footing. Seconds passed—one heartbeat, two—long, strung-out moments of utter astonishment. And then I was falling, tumbling into the waves with no more control than a rag doll.

Shocked—I couldn't remember the last time I had actually wiped out—I kicked hard, tried to scissor my way back to the surface.

I didn't move—*couldn't* move.

My legs had gone completely boneless, flopping helplessly in the water no matter how hard I struggled to move them.

My heart pumping like a piston at full speed, I tried not to freak out. *No big deal*, I told myself, clawing at the water with curled fingers. It wasn't the first time the ocean had tried to hold on to me. I knew what to do.

Using my hands to spin myself around, I kept my face turned toward the surface and started the long trek back up to air.

One foot, then two—it was hard going but I was rising. Relief filled me. *See, Tempest*, I told myself. *You can do this. Just another day in the—*

The undertow grabbed me.

I froze for a few crucial moments, my brain and body simply shutting down despite the adrenaline slamming through me.

The riptide swirled and danced around me.

Pulled at me with greedy fingers.

Tossed me around like I was nothing more than random driftwood.

And still I couldn't move, couldn't respond.

I was dragged deeper, into colder water, the ocean crushing in on me from every side while wave after wave plowed into me, over me.

Through me.

And that's when it really hit me—*I was trapped*. One more victim caught in the brutal grasp of the Pacific at dawn.

Panic exploded inside of me, stealing what little breath I'd managed to grab before plunging beneath the icy water. My heart beat double time and my lungs ached like I'd run a marathon, straight up the Himalayas.

As I continued to sink, her eerily beautiful face floated in front of me. Her voice was in my head, her hands on my body. I didn't know exactly who she was, but some primal part of me recognized her. Remembered her.

It was the wake-up call my sluggish mind needed.

Focus, I told myself fiercely.

Use your arms.

Paddle up!

But my body refused to do what I told it to. I was sinking fast and the harder I fought, the tighter the ocean's hold on me became.

Currents battered me from every side, tumbled me head over heels—again and again—until up was the same as down and I had no idea which way to go. And still I fought, clawing my way through the water, determined to break free.

But it was too late. Things were going gray, my air running out.

For the first time in my life, I was truly afraid of the ocean.

Afraid of losing myself.

Afraid of dying out here, when I'd sworn, since I was eleven, that I would always make my way back to land.

Rage burned through me. I didn't want to die—not here, not like this. I didn't want to give my body to the greedy Pacific that had already taken so much from me.

I *wouldn't* give in.

One more time I tried to kick.

One more time, my legs refused to respond.

Fear took over, clawing my insides like a crazed animal, stealing my concentration as surely as the ocean was stealing my life. Desperate, devastated, I began to cry—great, gulping sobs that turned the world ever darker as I sucked water into my starving lungs.

Daddy, I'm sorry. I didn't mean to leave you like this. Not again. Not like her.

The words echoed inside of me—a prayer, a plea, a cry for absolution as I gave myself up to the water and whatever it had planned for me.

That surrender must have been what my body was waiting for—the end of the struggle between what my mind wanted and what my body knew—because as soon as I gave up control, as soon as I stopped fighting, a strange force took me over.

My legs fused together in a bond that was both terrifying and primordially familiar—blending seamlessly into one as if they had been waiting my whole life to do just that—and with a few powerful kicks that were more instinct than design, propelled me straight to the surface and into Mark's waiting arms.

"God, Tempest, are you all right?" His brown eyes were frantic as they searched my face, and the hands he ran over my body were just a little too rough, a little too shaky.

I started to tell him I was fine, but I wasn't. No matter how hard I tried to breathe, my lungs simply wouldn't work. The same salt water that had shocked my body into action had also filled my lungs. And it was drowning me still, though I was now above the surface.

"I've got her," Mark yelled, waving wildly, before he wrapped one strong arm around me and started towing me in.

"It's okay, babe, I've got you," he repeated again and again while his powerful kicks torpedoed us closer to shore. "I've got you now."

Trying to make things easier for him, I forced my body to

limpness despite the terror still racing through me. Too bad I couldn't just as easily force my water-filled lungs to accept the oxygen I so desperately needed.

I was going to drown—not in the depths of the ocean, but in my boyfriend's arms on the way back to land.

It would have been ironic if it wasn't so damn frightening.

About halfway to the beach, my messed-up body finally figured out where it was and I started to cough, my paralyzed lungs unfreezing in one giant spasm that shook me from the inside out.

I heard Mark curse under his breath, his arm tightening around my middle as I jerked against him. "Come on, Tempest, we're almost there. Stay with me just another minute. Just another—"

Then we were in the shallows and someone was pulling me from Mark's arms, wading through the waist- then knee-deep water. I struggled to open my eyes through the coughing spasms—to see who was carrying me—but trying to breathe through the pain was taking all my effort.

And then some.

A part of me was aware of being laid on the sand, of gentle hands rolling me onto my side. But deep coughs continued wrenching their way through me, the world once again going gray around the edges as I battled to pull air into my burning lungs.

A random series of inventive Australian curses split the air—it was my best bud, Logan, who had carried me the last few feet to shore. And it was his giant hand that hit me right below the center of my back.

Stop, don't—

15

I tried to protest, but nothing came out.

Tried to fight the bizarre and sudden attack, but I was too weak to do anything but moan.

His hand hit my back again and again, until—*finally*—I started to puke. Struggling to my knees, I attempted to hide my face—I guess I was still aware enough to be embarrassed—but Logan refused to let me turn away. At least he'd stopped trying to drill a hole in my back with his palm; now the only thing racking my body was the spasms that emptied my lungs of water.

I coughed and puked, puked and coughed, for what felt like forever—I swear I must have brought up at least a gallon of water, maybe more—before I could draw my first real breath.

When I finally managed to suck in a strong lungful of air, it burned like hell itself. I tried not to freak out, reminded myself that a good saltwater ravaging could do that.

The thought didn't help much, especially as I started to remember everything that had happened when I was under.

Rolling off my knees onto my butt, I took inventory of my whacked-out body. Now that I was back on land, everything felt like it was working normally. Yet those minutes in the ocean were etched into my brain—as was the reality of what, just for a moment, I had become.

Panic set in all over again and I glanced down at my legs, hoping like hell I was back to normal. I was. My two legs were perfectly defined *and* separate, something I was incredibly happy about. When I tried to bend them they moved easily, following the commands of my brain as if the entire episode in the water had never happened.

Relief filled me at the comforting thought—at least until

Mark's voice penetrated my stupor, sounding dark and scared and more pissed off than I had ever heard it before.

"Tempest, are you all right? *Tempest?*"

When I didn't immediately answer, Mark crouched down next to me, his hands biting into my arms until it was all I could do not to wince. Not that it was his fault—it wasn't like he had a clue how sensitive my skin, and the flesh underneath it, was becoming. So sensitive that sometimes just the whip of the wind felt like a thousand leather straps flaying me and the soft cotton of my clothes chafed and burned with each shift of my body.

"Come on, Tempest, answer me." He shook me a little, but still I didn't answer.

What was I supposed to say—that with each day that passed I came closer to becoming what I hated?

That with each breath I took I could feel myself becoming less human and more *other*?

Or that I was afraid—deathly afraid—that in one week I would have webbed fingers, a scaly tail, and an overwhelming urge to plumb the depths of the ocean?

Since I could barely admit the fear to myself, I settled on an "I'm fine" that was about as convincing as it was truthful. But, hey, it was better than the alternative.

Anything was.

Chapter 2

❧

"Hey, man, back off. Give her a chance to breathe." Gentle hands pried Mark's frightened ones from around my upper arms, and looking up, I realized that I was almost totally surrounded. All the guys were there—Mark and Logan, Bach (who got his name because he rode the waves like Johann Sebastian composed music—beautifully), Scooter (don't ask), and Tony.

It might seem strange that I hang out with a bunch of guys a lot of the time, but I do it because most of my girlfriends aren't overly interested in getting up at five a.m. to catch waves for two hours before school. Brianne and Mickey (my best female friends) are much more interested in using the time to sleep—and do their hair—than they ever would be in surfing.

"I'm fine, Mark." Somehow I found a shaky version of my voice. "At least I think I am."

I sent him what I hoped was a reassuring smile, but he didn't look convinced—his too-white face remained livid with a fear he didn't even try to hide.

"So what happened out there, then?" This time it was Logan's voice, rough and just a little bit sexy, that asked the question. "It's not like you to take a tumble, Tempest, especially on a snapper like that."

I still didn't know what to say—didn't know what I *could* say. How did I explain something I wasn't even close to understanding myself?

What had happened out there was unlike anything that had ever happened to me before. Logan had said it himself: of all of us, I was the one least likely to grub like a beginner.

Least likely, hell. I'm pretty sure I'd been nine the last time I'd taken an unplanned header off my surfboard into the deep blue sea.

I knew I couldn't tell them what had really happened to me, knew they'd all think I was nuts if I even tried. Not that I'd blame them. A part of me longed for just such insanity.

Anything to make this less embarrassing.

Less frightening.

Less real.

Clearing my throat, which was no easy feat when it burned like I'd swallowed a shot glass full of wasabi, I tried to stick as close to the truth as possible.

Which was the best I could do, since I wasn't exactly good at lying. I could pretend with the best of them (especially to myself), but actually looking into the face of someone I cared about and flat-out lying—no, I totally sucked at that.

"I'm not exactly sure what happened. One minute everything was fine and then my legs went out from beneath me and the undertow caught me. Pulled me down." It wasn't exactly the truth, but it wasn't a lie either.

Again her face danced in front of my eyes, but I pushed it away, told myself that I was being stupid. My panicked mind had conjured her from leftover nightmares—she was no more real today than she had been six years ago when I had gotten tangled in a kelp bed at midnight. And yet, she'd seemed so real that I couldn't help wondering . . .

Forcing a smile, I looked into Mark's searching eyes and saw echoes of the same fear and anger and adrenaline that continued to race through me. "Hey, thanks for saving my life, by the way. I appreciate it."

He didn't say anything, but the glare he shot me told me to quit while I was ahead.

I chose to ignore it. "Seriously, though, I'm fine now." I met each set of concerned eyes in turn, then pushed lightly to my feet. It was a relief to find my body once again under my command—such a relief that I just might have been able to pretend those frightening moments, when I'd been sure I was going to die, had never happened.

I glanced around for my board, was thrilled when I saw it lying, discarded, next to Scooter's. "Thanks for catching my board, man," I told him with a smile.

He flashed me his lady-killer grin in return, though his green eyes still showed a little worry. "Are you kidding me? I couldn't let it get toasted—it's a *Brewer*."

The reverence in his voice as he said Dick Brewer's name was just one of the many reasons Scooter had never kept a girlfriend for longer than a few weeks—despite his gorgeous face; sexy, sun-streaked blond hair; and laid-back personality. But the simple fact was, no girl had ever meant half as much to him as catching a really good wave.

Now, that wasn't to say that I was knocking his awe for my board. It *was* incredibly sweet—especially since my dad had had it custom designed for my sixteenth birthday by one of the original, and best, surfboard gurus of all time. The fact that it was purple and orange—as well as perfectly balanced and formed— only made it that much sweeter.

The idea that in a week it might be completely useless made me dizzy all over again.

"True." I nodded at him, making sure to keep my face serious as I headed for my board. "But thanks, anyway."

"Where do you think you're going?" Mark asked as he came up behind me.

"Home." I glanced at the clouds. "It looks like the sky's going to open up any second. Besides, we'll be late if we don't hustle."

My words got the guys moving, exactly as I had intended them to. Most of us were already on probation for tardies— and though we didn't mind wasting away in detention if it meant catching some really great waves in the morning, it was sacrilegious to waste the afternoon surf for any other reason.

Even if that reason was my near drowning from bizarre and inexplicable circumstances.

After assuring themselves that I really was all right—for about the zillionth time—the rest of the guys scattered, leaving Mark and me alone on the beach. As I looked into his concerned face, I had the sinking feeling he wasn't going to be anywhere near as easy to get rid of as the rest of them had been. So I did what any self-respecting girl would do—I grabbed my board and booked it.

My house was just across the street from the expanse of loose sand we were standing on, and suddenly I wanted nothing more

21

than to get inside. To get as far from the ocean and Mark and what had happened as I possibly could. To have a few minutes alone so I could figure out exactly what *had* happened—and what I was going to do about it.

"Hey, wait up," Mark called, but I continued walking across the sand in a long-legged stride that was nearly a run, my surfboard bumping against my hip and thigh as I led a one-woman charge for my garage.

I was going to cry, I just knew it, and the last thing I wanted to do was break down in front of Mark. I never, never, *never* cried in public and I wasn't going to start now—not even if, in this case, "public" was the boyfriend who had just saved my life.

I knew I owed him a lot, knew he deserved more than for me to just dump his ass on the beach and run, but I felt like I was going to explode. Stuff like this wasn't supposed to happen yet. I wasn't ready for it, hadn't prepared for it.

Not that there was really a good way to prepare for drowning, but still. I needed more time and I should have had it. My seventeenth birthday was still over a week away. I'd spent the last year dreading February 27, and now it was turning out all that focus on a date was for nothing. My body—or at least this thing inside of me—wasn't playing by the rules.

I had just reached the sidewalk at the edge of our driveway when Mark's hand closed around my elbow. It was big and cold and wet, his fingers slightly calloused from years of carrying and waxing his board. For a second—one long, frightening second—I imagined what it would be like to sink into him.

To not fight.

To just *be*.

22

But since my mom left, I'd made it a point not to depend on anyone—except maybe my dad. It's too easy for someone to leave, to just walk away without a backward glance. Even Mark. Maybe especially Mark, since we'd broken up so many times before. Yet now, today, I wanted his comfort more than I could ever remember wanting anything.

Except leaning on him wasn't exactly fair—not when I couldn't tell him the truth. Not when my whole life could change in the blink of an eye, as today had proven.

Maybe, after the next few weeks or months were over . . . after all this just went away (please, God, let it go away)— maybe then I could relax enough to let my guard down with him. Until then . . .

I sighed. Until then, I had to hold it together. Keep the freak-outs to a minimum and my boyfriend's questions at bay.

"Chill, Tempest." He smiled at me then, that surfer-boy, endless-summer smile of his that had had young hearts all up and down this long stretch of coast beating too fast for as long as I could remember. Even mine.

Especially mine.

"The guys are gone and you don't need to put on the whole big, bad attitude for me." He stepped closer, crowding me in that way he had that either thrilled or annoyed me, depending on my mood. Today it angered me, because it was accompanied by a look that said he was going to push until he got answers, and after my tumble, I wasn't sure I was up to evading him. "You've got to be pretty shaken up—I know I am."

He had no idea just how shaken up I was, and I had no idea how to tell him. How could I when I'd worked so hard to make sure he never knew the real me? Never knew the secrets I kept hidden inside myself, secrets that I couldn't share with anyone.

It was hypocritical of me to blame him for trying to figure me out when I deliberately kept so much of myself a mystery. But I *did* blame him—it was easier than blaming myself.

Easier than blaming a mother who was never around to accept it.

Certainly easier than blaming fate or God or any other supernatural force out there that people thanked or cursed, depending on which twists and turns their lives took.

I'd never had that privilege, that choice between giving thanks or pleading for salvation. I'd been cursed from the day I was born—though I was too smart to sit around whining about it.

Usually.

"I *am* fine," I insisted. "It wasn't that big a deal." I was proud of how steady my voice sounded—maybe I was better at the whole lying thing than I thought.

"Yeah, right." Or maybe not.

But then, why was I surprised? Mark was a lot deeper than he looked—and a lot more observant. We'd been going out, off and on (mostly on), for two and a half years—had been friends a lot longer than that. He might not know all my secrets, but he did know me better than just about anyone.

A fact that was reflected in his brown eyes, as he stared at me worriedly. "You were underwater for a good three or four minutes." He reached up and tucked a wet clump of hair behind my ear, then leaned forward until his face was only inches from mine. My breath caught—like it always did when he was close—

but I did my best to ignore it. Now wasn't the time for hormone-induced weakness.

"I kept looking, but I couldn't find you." His voice broke and I realized, with a shock, that he had tears in *his* eyes. My resistance melted, even as I told myself to stay strong. To hold myself, and my emotions, in check. "You were right next to me one second and then you were just gone. I really thought you were going to drown."

I didn't know what to say. I wanted to laugh, to make a joke out of everything—I probably would have if my life hadn't just taken the mother of all turns into the land of the abysmally unfunny.

Then Mark was dropping his board, wrapping his arms around me, and pulling me into his chest like I belonged there. Though I told myself I didn't need it, *didn't need him*, it was all I could do not to cling. He smelled so good—a strange combination of sandalwood and salt water that was uniquely Mark.

I took a deep breath, held that scent in my lungs for long seconds as I tried to inhale the normalcy that made up his very essence. The normalcy I craved like a junkie with an open, aching vein.

He held me for a while, his wet-suit shirt cold against the bare skin of my stomach. I wasn't wearing a wet suit—I didn't need one in the ocean, no matter how cold it got. But here on land I was freezing, as usual. These days I almost always was when I wasn't in the water—and the shock of nearly drowning had only made the cold that much worse. If I stayed against Mark, let my body absorb the coolness of his, I would pay for it later.

And yet, I couldn't force myself to move, to let him go. The chill of his body against mine was no match for the ice scraping me raw from the inside out: frigid, frozen, frightening as hell. I'd like to blame it on my near-death experience, but once again, that would be a lie. The iciness had been growing in me for a while, getting a little worse every day until I swore I could feel my humanity slowly freezing beneath the onslaught.

My knees trembled.

I rested against Mark for as long as I dared—until my teeth were chattering and I was sure my lips were the same color as the Pacific. Then I took one last sniff, one last moment of comfort, and pulled away.

"Look, I gotta go in," I told him, working to keep my voice even.

"I know." Once again, his lips turned up in that bad-boy grin of his—the one that had first attracted me because it was so very different from my own restrained smile—and he said, "Are you going to make an appointment with the doctor? Get checked out?"

"No!" It was almost a shout and I felt guilty when I saw him rear back in surprise. But going to the doctor meant telling my dad and I couldn't—wouldn't—put him through that. Not now, when my seventeenth birthday loomed over the house like a particularly unwelcome specter.

I worked to soften my voice. "I'm fine. Just a little shaken up."

"Tempest." He didn't look convinced.

I shook my head, utterly exhausted by the whole situation. "I can't do this now, Mark."

His jaw tightened and as I stared at him I realized, with more than a little shock, that he wasn't going to let this go. Not now. Not this time.

"It's never *now*, Tempest. That's the whole problem." His hands clenched into fists. "You always put me off, always tell me we'll talk about it later. But we never do."

"Mark." I reached out, put a hand on his shoulder. "It's comp—"

He shrugged off my hand. "Don't tell me it's complicated. I'm not an idiot. And don't just ignore me like you usually do." He glanced over his shoulder at the ocean, and for the first time that I could remember, he looked angry. Really angry. "Do you actually think I'm so stupid that I don't know something weird happened out there? Something screwed up?"

My stomach tightened. "I don't know what you mean. The wave—"

"Yeah, right. The wave." He shoved his hands into the pockets of his board shorts and stared at me with an intensity that had my heart threatening to pound right out of my chest. "The day a wave like that knocks you around is the day I eat my freakin' surfboard. I'm not an idiot, Tempest."

"I never said you were."

"Of course not. You just treat me like I am."

"I *really* don't want to talk about this." I forced the words past my still-tight throat.

"Well, I do." His jaw was clenched, his eyes a deep, molten chocolate. "You tell everyone I'm your boyfriend. You tell *me* that you're crazy about me. But you don't trust me for shit."

"That's not true," I insisted, with a lot more confidence than I was feeling.

"No?" he asked. "Then prove it." Yanking his hands out of his pockets, he wrapped them around my upper arms and shook me a little. "Tell me what happened out there. Tell me why you won't talk to me. Tell me what's going on with you—for once. Do I have to beg?"

He wasn't rough, but pain shot down my arms at the first squeeze of his fingers. It took my breath, had me struggling for air for the second time that morning.

"Nothing's going on," I repeated, but I could barely choke out the lie. I was disgusted—with myself, with him, with the whole crazy situation. And it pissed me off that he was pushing me to talk to him about stuff even I didn't understand.

I fought to keep the anger out of my voice as I glanced over his shoulder at the ocean that had just begun to roar and thrash. Storms were rare on this stretch of beach, even in winter. But when the Pacific decided to put on a show, it did it with a lot of style. "Besides, we don't have time for this. If you don't beat the rain home, you'll be screwed. Traffic—"

He dropped my arms like I'd burned him, started to back away even as he stared at me incredulously. "That's it? Seriously? 'Go home, Mark, it's going to rain'?"

"I don't know what you want from me!" Frustration had tears burning behind my eyes.

"Bull. You know exactly what I want from you. You just don't want to give it to me." He bent down, picked up his board. Started to walk away.

Shame skated through me. No matter how annoyed I was at him, I didn't want him to leave—not like this. Not when he was this upset with me. Mark was the best, most normal thing in my life, and the thought of losing him . . .

"Mark. Please." I crossed the distance between us at a run, threw my arms around him, and held on tight. It was another shock to realize he was shaking even worse than I was.

28

Standing on tiptoes, I started to brush my lips across his in a soft, comforting kiss. But he wasn't looking for comfort, or for softness. Dropping his surfboard on the pavement once again, he fastened his hands on my shoulders and pulled me closer to him with an urgency I'd never felt before. And in that one instant, the kiss I had meant to reassure turned into so much more.

As his lips moved against mine, I could feel his worry and his desperation. His driving need not to let me out of his sight. And though I told myself I wanted nothing more than to get away, I couldn't help responding to him.

Wrapping my arms around his neck, I kissed him until both of us were breathing funny and my legs were once again threatening to go out from under me.

Kissed him until I could barely remember my own name, let alone everything I had to face in the next few weeks.

Kissed him until nothing mattered but the two of us and the way we made each other feel.

And then he was pulling away, grabbing his board and heading down my driveway with a stride that said he was still angry. Still hurt.

"This isn't over, Tempest." He tossed the words over his shoulder. "Not by a long shot."

As I watched him go, I wondered if it ever would be.

Chapter 3

❧

I stared after Mark until he was little more than a speck on the horizon, so many emotions bouncing around inside of me that I didn't know which ones to concentrate on. Fear, worry, disgust, anger, desire, confusion, love. They mixed together until I wanted to scream.

But since that wasn't an option—at least not at seven a.m. on my sleepy little street—I tried to put our fight out of my mind as I grabbed my board and headed up the driveway. As I walked, I stared at the huge steel and glass house I'd lived in my entire life.

My dad had designed it for my mom right after they'd found out she was pregnant with me; to this day, he swore it had been a wedding present for her (yes, she was pregnant when they got married), but I knew the truth.

This house, the only one of its kind in the neighborhood, was just one more of my father's desperate, pathetic attempts to prove to my mother that she wasn't trapped. I guess he'd figured if every room in the house had at least one whole wall of glass that overlooked the ocean, she wouldn't feel landlocked, wouldn't feel cornered.

He'd been wrong—but then, when it came to Mom, he'd been wrong about a lot of things. We both had. Nice to know I was continuing the family tradition in my relationship with Mark.

Furious with myself and my too-pushy boyfriend, I dropped my board on its stand in the garage—right next to my father's—and headed into the backyard to the shower Dad had had installed next to the back door, so we didn't track sand from the beach all over the floors inside.

As I showered in the hottest water my sensitive skin could stand, I did my best to block out the roars of the omnipresent ocean. I wasn't successful—I never was—and after I'd wrapped myself up in the fluffy black robe I always kept near the shower, I wandered into the house and down the hall to the kitchen where I poured myself some pineapple juice. Then I stood at the huge, seamless pane of glass that ran the full length of the room, sipping my juice and watching as the Pacific whipped itself into a frenzy.

Under my gaze, waves crashed and rolled, kicked up spray and churned the ever-changing surface of the ocean into shapeless foam. The water was darker now, more gray than blue, and I shivered as I watched the rain roll in. It was a good thing I hadn't been out there as the storm approached—I might never have made it back to the surface.

Lightning flashed above the water and I felt it inside of me, felt its call as surely as if it had said my name. It wrapped itself around me—around my heart, my body, my very soul—and tugged until I didn't know if I could resist it.

Didn't know if I wanted to resist it—even after everything that had happened.

The thought had ice slamming through me all over again, as if the hot shower and heavy robe had never happened. As if my father didn't have the thermostat set at eighty-two in a last-ditch effort to keep me warm.

"Tempest, can I have pancakes for breakfast?" My eight-year-old brother's voice intruded on my pity party.

"It's too late for pancakes, dork. You slept in." I turned in time to watch my thirteen-year-old brother, Rio, shove our younger brother, Moku, into a kitchen cabinet, hard.

For a second it looked like Moku was going to object—his lower lip quivered with the need to cry foul—but in the end he kept the pain to himself. Like he always did, as if he was afraid no one would be there to kiss it away.

It wasn't hard to figure out where his neuroses came from.

My heart hurt for him, this kid whom I had had such a big hand in raising. Nine years younger than me, he'd been two when my mom had ditched us and my dad had fallen apart. If this thing happened, if I ended up like my mother, what was going to happen to him? Who would take him to school and read him a book before bed and cuddle with him in the middle of the night?

Who was going to defend him from Rio, who took a savage delight in torturing him whenever our father's back was turned?

"Cut it out," I told Rio as I reached into the fridge for the lunches I'd packed for them the night before.

"Cut what out?" His face was the picture of innocence.

"You know what." To make sure he got my meaning, I knocked into him with my shoulder as I crossed to the table.

"There's cereal for breakfast, Mo. But I'll make pancakes for dinner, how's that sound?"

"Yummy!"

Behind him Rio made a gagging sound, but I chose to ignore him. It was that or start the morning with yet another fight.

"Why do you have to be such a dork?" Rio asked Moku with a big-brother smirk.

"Why do you have to be so mean?"

"I'm not mean, just honest."

"Knock it off." My dad breezed into the kitchen, dressed in his normal work attire of board shorts and an electric yellow surfing tee. Looking at him like that, it was hard to imagine he was the president of a company that had worked its way onto the Fortune 1000 list three years before and was steadily rising in the ranks. "Morning, Tempest."

"Morning, Dad."

"How were the waves today?"

"Good." I concentrated on pouring Mo his Froot Loops and prayed my dad wouldn't notice the tension in my voice.

"Really?" He was looking out to sea. "Looks kind of rough."

"That just kicked up," Rio said quickly, his mouth full of Cocoa Pebbles. "It was pretty calm earlier."

I glanced at him, saw him staring at the waves with a concerned look that was at odds with his normally obnoxious behavior. And suddenly I knew he'd seen what had happened—had watched from his room as I'd almost drowned.

No wonder he was being a bigger pain in the butt than usual. He must have been panicked—we might not always get along, but we stick together. After Mom left, we'd had little choice.

I tried to catch his eye, but he wouldn't look at me.

"Good." My dad kept watching the waves and I tried to pretend I didn't know what he was looking for. But that was just one more lie—he was looking for the same thing he was always looking for: my mother. Too bad he hadn't figured out what the rest of us had: that after six years, it was pretty much a lost cause to expect her to swim on home and take up where she'd left off.

Finally, he forcibly jerked his attention away from the window and focused on us instead. "Tests today?"

"Spelling," Moku said proudly.

"You know your words?"

"Tempest quizzed me last night. I got them all right."

My dad shot me a grateful look. Moku had ADHD and was in the middle of being tested for dyslexia. Trying to get him to spell words was more painful than having your wisdom teeth yanked out—without anesthesia. My dad tried to work with him too, but it was rough going. Mo just responded better to me.

One more reason this whole nightmarish birthday thing just plain sucked.

"I've got a math test today," Rio volunteered. "I'm going to ace it."

"You studied?" my father asked incredulously and I couldn't blame him. Rio was about as interested in school as I was in quantum physics.

"What? Like that's so hard to believe?"

"Yes." My dad and I answered in tandem, but then I remembered the cute blonde Rio had been sitting with when I'd picked him up from school the day before. Her arms had been loaded with books—maybe he was trying to impress one of the smart girls. It would be a nice change of pace.

"Whatever." With a shrug, Rio slid his bad attitude back into place.

"How about you, Tempest?"

"Not until next week."

"How's the college search going?"

"It's not." My voice was flat, angry, but I couldn't help it. At the rate things were going, I'd never get the chance to go to art school. Never get to paint in Paris . . .

I slammed the door shut on the self-pity before I made myself sick. Seriously, nobody likes a whiner.

"All right, then." My dad backed off.

In the hallway my mother's grandfather clock—the one she'd insisted on having and the one my father kept just in case she ever came back—chimed seven times, prodding us all into action.

"Tempest, I'll drop Mo at school today if you can take Rio. I have an early meeting set up."

"Hear that, shrimp?" I deliberately used the nickname Rio hated. "I'll be ready in ten minutes, so get your butt in gear." On my way out of the kitchen, I slipped Moku's lunch into his backpack, then ruffled his hair affectionately. "I'll pick you up after school."

"For pancakes?" he asked eagerly.

I laughed. "For pancakes."

But once I was on the stairs, heading toward my room, my smile slipped. I was frightened—frightened for myself and frightened for my family. What would happen to them if I couldn't resist the change?

Sure, my mind chose humanity—like it always had. But my soul, my treacherous soul, *yearned* for the absolute freedom of the Pacific.

For a girl who had always prided herself on her mortality, the betrayal cut like the sharpest of knives.

And my painting? If I went too long without putting brush to canvas, I felt like a part of me was missing. The idea of disappearing under the waves, of never again creating something, had me twisted into knots.

Because I couldn't change the past—or, I was afraid, the future—I tried to put it all out of my mind and concentrate on the present instead.

If I didn't hustle, I would be late for school. Yet even as I yanked on my favorite pair of perfectly faded jeans, I couldn't help looking at the storm-tossed Pacific one more time. And wondering where I'd be next year.

Next month.

Next week.

The fact that I didn't know—for the first time in my sixteen years of existence—scared me to death.

By the time I got to school, after dropping Rio at junior high, I had only enough time to find a parking spot—about a million miles away, of course—and then book it to class before the second bell rang. First period was AP Chem with Mr. Hein and he was even more of a stickler when it came to the tardy policy than the other teachers.

One second late and he started filling out a detention slip and he didn't really care what excuse you had. Unexpected female emergencies went about as far with him as stories of flat tires did. I should know: Brianne had tried them both this year, along with a whole host of more inventive excuses that had also been shot down as the school year progressed.

Which was why I was completely out of breath—not to mention soaked to the skin from the untimely winter storm that had hit just as I'd pulled into the parking lot—by the time I slammed through the open door of Mr. Hein's chem lab one second before the tardy bell rang. I was glad I hadn't bothered with more than lip gloss and a ponytail—any other efforts would have been completely washed away.

"Good morning, Tempest. So nice of you to join us today."

"Sorry," I gasped as I squished my way to my desk in the center of the second row, right in front of Bri and next to our other friend, Mickey (yes, like the mouse—long story short, her mother went into labor at Disneyland). "Traffic was—"

"Mmm-hmmm," he interrupted, letting me know without words that my excuse—no matter how true—was no more believable, or important, than Bri's fictitious ones were.

"This week we're going to talk about the structure of matter," he droned. "I want to start with the different types of atomic bonding . . ."

"Good waves?" Bri whispered as I took my seat in front of her.

"Bad traffic." I pulled out a notebook and started to take notes on ionic and covalent bonding, even as I tried to ignore the chill working its way through me. I wasn't sure how I was going to make it until my clothes dried—right now I was so cold that it felt like my very bones would shake apart. Add to that the fact that my neck felt like it was on fire—heat and pain licking their way from behind my ear to the top of my shoulder—and it promised to be one hell of a day.

"Here." Mickey slipped off her leather jacket and handed it to me. "Your teeth are chattering. Again."

I wanted to refuse—it looked expensive and I was so wet I was afraid I'd ruin it—but she was right. My teeth *were* chattering, my hands trembling so badly I could barely take notes. "Thanks," I whispered as I slipped into it. Immediately her body heat started to dispel some of the chill. It didn't warm me— nothing could do that these days—but at least the cold was almost bearable.

Chem dragged, like it always did on non-lab days, and by the time the bell rang I was sure I'd have nightmares about the chemical bonding of atoms. I could see the whole thing now—me running screaming through a dark hallway while elemental compounds with huge teeth and sharp claws chased me down.

What did it say about me that the prospect was a lot less daunting than what I actually had to face in the next few weeks?

Shoving the thought away—there wasn't anything I could do about it, anyway—I started to shrug out of Mickey's jacket. I was almost dry and only reasonably cold, so I was pretty sure I could make it through the rest of the day without it.

But she gestured for me to keep it. "You can give it back at lunch. Your shirt is still pretty damp and it's kind of . . ."

Her voice trailed off and I glanced down, shocked to realize she was right. My shirt was clinging to my chest like it had been painted on, and the fact that I was still too cold was . . . more than obvious. Mortified, I pulled the jacket closed again and cursed my mother—and the freaky metabolism she'd given me— for what had to be the millionth time.

Too bad it didn't do me any more good this time than it had the other times.

"Thanks," I said, gathering up my books and heading for the hallway with an awkward little wave.

I was in a bad mood and I didn't want to see anyone. My underwear was wet, I looked awful, and to top things off, my neck still hurt like crazy. I ran my hand over the part that ached and it did feel a little warm. I nearly snarled at the thought—getting sick after everything else that had happened today would just be the icing on the crappy cake that was my life.

Not that I had time to dwell on it. It was still raining, so things were an absolute disaster. Because it's sunny in San Diego something like three hundred days of the year, most of the high schools are built with outdoor hallways—and ours is no exception. The areas close to the buildings were covered, but trying to fit three thousand adult-size students under a series of narrow overhangs was impossible.

That didn't stop most of us from trying to squeeze under, which led to major traffic jams, assorted pushing and shoving, and at least one or two fistfights on every rainy day.

A year ago, I would have preferred walking in the rain over trying to maneuver my way through the sardine-can passageways, but a lot had changed in a year. Now the idea of getting soaked to the skin—again—was almost as unappealing as the idea of giving up everything and jumping into the ocean like my mother had so many years before.

"Hey, watch it!" I heard Bri yelp from behind me, and I glanced back in time to see some freshman jerk cop a feel as he scooted past her. That was yet another hazard of rainy days: dorks with more hormones than sense. At least she'd gotten in a lick of her own, I noticed with satisfaction. The guy who'd grabbed her ass was now walking with a very pronounced limp.

That was just one of the many things I liked about Bri. Despite the fact that her perfectly styled blond hair, cute face, and bright blue eyes made her look like the quintessential cheerleader, she was more than able to kick a little ass when the occasion warranted. Unfortunately, the occasion warranted it quite a lot at our school—I kept telling her a well-placed piercing or a couple of tattoos would take care of the problem, but she just rolled her eyes and gave me her patented our-bodies-are-temples speech.

I might have agreed with her, if my temple hadn't been on the verge of completely and totally wigging out.

"Ugh," Bri said as she elbowed her way through the masses to walk next to me. "I can't wait until we graduate. I am *so* over high school guys."

"We've still got a year and a half until that glorious day. Don't be letting the door hit you quite yet."

She snorted. "Easy for you to say—you managed to snag one of the best guys in this place. So please, have some pity for the rest of us."

I kept my mouth shut as we continued weaving our way across the campus to the liberal arts building and our American Lit class. It's not like I could argue with her—Mark was definitely one of the coolest guys in school. He wasn't part of the super-popular, clonelike in-crowd—that group was made up of La Jolla High's football, basketball, and baseball stars and the cheerleaders who dated them—but he was definitely sought after.

He was too hot and too good of a surfer not to be. And, much more important, he cared about me and treated me right. Sure, he had a temper and sometimes he saw more than I was comfortable with, but he also had a really good brain under all

40

that shaggy, sun-bleached hair. If only I could get him to stop pushing me to tell him everything, to stop being so possessive, things would be perfect.

"So, how'd the surfing go today?" Bri asked as we were swept along in the endless tangle of adolescent bodies.

"Like you care." I rolled my eyes at her and winked so she'd know I was joking.

"Hey, I like to surf. I'm just not obsessed, like some people I know."

"It's only obsession if you can't control it."

"Spending every spare minute of your day on a surfboard seems obsessive to me." She narrowed her eyes. "And you're dodging the question. What happened out there?"

I gave in to the inevitable—the guys may not have said anything yet, but it was just a matter of time before everyone knew. "I totally grubbed, hit the water hard."

"No way!" The look she shot me was pure astonishment, mixed with a lot of disbelief. "You *never* do that."

"Well, I did it today—so hard that Mark had to fish me out of the chowder and tow me back to shore like a total frube."

With her usual impeccable timing, Bri grabbed my arm just as we passed our classroom and yanked me out of the crush and into the door of Mr. Keppler's American Lit class.

I swear, the girl was a general in a former life: when she has her mind set on something, she runs over whoever or whatever is in her path. I'd spent the first year of high school following along behind her, trying to figure out how to do what she did. Finally I just gave up and let her take the lead—it worked out much better for both of us.

"So, are you okay?" she asked as we found our seats on the right side of the circle.

Yes, Mr. Keppler arranged our desks in one big circle, so we could all stare at each other while we "ruminated" on the literature of the day. And most days, he even sat with us. If he wasn't a complete and absolute Greek god, it would be totally nerdy. As it was, Bri and I reaped the benefits because she'd managed to snag us seats directly across from his desk on the second day of class. I couldn't begin to add up how many class periods I'd spent staring at him instead of thinking about a bunch of dead guys who wrote stuff long before I was even born.

"Yeah, of course." I slid into my seat—which had the added benefit of being right in front of the heater—and took my first easy breath since getting to school that day. Another big plus for Mr. Keppler was that he always kept the classroom warm, unlike Hein, who I swore was half Eskimo. "It was no big deal."

"It was a very big deal." As he sank into the desk on my left, Mark yanked on my ponytail like he always did. "She nearly drowned."

I was so relieved that he was behaving seminormally that it took me a minute to realize he *wasn't*. He hadn't kissed me, hadn't smiled at me, hadn't said a word to me. Instead, he was talking to *my best friend* like I didn't even exist.

"Oh my God!" Bri sat up straighter, her narrow eyes cataloging every inch of me for injuries. "I can't believe you didn't say anything!"

With worry over Mark gnawing at me, I didn't bother to answer. What was I supposed to say anyway—that I had started turning mermaid today and then nearly died because I couldn't get my body to work right?

That would go over really well, especially with the men in the little white coats. I glared at Mark, tried to make him look at me, but he just pretended I wasn't there. Again.

Suddenly, Bri gasped like her visual search had actually found something.

"Hey, what's wrong with your throat? Did you cut yourself?"

She leaned forward to get a closer look, but I slapped my hands over my neck—right at the spots that had been burning since I'd gotten to chemistry an hour before.

As I ran my finger over them, I realized with some shock that the skin right below my ear was no longer smooth. It was bumpy and raised and had a small slash beneath the bumps that was much too precise to be random.

"Did you get hurt after all?" Mark leaned toward me, suddenly remembering I was there now that it looked like something might actually be wrong with me. "Let me see."

I kept my hands where they were while my mind ran in a million different directions at once. With everything inside of me, I prayed for the cuts to be nothing more than collateral damage from my tumble in the ocean. But as I ducked my chin and fumbled in my purse for the mirror I always kept in one of the pockets, a bunch of other explanations went through my head. None of them was comforting.

I pulled out the mirror and held it up to my left ear, trying to look at the odd bumps without letting Mark or Brianne see. But as I got my first glimpse of the strange little slash in the mirror, my heart literally skipped a beat. Then two.

Trying (and failing) not to freak out, I frantically switched the mirror to my right side, only to see the same thing there. A short (no more than three-quarters of an inch), shallow cut ran directly beneath each of my ears. The cuts gaped a little on each side, despite the fact that they looked fully healed—there was none of the redness or dried blood that you would expect from a new injury.

My hands started to shake—so noticeably that I made myself dump the compact back in my purse. Mark and Bri were staring at me like I'd lost my mind, but I didn't know what to say to them, didn't even know if I could look at them.

I hadn't cut myself in the ocean, hadn't hurt myself and been unaware. No, nothing that simple would do for me. Instead, it was a million times worse.

No, make that a *billion* times worse.

Because one look at the slightly raised, slightly open slices and I knew exactly what they were. After all, I'd seen them before— every day of the first eleven years of my life—on my *mother*.

The short yet rocky journey between my life and complete and utter insanity had just been fast-tracked. Sometime between checking myself over in the mirror before leaving the house and right now, I had grown *gills*.

Chapter 4

Gills? The horror of it reverberated in my head like a gong gone wild. I had *gills*?

I stroked the little slits with my fingers, told myself there had to be another explanation, but even in shock I was smart enough to know that self-delusion could only get me so far. Especially with my boyfriend and best friend staring at me as if I'd been hit in the head by my surfboard one time too many.

Not that I blamed them.

"What's wrong?" Bri hissed as Mr. Keppler started taking attendance.

I pulled my shirt collar up to cover the evidence that I was something more—or less—than human. "Nothing."

The look she shot me said she didn't believe me any more than Mark had.

Ducking my head, I did my best to look normal—but how could I? So far that morning I'd sprouted a tail and then gills, not to mention the fact that once again I was so cold I had to lock my jaw to keep my teeth from chattering an entire symphony.

Yeah, I was perfectly normal. For a *freak*.

Mr. Keppler's class, which usually passed so quickly, dragged by with the excruciatingly painful slowness of a root canal. As he droned on about *The Great Gatsby* and glasses and the Valley of Ashes, all I could think was that my life was over.

I was sixteen and everything I knew, everything I wanted out of life, was going up in flames around me—and there wasn't anything I could do to stop it.

Any more than I could stop myself from stroking a finger across my new gills, hoping that—like the tail—they would disappear in a matter of minutes. So far all the wishing in the world wasn't getting me anywhere.

Panic, disbelief, and horror warred for a place within me, and I steadfastly tried to ignore them all. But they were insidious, all-consuming, and soon it took every ounce of concentration I had to sit still and wait for the stupid bell to ring.

Worse, cutting through all the other screwed-up emotions was one more—one I would have sworn that by this time I was incapable of feeling.

Betrayal.

My mother had left each of my brothers and me a letter when she took off for oceans unknown. Mine explained that one day I would have a choice as to what I would become. She'd said the changes wouldn't start happening until I turned seventeen. That after my birthday I would have an overwhelming craving for the ocean, one that would be hard to resist. And that I would have three months to make a choice about how I wanted to live the rest of my life.

This didn't feel like a choice—more like my body had been

hijacked by fate and my brain was just along for the ride. Leave it to Mom to omit the most important, and most difficult, parts of the equation. I had read that letter so many times that I had it memorized even now, years later, and I know for a fact that she had never mentioned any uncontrollable physical changes in there. I definitely would have remembered if she'd told me about any of this.

Of course, she hadn't exactly given me a bunch of clues for how to handle things either. I mean, seriously. If I now had gills—not to mention a tail that came and went at inopportune moments—who knew what else was going to happen to me in the next few weeks, and how the hell I was going to hide it? If the gills stuck around, did that mean that soon I would stop being able to breathe air?

A series of shudders that had nothing to do with the cold worked their way through me.

The second the bell rang I was out of my seat, my backpack dangling from numb fingertips as I hurried across the room. "Hey, Tempest, where's the fire?" Bri asked.

"I don't feel so good," I told her, not completely untruthfully. "I think I'm going to hit the bathroom before next class."

"You want me to come?"

"No! I mean, I'm fine. Just a little nauseous. It's above and beyond to expect you to listen to me hurl."

I hightailed it out of the room before she could say anything else—or worse, Mark could. But I wasn't headed for the bathroom, or my next class. No, I was on my way to the parking lot like the hounds of hell were after me. Normally, I would never consider ditching third period—art was my favorite class, by far.

But today wasn't a normal day, and detention or no detention, it was turning out to be a great day to be anywhere but here.

⬧

Two hours later I was cruising the topsy-turvy highway that ran along the beach in Del Mar, despite the rain that was still coming down in torrents. I had the heat turned up and my heaviest jacket wrapped around me and still the chills racked me.

Shit. Was this how I was going to spend the rest of my life? Freezing my ass off and hiding from the world?

I took a curve too fast, but I'd had superquick reflexes since birth—an interesting by-product of the whole mermaid thing—and the car didn't so much as slide. I took the next curve even faster.

I was being careless, reckless even, and I tried to work up the will to care. But the road was deserted—as it always was during a thunderstorm—and the only life I was risking was my own. Right at the moment, it didn't seem like such a bad gamble. After all, if things continued the way they'd been going, I'd be shark bait in a matter of days anyway.

Still, as the weather grew worse, I slowed down. Took a couple of curves at a more sedate pace before pulling to a stop by the side of the road.

I don't know how long I sat there, listening to the hollow drum of the rain against my roof and the roar of the angry ocean. It was really pouring now, the water coming down in great sheets that coated my windshield and kicked up the surf to dangerous heights. The waves coming in were monster huge and menacing as hell.

I longed to ride them, though my father had expressly forbidden me to do so. He so rarely put his foot down about anything that I tended to listen to him when he did—especially when he told me stories of friends he'd lost in just such conditions.

The stories had frightened me, as he'd meant them to, but today fear wasn't enough to stop the yearning, the bone-deep desire to throw myself into the roiling ocean and just let it have me.

I still don't know what possessed me to do what I did next. Ignoring the rain, ignoring the cold, ignoring my chattering teeth and half-frozen appendages, I climbed out of the car and let the rain and the wind wash over me.

It tore through my hair, whipped against my tender skin until tears of pain rolled down my face. Lightning rent the sky, flashed above the ocean like a bomb exploding mere moments before thunder shook the ground. And still I stood there, refusing to get back in the car where it was safe.

My name wasn't Tempest for nothing.

Unwilling to give in to the wind or the rain or the voice in my head that warned me away, I staggered toward the water. It seemed a better idea than throwing the mother of all temper tantrums and screaming "it's not fair!" at the top of my lungs.

Life's not fair, little girl. For the first time in years, I heard my mother's voice in my head. *Sometimes you've got to make the best of what you've got.* The advice might have meant more if it hadn't come from a woman who had run away from every responsibility she'd ever had.

There was a rocky slope between me and the beach, and I stumbled down it—slipping and sliding with single-minded intent. I wanted only to get to the water. To feel the ocean lapping at my feet, before it surrounded my frail, human body. To be free in a way I couldn't be when I was on land.

I spilled down the last few yards, tumbling onto the beach—and my ass—as my legs went out from under me. I hit the ground hard, so hard that I didn't immediately climb back to my feet. I just sat there in the middle of the storm, the sand cold and squicky beneath me, and let the rain have me.

I was colder than I'd ever been—nearly frozen—my body struggling to regulate itself in the downpour. Another gift from dear old Mom, this inability to control my own body temperature except in the water. Not for the first time, I wondered if I really was as cold-blooded as I felt.

A hint of color in the middle of the blue gray waves caught my eye, had me convinced I was imagining things. Except when I looked again, it was still there—a flash of red in the middle of the bobbing, threatening waves.

The rain was still coming down hard, so hard that for a minute I was sure I was only seeing the reflection of light through water, like a rainbow. But there was no sun and little light out here in the middle of the storm.

I jumped to my feet, wiped the streaming rain out of my eyes, then cupped my hands around them in an effort to keep the water out as I tried to find that little dot of crimson again.

There it was—my heart beat double time as I realized what I was seeing. *Someone* was out there. Someone was swimming in the seething, storm-tossed waters.

What a moron, was my first thought.

My second thought was that there was no way he was going

to make it back to shore. Not in the middle of all this. He was going to drown trying.

I fumbled for my cell phone, started to dial 911—in the winter there were no lifeguards on these beaches—even as I kicked off my shoes, some unconscious part of me already preparing to plunge into the water to try and save the idiot.

Only, as precious seconds passed, I figured out he didn't need saving. Before my pissed-off, terrified eyes, he stood straight up in the middle of the thrashing waves.

For one brief, bizarre moment the water was so high that it looked like he was hovering on the surface of the waves—literally walking on water.

But then the wave crested and I realized he was actually surfing the monster waves, his board cutting through the disturbed water like a knife through soft-serve ice cream. His red swimsuit was a beacon of insanity.

My God, was all I could think as I watched him maneuver through the waves like a maestro.

My God, he was good.

And my God, what I wouldn't do to be out there with him—suicide or not.

The waves bucked and roiled around him, but you would have thought he was having a picnic out there amidst all that crashing. He never faltered, his body staying in perfect form as he rode the wave in much farther than even I would have been able to on my best days.

When he finally dropped back down to the board, I was as disappointed as I was relieved. Watching him had been like watching art come to life.

I started across the squishy, waterlogged sand, unsure what I was going to say to the guy. But approaching him was almost a compulsion, one I had no desire to resist.

We made it to the water's edge at the same time. I stopped uncertainly as I got my first real look at him rising out of the ocean like Poseidon himself, all muscles and wet, sleek, tanned skin.

He towered over me despite the fact that I stand close to six feet, without shoes. And he was gorgeous—so gorgeous that I couldn't help staring at him. Thank God he didn't seem to mind, and was in fact studying me right back.

He had a fallen-angel face that was as compelling as anything I had ever seen. Perfectly chiseled, amazingly crafted, he was so beautiful I almost wanted to reach out and touch him, just to ensure that I hadn't made him up in all my topsy-turvy angst.

His too-long black hair hung in watery clumps around that face and his smoky eyes watched me with a sexy intensity that belied his easy grace on the surfboard. He wore a strange necklace, a rawhide band with some sort of pouch attached to it, and his biceps were covered with oddly glowing black tattoo bands in an intricate pattern of symbols I had never seen before, and which certainly didn't seem normal. It was a design that was echoed beneath his muscular pecs and—I saw when he dropped his board—across his broad shoulders as well. My fingers itched with the need to paint him.

Who was he and why had I never seen him out here before? A guy that surfed as well as he did would have to ride the waves a few hours every day to stay at the top of his game. This wasn't my normal beach, but I surfed here enough to recognize most of the hard-core wave riders.

"Hey," he said with a grin. "What are you doing out here? It's pretty crazy today."

My heart stuttered. "That's what I was going to ask you. Who tries to surf in this?"

He shrugged good-naturedly. "Someone who knows what he's doing."

"Or someone with a death wish. You could have died out there!" I couldn't believe the words coming out of my mouth, or the shrewish tone they were delivered in. What was wrong with me?

"I started out before it got this bad. I wasn't expecting it." He shivered and it registered for the first time that he wasn't wearing a wet suit.

"I'm sorry. You must be freezing." I stepped back to let him pass, but he didn't move, just stared at me with those intense eyes that made me both fluttery and strangely relaxed at the same time.

"I'm cool."

"Don't you want to get out of the rain?"

"I like water. Don't you?"

My stomach somersaulted, though I didn't know if it was because of the knowing way he'd asked the question or because part of me wondered how his lips would feel against mine. I think it was probably a combination of both.

Mark, I reminded myself, as I took one giant mental step back. Despite our earlier fight, I was pretty sure he wouldn't appreciate me ogling some other surfer. Especially one who looked like this.

The relaxed feeling left as easily as it had come.

"Hey, are you okay?"

"I'm fine." Why did people keep asking me that? Did I really look so bad?

His voice was gravel and salt water and warm, sweet syrup combined when he said, "Your lips are blue and you're soaked to the skin. But other than that, you look great."

He'd answered my question so casually that it took me a minute to realize I hadn't actually said it aloud. I did freak out then, stumbling away from him like he'd suddenly grown six-inch fangs.

"I need to go."

"Okay." He glanced toward the road. "Is that your car up there?"

"Yes." I slipped my hand into my pocket, prepared to dial 911 for entirely different reasons this time.

"I'll walk you up—the rocks around here get pretty slippery in the rain."

I should have protested. I mean, I didn't know this guy at all—and no matter what he said, he wasn't from around here. He could be a crazed serial killer who picked his victims from isolated beaches. But the second he touched my elbow, a strange warmth spread through me and I found myself walking with him despite the voice in my head screaming no, no, no!

He helped me up the slope I had stumbled down earlier, his support making the ascent much easier than it should have been. I glanced at him from beneath my lashes, then stared, transfixed, at the way his muscles bunched and flexed as he moved.

What was wrong with me, I wondered again. It wasn't like I'd never seen a muscled-out guy before. I mean, Mark was pretty well built—as were Logan and Bach and the others. They all had six-packs and rock-solid biceps, so what was so special about *this* guy?

Why was he having such an odd effect on me?

When we got to the top, he pulled his hand away from my arm, and the comfortable warmth immediately dissipated, leaving me cold.

Lost.

And strangely uncertain.

Despite the riot of feelings rocketing through me, I made no move for the safety of my car. I just stood there, watching him watch me and wondering what was supposed to happen next.

"It was nice meeting you . . ." His voice trailed off questioningly.

"Tempest. My name is Tempest."

"And I'm Kona."

Kona. I turned the word over in my head. "You're Hawaiian?"

"Something like that," he said with a smile.

"Samoan?" My dad had taken us on a tour of the Pacific Islands during last year's summer vacation. I had loved every part of it, especially the crystal-clear water and glassy waves.

"I'm a little bit of everything—I don't really try to label it."

I flushed. "Sorry. I didn't mean to insult you. I went to a bunch of the islands last year and really loved them. The people were fabulous."

"I wasn't insulted." He reached for my hand this time, stroked the inside of my wrist with his thumb. Normally I would have taken a swing at any guy besides Mark who'd touched me like that, but there was something compelling about Kona, something that made his touch feel safe instead of threatening. "Which one was your favorite?"

The feel of his skin sliding against mine had my breath catching in my throat. I tried to answer the question, but the string of words that had come out of his mouth made no sense to my oversexed brain. "What?"

"The islands? Which one did you like?"

"All of them." I told myself to pull my hand away, but once again my body and my mind weren't on the same wavelength. Only this time, the lack of communication didn't seem so bad. "Each one had something different. But I guess I liked Fiji the best. Tahiti and Bora Bora were so crowded."

"Wow, you really made the rounds."

"My dad was a professional surfer for years. Every summer we go someplace we can catch good waves." Someplace where we might spot my mother, but I didn't tell Kona that part. My dad's little obsession was no one else's business.

"That's cool. You're pretty lucky."

His words snapped me out of whatever weird trance I'd been in since I'd first seen him—with my loss of humanity looming over me like Godzilla over Tokyo, I felt anything but lucky.

I pulled out my cell phone, pretended like I cared about the time. "I've gotta go."

"What's the matter? You turn into a pumpkin at twelve twenty-five?"

"How'd you know what time it was?" I looked him over—the only thing he was wearing was a pair of red and white board shorts, no watch or cell phone in sight.

"You didn't answer my question."

"You didn't answer mine."

"It's a gift."

"What is? The time thing or the dodging questions?"

"Both." Kona smirked a little.

I couldn't decide whether he was laughing at me or not. My spine stiffened at the thought and I pulled away, digging my keys out of my back pocket where I'd shoved them. "Anyway, thanks for the help up. Maybe I'll see you around sometime."

His amusement grew more pronounced at my obvious brush-off. "I think you can count on seeing me again, Tempest."

His words had me flushed all over again, but for different reasons this time. Which was completely ridiculous. I cared about Mark. I wasn't looking for something—or somebody—new.

Still, when Kona turned away and started walking down the road in the opposite direction, I called after him. "Hey!"

He turned, one eyebrow raised inquisitively.

"Where's your car?"

"I like to walk."

"It's raining." God, I sounded so lame. But it sounded worse to say what I was really thinking, that some reckless driver like myself could come barreling around one of the curves at any minute and wipe him out.

My lameness didn't seem to bother him, as he walked a couple of steps back toward me. "It would be raining whether I had a car or not." He glanced at the still-pouring sky. "But you be careful. The roads are slick."

"Do you need—" I bit the words off, horrified at the fact that I had almost offered some guy I didn't know a ride. Where was my sense of self-preservation?

He just waved and started back down the road.

"Kona!" I called after him again. This time he didn't turn around, didn't even pause in his trek up the sleek, treacherous road.

I watched him for a minute, two, until the rain made it harder and harder to see. Blinking rapidly, I rubbed the water out of my eyes, wanting one more clear picture of him for my mental scrapbook. But when I looked again, he was gone. I narrowed my eyes, looked for that telltale flash of red. There was nothing—he had disappeared as if he had never been.

It wasn't until I was in my car, fumbling with the controls for my heater, that I realized the whole time he'd been touching me, I hadn't felt the cold.

Chapter 5

That night, and every other night for the rest of the week, I had strange dreams. Each one started out the same way. I was surfing a really wicked barrel and doing a hella good job of it. I was right in the center of the glass house and there was water all around me—above my head, below my board, on either side of me. Only the path in front of and behind me was clear.

I rode the tube all the way in and was having a really great time doing it, but instead of ducking out like my dad had taught me, I got caught inside as it crashed around me. I tried to find my way out, tried to get back to shore, but the water kept pulling me down—deeper and deeper below the surface.

I didn't need a degree—or three—in psychology to know that if I told anyone about the dream, they would say it was a by-product of my near-drowning experience. And they'd probably be right. Except, and this was the kicker, even if the dream was partially because I'd almost drowned, it was also about a lot more.

Just how much more was what had me staring at the ceiling in the middle of every night, willing myself not to sleep. Of course, every night I eventually lost the battle and was sucked, not just below the surface, but into a world I had never let myself imagine.

My mother was there, as were any number of other mermaids—and Kona. They darted in between wreckages of old planes and ships on the ocean floor, played with colorful schools of fish and with each other, built towering castles of coral and sand.

In general, it should have been a reassuring dream, a promise of happiness to come if the worst happened and I lost my battle for humanity. But underlying all the bright colors and laughter was a darkness that terrified me. One that seemed to creep over the ocean floor, enveloping everyone and everything in its path.

I'd felt that darkness twice before: That long-ago night when I was ten and had come face-to-face with a creature I couldn't hope to comprehend. And last week, when I'd fallen off my surfboard and nearly drowned.

That I was feeling it again now, when so much was on the line, made me wary—even in my sleep. The fact that Kona was somehow wrapped up in it—even in my subconscious—only made me more nervous.

I woke up at the same point in the dream every time, with my heart pounding too fast and inexplicable tears sliding down my cheeks. It was frightening as hell. Before this week started, I could count on one hand the number of times I'd cried since my mother left us, but these days it was like I had sprung a leak.

I hadn't had any more freaky incidences—while I was still freezing all the time, my tail hadn't come back. And nothing new had occurred. If it weren't for the gills that refused to go away, I could almost convince myself that everything that had happened recently was just part and parcel of my recurring nightmare.

But the gills *were* there, and anticipating something else happening—something worse—was like waiting for the other shoe to drop at any time. Was there any wonder, then, that I wasn't sleeping much? Or that I was walking around jumping at shadows?

"Hey, Tempest," my dad called. "Mark's here. He wants to know if you're going out with them today."

A week ago, Mark wouldn't even have had to ask—I would have been waiting outside for him, board in hand. But the tension between us still hadn't played out—neither of us had been willing to back down—and we hadn't spent much time together the last few days. Still, he'd stopped by every morning for the last five days, even though I'd turned him away each time.

My body longed for the ocean, but for once my brain was firmly in control. And there was no way I was going back in that water and risking becoming a mermaid once and for all.

"Tempest?" my dad called again.

"Tell him I'm sick."

The door opened. "*Are* you sick?" My dad's face was concerned as he looked me over.

"No."

"Oh." There was a long pause, followed by an even longer throat clearing. "Did you two have a fight?"

"No." Seeing as how Mark and I had avoided each other altogether for the last few days, fighting with him again hadn't really been an option.

"Did something else happen, then?"

61

My eyes shot to his. "What do you mean?"

"I don't know. You've been acting kind of strange lately and you look exhausted. I thought maybe . . ."

"Maybe what?"

"I know we haven't talked about this. That's my fault. But your birthday's in a few days and your mom's letter—"

"I don't want to think about that stupid letter." I climbed out of bed and smoothed the sheet and comforter back into place.

I didn't usually make my bed, so the fact that I was doing it today probably wasn't lost on my dad. But then, he'd never been as easy to fool as most of my friends' parents were. It probably came from all those years hanging out on the pro-surfing circuit, partying and chasing girls.

He always told me he'd never really been into the life, but I'd seen the old surfer magazines and looked through the scrapbooks my mom had kept from before I was born. In each of them, he was always right in the thick of things—usually with my mom. The weird thing, though, was how happy he looked in the pictures. How happy they both looked.

"I know you don't want to think about it, sweetheart. But we don't have a choice. Things are going to change soon. You can't hide forever."

"Nothing's going to change," I answered. I already mentioned that I was the queen of denial, didn't I?

He watched me for a minute, then crossed the room and pulled me in close for a hug. It was one of those strong, all-powerful hugs I remembered from my early childhood—the kind that smelled of salt water and Tommy cologne and made me feel incredibly safe.

Like a child, I clung to him for a second, trying to hang on to everything that I had right now. Trying to remind myself once and for all why I was going to resist the lure of the sea. Here on land I had my family and Mark and Brianne and Mickey and Logan. I had school and surfing, parties and painting. Art school and studying abroad.

What exactly did I have waiting for me out there anyway? A mother who hadn't cared enough to stick around—or to come back and help me through a transition I so totally didn't want to make?

Randomly, Kona's face rose in front of my eyes—intense and beautiful and full of an ancient knowledge I couldn't hope to understand. I hadn't seen him since he'd all but disappeared during the thunderstorm, but then it wasn't like I'd exactly been looking for him. I'd been avoiding the beach like I would a particularly nasty bit of flotsam.

That hadn't kept me from thinking about him, though, even when I was awake. The night before last I'd even looked up the origin of his name on one of those baby sites. I had been right—it was Hawaiian, and it meant "island wind" or "storm."

The name—and its meaning—seemed to fit him perfectly. Maybe too well. Like a powerful storm, he had disrupted my life from the moment I first saw him. His presence was an all-encompassing thing, until I felt almost like I was moving back and forth at his whim.

"Tempest. You can't hide from this."

My dad obviously didn't know me as well as he thought he did—if my transition was the thousand-pound purple gorilla in the room, then I was more than okay with pretending bananas didn't exist. "I won't be mermaid, Dad."

63

"How do you know that? You love the water—you have the most natural affinity for it that I've ever seen. You might very well have your mother's genes—"

"If I do, then that's all I have from her and genes aren't enough. You know what she said. I get to choose and I will *never* choose to be like her."

"Sweetheart." He tucked a strand of hair behind my ear. "You see everything in black and white. You always have. But life isn't like that."

I stood up, made a beeline for my closet. I couldn't stand to listen to him, didn't want to hear any more. It wasn't like I didn't know the lecture by heart—every time my mom came up I got the shades-of-gray speech. If I had to listen to it today, I just might lose my mind.

How could he be so understanding? She'd run out on him and my brothers and me like we were nothing more than a temporary family. One that stood in for the real thing while she experimented with life on land. In my book that was unforgivable, and I absolutely, positively would not become like her.

I refused to ever be that selfish.

Besides, how was my dad going to manage on his own? Working together we could barely keep up with Moku and his problems. How much worse would his disorders get—how much worse would *he* get—if I disappeared from his life as suddenly and completely as my mother had?

Yanking my favorite swimsuit off a shelf, I slammed into the bathroom. "Tell Mark I'll be out in five minutes." Anything was better than sitting here listening to my dad fumble for answers— let the ocean do its worst. I was strong enough to take it.

It was more like ten minutes by the time I had finally collected my board and made my way to the driveway, where Mark was waiting. He looked as good as ever, his shaggy blond hair almost obscuring his dark brown eyes from view. His midnight blue wet suit was rolled down so that it rode deliciously low on his hips, and if things had been better between us I would have gone straight for a lip-lock. As it was, I settled for a nod and an escort to the water.

He didn't say anything as we walked, just strolled along beside me as if we had all the time in the world. I didn't speak either, more because I didn't know how to reach out to him than because I didn't have anything to say. The problem wasn't that there was nothing to say, it was that there was too much and I didn't have a clue where to begin.

"I'm glad you came." The words were low, uncertain, and I could almost pretend I'd imagined them if not for the fact that he was staring at me with a million times more intensity than an early-morning dawn patrol.

"Me too. I've missed it."

"I've missed you."

My heart—and my resolve—melted. "Mark . . ."

"You don't have to say it back." But his smile was pained, the look in his eyes intense.

"I did miss you—a lot."

"So why'd you stay away?"

"I don't know. I've just been really busy." The lie stuck in my throat.

The look he shot me told me my lying skills hadn't improved in the last few days. "I totally understand if you're nervous about getting out there again. That spin would have shaken up any of us, Tempe."

"I'm not afraid of drowning." That at least was the truth. "I just haven't had a lot of time."

"That never stopped you before."

Exasperation curled through me. "I didn't come out here to get the third degree, Mark."

"You've avoided me for almost a week and now you jump down my throat when I try to talk to you? What's that about?"

"Nothing. I just want to surf, okay?"

His jaw clenched and I thought for sure we were in for a doozy of a fight—Mark and I weren't on-again, off-again for nothing—but he managed to swallow whatever objection he had. "Well, let's do it then."

I nodded, then braced myself before looking out to sea for the first time since leaving my house. Dawn was just beginning to streak through the inky darkness; its fingers of red and orange wound through the night sky like fancy ribbons. Everything inside me strained toward the water, and I yearned to paddle farther out than I'd ever been before. To just sink below the surface and get lost for all time.

That wasn't going to happen, though. I refused to let it, refused to want it no matter how my treacherous body seemed to feel. I would take this slow, and when it was time to head back to shore, I would do so.

"Hey, there's my girl." Logan slung a wet arm across my shoulders and I realized how late Mark and I were. The guys had already done at least one run.

"Actually, she's *my* girl." Mark's voice was teasing, but the look in his eyes was anything but.

"How's the water?" I ignored Mark, leaning into my friend with a grin. Being around Logan was like that—no matter how grumpy, sad, or pissed off you were, when he was around it was almost impossible not to smile. Even the discomfort of his arm against my sensitive skin was worth it.

"Dude, it's going off! Best conditions I've seen all week."

"Excellent."

"So, where you been?" He nudged me closer to the shallows.

"Busy."

"Too busy to surf?" He clutched his chest in mock horror. "Blasphemy, I say. Blasphemy!" His Australian accent made the word sound hilarious and I started to giggle. I couldn't help myself.

"I know," I answered, striving for deadpan. "It was a nightmare."

"I bet. Being landlocked is my personal idea of hell, you know." He glanced down. "New swimsuit?"

"It's the same one I wear almost every day."

"Then maybe it's you? Something looks different."

I glanced down in a hurry, horror-stricken at the idea of yet another change creeping up on me before I could prepare for it.

"She looks fine to me." This came from Mark, who rubbed a hand over my lower back in soothing circles as he eased me away from Logan.

Typical Mark. That was just one more reason we kept coming back to each other, despite the arguments and accusations. No matter how upset he was with me, he always had my back. And I always had his.

"It's probably the lack of ocean water," I joked. "Four days without it and I'm all dried out."

"So, does that mean you're ready to do this thing?"

"Absolutely."

"Last one in is a Barney!" Logan started toward the ocean at a dead run.

Mark and I took off after him, and by the time I reached the water I was laughing like a crazy woman. I couldn't help it—it just felt so good to be out there, doing what I loved, that I couldn't believe I'd let fear keep me away for the better part of a week.

The others joined in, and as we paddled out together it was like I'd never left.

"Yo, Scooter, what happened to you out there? Too busy worrying about your looks to catch a wave?" Bach called.

"You dropped in on me—it was back off or run you over."

"The day you can run me over, bro—"

"Shoulder hop me again and I'll show you what I can do."

"Oooh, I'm scared."

"You should be. I—"

"Are you two done yet?" This from Logan.

"Almost. Why?" Bach glanced back at him.

"Because you're about to get worked."

"What?" His head spun forward. "Oh crap!"

The wave crashed over him, spinning him surfboard over heels, and then we were all ducking through it or going over it—waiting on the monster wave we'd been watching from way back.

"Hey, Tempest, you ready?" Mark called.

"Never more." It was true—for this one moment, I felt great. My body was doing exactly what it was supposed to do and I could almost feel the wave beneath me.

"Here it comes!" yelled Scooter.

I watched as the guys took off, one after another, but still I waited. It didn't feel right yet, didn't feel—

Yes! There it was! I pushed up and it was magic—one of those rides where everything just comes together like it was meant to be. I found the sweet spot right off, and I swear it was like I was flying. And when I managed to pop a monster aerial, I really was flying for a few, perfect seconds. The guys roared in approval as I rode the wave all the way in—long after they had dropped out.

I reached shore before them, but I was alone less than a minute before Mark grabbed me in a gigantic bear hug and swung me around. "That was fantastic! You got crazy huge air."

"What can I say?" I laughed. "Some people got it—"

"And some people don't," said a voice behind me.

I froze at the interruption, every hair on my body standing straight up in red alert.

"Yo, man, how's it going?" Mark set me back on my feet and extended a friendly hand over my shoulder.

"It's going. Obviously not as well as it is for her, but it's going."

"No doubt. My girl's got mad skills."

"That she does."

I still hadn't turned around, and Mark was looking at me strangely, so I faked an interest in a make-believe ding on my surfboard.

"Hey, Tempe, I want you to meet this guy. He's been surfing with us the last couple of days and his skills are as crazy as yours."

His friend laughed, a low, warm chuckle that had my blood running hot and a bowling ball weighing down my stomach.

My joy at being in the water drained away as quickly as it had come and suddenly, I wanted to be anyplace but where I was.

But since the ground opening and swallowing me whole wasn't really a viable option, I braced myself and slowly turned to face the newcomer—already convinced of what I would see.

Sure enough, standing next to Mark with a grin as wide as the Pacific was a tall, bronzed, well-muscled guy with dark hair and wild, wicked eyes. The same guy who'd been haunting my dreams—and my nightmares—for the last four days.

"Tempest, this is Kona. Kona, my girl, Tempest."

"It's good to meet you," Kona said, tongue totally in cheek. "Mark has told me a lot about you."

He reached for my hand and as our fingers touched, I felt a jolt deep inside myself—as if the two halves of my world had just violently, irrevocably collided.

Chapter 6

I wanted to snatch my hand back.

Wanted to go on holding his hand forever.

Wanted . . . so much that I wasn't sure where to start or how to ask for what it was that I needed.

"Yeah. It's good to meet you too."

His thumb rubbed across the back of my hand, causing shivers to run up and down my spine like little windswept feathers. I braced for the pain I always felt when someone touched me these days, but there was none. Only a pleasure so intense that I wasn't sure how to handle it.

"So, are you ready to go again?" Mark asked, his eyes darting between us like we were players at a tennis match. I could see them darkening with suspicion, and I pulled at my hand, trying to get Kona to let it go before Mark turned all macho he-man on me.

Kona's fingers slowly released mine, but not without a final squeeze that had my breath catching in my throat. *How can this be happening?* I wondered crazily. More importantly, *why* was it happening? And why now, when I already had more than enough changes to focus on?

"Are you?" Kona's voice was a little raspier than it had been, his eyes just a little darker—as if the contact between us had affected him as well.

"Am I what?"

"Are you ready?"

The words hung in the air between us—trapped—and it was like he could see inside of me. Like he knew so much more than I did about . . . everything.

"Ummm—" Did I mention that I'm not the most articulate person at the best of times, and under pressure, my words dry up as completely as the desert during a sandstorm?

"Of course she's ready." Mark wrapped an arm around my shoulder, bringing me against his body, and for one irrational second I felt like a bone being pulled in different directions by two slavering, growling dogs. Except both of these guys still had smiles on their faces. "Right, Tempest?"

"Yeah, of course." I gave him the answer he wanted, but it was just another discernible lie. I wasn't ready to go into the ocean again, not with Kona watching every move I made. But Mark couldn't see inside my head and as he pulled me toward the water, pain ricocheted down my arms.

Again, I wondered at the differing sensations. Pain from Mark, the guy I was pretty sure I loved and who I felt secure around. Pleasure from Kona, the guy I didn't know how to respond to and who I certainly didn't trust.

Mark propelled me down the beach until the surf danced around my ankles and licked at me like a hundred tongues of fire. Something was coming, it seemed to tell me as it burned

72

where it normally soothed. Something big, and I couldn't hide from it anymore.

As if I had ever been able to.

We started paddling out, and within seconds Mark was ahead of me, his whipcord-lean body stretched out over his board like an offering to the surf gods. Normally I would be right there with him, pushing into the water—desperate for the next big wave— but instead I hung back, hesitant to push off with Kona so close.

I expected Kona to take off with Mark, but he stayed beside me, content to move with the ebb and flow of the waves instead of cutting his own way through them.

"What are you doing?" I whispered, when I was sure Mark was out of earshot.

"What do you mean?" He paddled closer until his board was nearly touching mine. It was a deliberate attempt at crowding and one I would normally have called anyone on, but today—with him—I let it go. I had more important things to worry about.

"Come on. You didn't just show up at this beach accidentally. You came for a reason."

"And what reason would that be, sweet Tempest?" He lifted one eyebrow in a way I found ridiculously hot.

"That's what I'm asking you!"

"That doesn't seem right." An unexpected swell came up, had both of us clutching our boards to keep from grubbing. "If you're going to assign dark intentions to me, I think you should be brave enough to admit to them."

"Can't you just once answer a question without dodging around it eighteen different ways?"

"Where's the fun in that?"

"See what I mean?" I glanced away from him, watched as the

wave began to set up. Panic, cold and clammy, raced down my spine as images of tumbling beneath the water bombarded me from all sides. "You never just tell the truth."

He studied me and for once there was no humor in his expression. "That's an interesting complaint coming from you, Tempest. Besides, the truth is a nebulous thing. If you get too much too quickly, it feels like the top of your head is blowing off."

"It feels like that already." I braced myself, prepared to push up.

"It's only going to get worse." He flexed his biceps and I realized that his tattoos looked like they were glowing, just as they had the first time I met him. There was something strange about them, that was for sure . . .

The observation had my stomach cramping up. "What does that mean?"

"What do you want it to mean?"

"You're doing it again."

"Doing what?

"Talking in circles."

His smile was wicked hot when he answered, his eyes pure silver, sexy and bottomless. "You want direct?" At my nod, he continued. "You'd better pay attention or it'll be my turn to fish you out from the deep."

"What—"

But he was already up, and I scrambled to follow suit before I got rolled. As the wave crested, I managed to stay on my board—barely—but it wasn't my most successful ride, by any means. I was too busy watching Kona ride the wave like he was born to do it.

Who is he? I wondered for at least the millionth time.

Friend or foe?

Mermaid or human . . . or something else entirely?

And perhaps most importantly, *what did he want from me?*

When I got back to shore, Mark was waiting—and so was Kona. "What was that?" Mark teased as he pulled me close. Too close. I forced myself not to struggle away from him.

"That was me doing my best impression of a Barney."

"Or your worst," Kona added. "Depending on how you look at it."

I ignored Kona, kept my gaze firmly on Mark. "I'm having trouble finding my sea legs these days."

"It's all good." Mark nodded toward the ocean. "You ready to go again?"

"I think I'll sit this one out." I settled onto the sand, my board next to me. "But you go ahead—I love to watch you surf."

"I'll wait with—"

"Go! I'm just going to hang for a few minutes and I'll do the next one with you."

"Come on, dude!" Bach's voice drifted back to us from where he stood in the shallows. "It's setting up."

I shoved Mark toward the water. "Seriously, go!" I waved at Kona. "And take him with you."

"I'll be right back." Mark dropped a quick kiss on my lips that felt more like a brand than a sign of affection, then hurtled down the beach toward the water, Kona hot on his heels.

It was a joy to watch them move in tandem—light and dark, security and danger. Familiar and . . . I didn't know how to end the thought as something about Kona felt even more comfortable than Mark, so I just let it go.

Right before they hit the water, Kona stopped. He said something to Mark I couldn't hear, then settled on the sand at the
water's edge. Why wasn't he going? Why had he chosen to hang
out on shore when he could be surfing?

Then he turned to me, pinned me with a look that had my
heart beating way too fast. It was a look that said everything and
nothing—a look that was irresistible because of the dichotomy.

Before I could figure out why I was doing it—or talk myself
out of it—I stood and headed toward him. It would be nice to
get my toes wet as I waited for Mark, I rationalized. That didn't
mean I had to talk to Kona at all. I could just—

He met me halfway and though he didn't touch me, I swear
I felt the slow skim of his fingers up my arm, over my shoulder,
down my back. It was like I was connected to him, and not just
physically. A part of me felt comfortable with him, like I could
lower my guard and let him see inside me in a way I never
could allow Mark.

I trembled even as I started to sweat in the cool morning air.

We settled on the sand without saying a word. Kona sat too
close to me and I let him—truthfully, I wasn't sure I wanted to
stop him. We weren't actually touching, but every breath he took
brought his shoulder within a hair's breadth of mine and I could
feel the heat radiating from him like a sun. Within a couple of
minutes I was toasty warm, the cold gone like it had never been.

"How are you doing, Tempest?" His words were quiet, his
voice low and sensual and anything but casual. I had to work to
keep my tongue in my mouth and my hands on my board even
as I realized he was looking for much more than a superficial
answer.

I refused to give it to him. Instead, I stiffened my weak spine and made like his voice—and the rest of him—had no effect on me. "I'm fine. Why?" I wouldn't turn toward him.

"Oh, I don't know. Maybe because you look like you could catch bullets with your teeth?"

"I always look like this."

"Poor Mark."

I did look at Kona then, pinning him with the glare I usually reserved for idiotic freshman boys who couldn't keep their hands to themselves. It had made more than a few cower in fear through the years.

Kona merely laughed. Hard.

It sounded like the ocean, like popcorn popping. Like happiness itself. I ground my teeth together so tightly that I swear I felt one of my right molars crack.

Why am I getting so upset? I wondered as I sprang to my feet and marched the last few yards to the water. It would have been a good exit if I hadn't tripped in the sand like a total frube.

He caught me before I could go down, and we stood there a long time, looking out to sea while the water—ice cold and soothing—tickled our toes. Finally, when I couldn't stand the tension for one second longer, I glanced at Kona, then froze at the picture he made. He looked different with the water touching him—less human, more magical.

Like he could take on an army and win.

The thought made my palms sweat, so I took a few more steps into the ocean, my muscles clenching so tightly that I worried briefly that I was going to cramp up.

Is he really glowing? I shot another look at him from beneath my lashes. No, of course not—it was just the sun shining off all that silky, raven black hair.

Then what? Something was different. Of this I was absolutely certain. "Are *you* okay?" I demanded, unconsciously echoing the question everyone had been asking me for the last five days.

"Yeah." His eyes smiled at me. "Why?"

"You look . . ." I stopped. What could I say that wouldn't sound totally lame?

"Yes?"

I didn't answer. Instead, I moved deeper, and the currents caught me—played tug-of-war. Pushed me closer to Kona then pulled me back. Again and again, until Mark shouted, "We're going again. Are you coming?"

His voice was strange, strained, and I realized I'd been paying far too much attention to Kona. I knew better—Mark had always been the jealous type, and obviously he'd reached his breaking point.

I couldn't help the way I responded to Kona, though—every inch of my body (and most of my concentration) was tuned toward him like he was a lightning rod. There didn't seem to be anything I could do about it.

"Are we, Tempest?"

My mouth was desert dry, so I just nodded.

"You bet!" Kona called back to Mark as he ran to shore to retrieve our boards. And then his hand was cupping my elbow, his strong, calloused fingers relaxed as he propelled me deeper into the surf.

The second he touched me that strange, tingling heat started again—warmth spreading through me, taking me over. Like a rogue wave—unexpected, frightening, dangerous.

But oh so exhilarating.

Pulling my elbow from his grasp, I tamped down on the feeling and pushed toward Mark, who was looking at me when he should have been looking at the wave about to take him out like a total newbie.

"Hey, watch out!" I called. "Mark!"

He just laughed and bodysurfed the thing—board and all. In that moment, his laugh was smooth, uncomplicated, beloved. I laughed with him.

It was either that or scream. Because the farther I got away from Kona—and the distraction he presented—the more I was feeling the elemental changes to my body. My chest was tight, the gills behind my ears straining to be immersed in the water. My skin, where the sun touched it, felt raw, and my whole body was one huge, vibrating guitar string. Waiting, just waiting, for the next note to be played.

I glanced down at the sea, watched as a wave stacked up. It was the one I wanted—a little swollen, a little out of control, a little too big for any sane person to catch.

It was perfect—especially since these days I was definitely on the shady side of sanity.

Pushing off, I rode my board the rest of the way, ignoring Mark's shouts and Logan's curses. My blood was humming in rhythm with the wave, my body literally quivering with excitement. As the wave continued to stack up, sea foam flew everywhere, hit me in the eyes, the mouth, the nose.

Don't let me wipe out, don't let me wipe out. The words were a mantra, running through my head again and again as I took off. If my legs wigged out this time, I had no idea what I'd do. No way Mark would buy another lame excuse, especially since we both knew I had no business surfing this wave. No one did.

"Breathe. Everything will be all right." Kona's voice was firm, solid. Something to hold on to in the raging maelstrom of the sea and my emotions.

I turned toward him, shocked that I could hear him from so far away, especially over the roar of the ocean. But when I looked, he wasn't speaking, wasn't even looking at me. For all intents and purposes, he was completely engrossed in finding the sweet spot of the wave we'd just dropped in on—something I should have been doing as well.

"Move forward a little or you'll miss it." Once again, I heard Kona's voice, felt the intensity behind the words. I followed his directions, focusing on the wave for the first time since I got out there. And of course, he was right—I needed to get going or I was going to end up wiping out again—this time from sheer stupidity.

For the next couple of minutes I forgot about my birthday, forgot about being mermaid, forgot about Kona, and just surfed the hell out of the wave. And when it was done, when we had both ridden the thing into shore (Kona making it even closer in than I could) I felt at peace for the first time in a very long time. Like my body belonged to me again.

Like everything was going to be okay.

Mark met me at shore and I let him pull me into a huge bear hug, concentrating on the feel of him against me, his breath sweet and warm and *normal* in my ear. "That was kick-ass!" he said, his lips skimming over my cheek and down my jaw.

"I know." I laughed up at him.

He pulled back with a grin, slung his arm around my shoulder, and propelled me up the beach toward home.

We were halfway there before I remembered. Stopping dead, I turned and searched the beach for Kona. He was nowhere to be found. "Where's Kona?" I demanded. I needed to thank him, needed to . . . I didn't know what I needed to do with him. But I burned with the need to see him again. To figure out how he'd managed to talk to me over the roar of the ocean.

"Why?" Mark said, his smile gone so fast it was like it had never been.

"I don't know. I just thought I'd—" I stopped, unsure of what to say, especially when confronted by the tension that had invaded Mark's body.

"He ducked out a few minutes ago," Logan said as he walked by on my right, saving me from having to come up with an answer for Mark.

"Did you see him go?"

He shot me a funny look. "No, but I don't think he sprouted wings and flew away, do you?"

Logan's words sparked the memory of when I'd first met Kona, when he'd all but vanished in front of me. Wings? Did I think he'd grown wings? Of course not.

But scales were a whole different story.

PART TWO

Take Off

❧

The cure for anything is salt water—
sweat, tears, or the sea.
ISAK DINESEN

Chapter 7

I looked down at the piece of pizza with the works and knew I couldn't eat a bite. Not tonight, not now, when my seventeenth birthday was a few short hours away. Shoving the plate back, I tried to act naturally when Mark gave me a concerned frown.

"What's wrong, Tempest? You've been acting funny all night."

"I'm not hungry."

He stared at me incredulously, and I understood his shock. For the last six months I'd been ravenous, eating everything I could get my hands on without ever gaining an ounce. Most girl-friends let their boyfriends have the last piece of pizza in the box, but with Mark and me it had been the other way around for a while now. Yet tonight, I couldn't even work up the will to eat one piece, let alone my usual four.

"Are you sick?"

"No." I snapped out the word, annoyed beyond measure with people asking me if I was okay or sick or upset or whatever.

Mark reared back at the ugly tone in my voice, a quick flash of hurt crossing his features before he could hide it. Right away

I felt like a bitch, particularly since I'd spent most of the last week thinking of another guy.

Thinking of Kona.

"I'm just hyped up, I guess," I said in a more even tone. "With my birthday tomorrow and everything."

Mark grasped the lifeline gratefully. "So, what do you think your dad's going to get you this year? It'll be hard to top the Brewer."

"I don't think he *can* top the Brewer—it's the best present I've ever gotten."

"Well, yeah. It's totally wicked."

That was one of the great things about having a boyfriend who was as obsessed with surfing as I was. Another guy might get bent out of shape that I liked my dad's gift better than his, but Mark understood.

In the surfing world, not much could top a custom-designed Brewer—not even the brand-new iPod Mark had gotten me last year when I'd lost mine in the ocean days before my birthday. He'd loaded it with all my favorite songs, had even programmed special playlists into it for me. It had been a perfect gift for me and I loved it—just not as much as my board.

Mark started on his third piece of pizza, and I glanced around the parlor we'd been going to for as long as we'd been dating. Tonight it looked a little different—the red-and-white-checked tablecloths were a little fuzzy, while the pizza- and Coke-shaped neon lamps on the windows were so bright they hurt my eyes. And the familiar smells—garlic and tomatoes and Italian spices mixed with the briny scent of the ocean—had me feeling a little sick.

Was it just my mind playing tricks on me or was something going on with my senses? Was the change starting to happen?

"You ready to go?"

Mark was staring at me with an unusual exasperation, and when I looked at the table I realized why. He'd finished the pizza and paid the check, all while I was taking a little side trip to la-la land.

I grabbed his hand and let him pull me to my feet. "Sorry I haven't been the best company lately," I murmured lamely as he guided me out of the restaurant.

"I'm getting used to it," came his cryptic reply.

"What does that mean?"

He shook his head. "I don't want to argue, Tempest."

"You could have fooled me." I felt like a jerk even as I said the words, but I couldn't pull them back. A part of me was spoiling for a fight and was really hoping that Mark would give it to me.

But he merely shook his head and started toward his bike, a tricked-out Ducati Streetfighter S that had been his seventeenth-birthday present. He loved the motorcycle, but I knew he'd trade it for my Brewer in a heartbeat.

"What movie do you want to see?" he asked.

"I picked last time."

"Yeah, but it's your birthday tomorrow. I figured I could be a gentleman and let you choose tonight."

"And then you get to choose the next two times, right?"

"Three actually. The offer comes with interest attached."

I laughed. "Of course it does."

He drove too fast, as usual, and we got to the theater in record time. I ended up choosing an action movie that I knew Mark had been anxious to see. There was nothing I really wanted to watch and anyway, it wasn't like I was going to be able to pay attention. It had taken all my effort to keep up my end of the conversation while we were in line.

As the movie raged around us with exploding buildings, car chases, and gunfights galore, I cuddled into Mark and simply concentrated on how good it felt to be curled up next to him, despite the prickles of pain caused by the brush of his hand on my bare skin. His arm was warm and comforting around my shoulders, his chest firm against the back of my shoulder. He smelled like pizza and the ocean and the cologne I had had made especially for him.

I never wanted the movie to end.

But the two hours flew when I wanted them to drag and after the mother of all fight scenes, the film ended with the good guys bloodied but victorious. If only things were as black and white in real life.

Mark drove us home slowly, and I tried to stay relaxed, but the closer we got to my house the more freaked out I got. It was eleven thirty. My birthday was less than one hour away.

Would I change, like Cinderella, as soon as the clock struck midnight? Or would it happen later, in the light of day?

Would I get a choice, like my mother had promised, or would the mermaid thing just happen?

"Tempest." Mark's voice was impatient and a little annoyed, and I realized we were parked in front of my house. He'd turned off his bike and was waiting for me to climb down. "Hello? Tempest?"

"What?"

"You did it again—I swear, you were a million miles away."

"Sorry." I was beginning to sound like a broken record.

"Do you want to go in, or walk by the beach for a little while?"

For the first time that I could remember, I didn't want to be near the water. The idea of walking on the sand and letting the ocean kiss my toes made me tremble—not now, not tonight. It had taken enough from me. The idea of it taking what might be my last moments with Mark was too much for me to handle—or accept.

"Let's go inside."

He seemed surprised by my answer, but he didn't argue. Instead, he waited for me to get off the bike, then followed, his arm around my shoulders as we walked toward the front door.

The proprietary way he held on to me was suddenly annoying, though I wasn't sure why. Usually I liked the way Mark was a total gentleman—he always held doors for me and let me go first, always made sure he was the closest to the curb when we were walking on the sidewalk. It made me feel good to know that he was thinking of me, but something about the way he was wrapped around me—like he was afraid I would run off— bothered me. The fact that his fears were justified only made the whole thing more irritating.

I wrenched my elbow from his grasp, then shouted "I'm home!" as soon as the door closed behind us. I had no doubt my dad was waiting up for me.

"Okay," came my dad's answer from his office at the top of the stairs. "Tempest—"

"Mark's here." I cut him off, not sure what he was going to say but certain it was about my birthday.

My dad poked out his head, still looking every bit the quint-essential surf bum despite the fact that he was almost forty-five years old and the head of a very successful surfing gear and clothing line.

"Oh, all right then." He gave me a meaningful look. "But come see me before you head up to bed."

"Sure."

I turned back to Mark, strangely unsure of what to do with my hands. Despite my annoyance, I wanted to wrap them around him, to hold him to me as tightly as I could until the clock struck midnight and whatever was going to happen, happened.

I settled for shoving them in my back pockets.

"Do you want a soda or something?" I asked into the suddenly awkward silence.

"Nah, I'm good." Mark stretched out on the sofa, like he usually did at my house, and I perched in the corner—as I usually did. I reached for the remote control, but he stopped me.

"Come here." Mark's eyes were heavy lidded, intense, and I felt an answering warmth start inside me. Scooting closer, I went willingly into his arms.

His breath was coming hard and fast as he skimmed his mouth over my forehead and down my cheeks to my mouth. "I love you, Tempest." He said the words against my lips, but I felt them in every part of me. His voice was soft, yet it held a con-viction I couldn't hope to argue with.

"Mark." I didn't know what to say, how to feel, with the intensity of his emotions laid out between us.

"It's okay. I know you're not sure you feel the same way. I just—"

In the hallway, the clock struck midnight. Heat worked its way through my body, a kind of sparkling warmth that lit me up from the inside. Was it the change or was it Mark? I didn't know and in those moments, I didn't care.

"I *do* love you. I love you so much, Mark." The words burst from me, and as soon as I said them I wondered why it had taken me so long to get them out. Mark was everything I wasn't—steady, sure, confident in himself and the world he lived in. I didn't deserve him, but I wanted him and everything he stood for. For whatever time my mother's legacy allowed me, I would take him.

I threw myself on top of him, suddenly unable to touch him enough. My hands skimmed over his shoulders, down his back, up his chest. I fumbled his T-shirt over the flat expanse of his stomach, relished the feel of his hot skin against my cold palms.

"Tempest!" He pulled me closer, glancing uneasily up the stairs as he did. "Your dad . . ."

I followed his gaze. The door to my dad's office was firmly shut and I knew he wouldn't bother me—at least not right now. Not on what might be my last night as a human.

"It's fine."

"I don't—"

"Kiss me." I didn't care if I was begging. "Please, Mark. Just kiss me."

And then he did, his mouth hungry and intense on my own. I wrapped my arms around his neck, plastered my body to his, and kissed him like the world was ending.

Kissed him like I would never get enough of him.

Kissed him and kissed him and kissed him until we both were hot and sweaty and more than a little breathless.

91

Mark pulled away first, his breath heavy and eyes dark. Setting me on the other side of the sofa, he reached into his jacket pocket and pulled out a flat, gold box. I was gratified to see that his hand was trembling when he handed it to me—that I wasn't the only one feeling out of control. I was so turned on and shaky that I felt like a snapper could not just knock me over, but bury me as well.

"What is it?" Was that my voice, I wondered wildly, all low and husky and sexy like that?

Mark's eyes darkened to almost black, and I realized that yes, I was the one who sounded like she'd just rolled out of bed.

"Open it and find out."

My fingers were clumsy as I fumbled the purple ribbon off the box. I didn't know what I was expecting, didn't know what I thought I'd see when I lifted the top. But nothing could have prepared me for what I found.

For a second, I thought the back of my head was going to blow straight off.

Shock ricocheted through me, had me dropping the box like it was a jellyfish about to sting.

Mark picked it up, looked down at the necklace inside, as if searching for what had set me off. "What's wrong? Don't you like it?"

What could I say? How could I not like it when any normal girl would be gushing like Old Faithful?

"Of course I do. It's beautiful."

And it was beautiful, absolutely stunning. I needed to reach for the box, needed to coo over the gift and let Mark fasten it around my neck. Needed to rush to a mirror and see how it looked.

But I could do none of that—not when I was shaking so violently I could barely hold it together. Not when my world felt like it had just caved in around me.

"Tempest?" Mark's voice was concerned. "I can get you something else. It's just that when I saw it, it made me think of you."

I looked down at the gold collar. It was designed to wrap around my neck like a lover's hand, the gold soft and supple and perfectly rendered so that the two ends almost met in front. One end was a beautifully crafted tail, dotted with purple and blue stones, which led into a flowing body that would wrap around my neck before the other end—which was a mermaid's face and long, ruby-encrusted hair—came to rest in the center of my chest.

"How could I not like it?" I whispered sickly, even as I reached for the box. "It's perfect."

I lifted my hair out of the way, let him secure the collar around my neck before dutifully crossing the room to look in the closest mirror. Mark followed, stopping behind me with his hands on my shoulders as we both gazed at my reflection.

"Wow!" he breathed. "It looks like it was made for you."

And it did. It really did. I stared at myself in the mirror and did my best not to scream.

I was afraid that once I started, I would never stop.

Chapter 8

❦

After assuring Mark I loved his gift, I walked him out to his bike and watched while he drove away. I knew he was confused, knew he'd expected to take up where we'd left off after he'd paused to give me my present, but the feel of the necklace hanging around my neck killed all of the heat he'd generated inside me.

The second he was out of sight, I ran upstairs and ripped the thing from my neck. I wasn't sure what bothered me more—that he saw through me well enough to see the mermaid part I thought I'd kept hidden, or that he'd been right: the mermaid *was* perfect for me—it looked absolutely fabulous around my neck. Like it was designed just for me.

I shuddered at the thought.

"Tempest." My dad opened my bedroom door a crack. "I wanted to talk to you for a few minutes."

"Not now, Dad."

"But we might not get another chance. I wanted you to know that I'll understand if you choose to go with your mother. I—"

"I won't." I walked over to stand in front of my mirror, started cataloging all the human attributes I still had.

"But if you do—"

"I won't!"

"Tempest, please, listen to me."

"I can't." I hated the tears that clogged my throat, but I couldn't stop them—any more than I could stop time from moving forward. "I can't think about it, Dad. I just can't."

He started to say something else, but must have thought better of it because in the end he merely nodded. "Okay."

"Okay."

His eyes met mine in the mirror. "Happy birthday, Tempest."

"Yeah," I choked out. "Thanks."

"I love you."

"I love you too."

I waited for the door to close behind him, then flung myself across my bed in a fit of rage. I didn't cry, not this time. The anger was too raw, too real, and for now I was all cried out.

A few minutes later my bedroom door opened again.

"Dad."

"I'm sorry. I can't just walk away and leave you in here when I know you're scared and miserable."

"I'm not—"

"Don't kid a kidder, sweetheart." He crossed to the bed and for the first time I realized he was balancing a tray with a teapot and two cups on it. He'd brought me hot chocolate—my favorite make-it-all-better drink from the time I was a little girl.

My heart cracked wide open and I threw myself at him, so hard I nearly knocked the tray right out of his hands.

He paused long enough to set down the chocolate and then his arms were around me, his chin resting on the top of my head as he squeezed me so hard I could barely breathe. But I didn't struggle—for now, the pressure felt more than good. It felt perfect.

"I don't want to go, Daddy. I don't want to go. I don't want—" My voice broke as he settled me on the bed and patted my back like he'd done when I was a little girl and had gotten hurt.

"Nobody's going to make you go anywhere, Tempest. You know that. Your mother said—"

I snorted. "Yeah, and she's just so reliable, isn't she?"

My dad sighed, long and deep like he was in pain, but he didn't say anything else. We sat there on the bed for long minutes, silent and still except for the rise and fall of our chests.

"Tempest, look at me."

I didn't want to, didn't want to see the disappointment and the pain in his eyes. But I knew that tone. My father didn't use it very often, but when he did, it meant he wouldn't tolerate disobedience. Reluctantly I raised my eyes to his.

"Being a mermaid isn't a punishment."

"Yes, it—"

"No, it isn't." He talked over my objection. "It's a gift, one that few people are ever granted."

"Yeah, well, they can take it back. I don't want it."

"You don't want it because you blame it for taking your mother."

"Like you don't?" The words burst from me. "She left you, left us, because of this thing."

"No. She left because there were things she had to do, things she couldn't do here on land. Things she had to be mermaid to accomplish."

"What kind of things?"

"Important things. Private things."

"Yeah, right. So private she couldn't even tell her husband and family about them? And you believe that?"

"I do."

I stared at him incredulously. "Why? She left you alone, with three kids to raise and no explanation. How can you believe in her?"

"Because I love her. And I trust her."

"That's bull."

His eyes narrowed dangerously. "Watch it, Tempest. She's still your mother—and my wife."

"Is she? Really? Then where is she? Because I thought a mom hung around. Thought a wife showed her husband her face occasionally."

For once my father was at a loss for words.

Finally, when I was sure there was nothing else to say, he murmured, "Maybe when the changes start to take place, she'll—"

My laugh was bitter. "I have *gills*, Dad. I grew a tail last week. I can barely stand to be touched and I'm so cold all the time I feel like I live in a freezer. I think the changes are already here."

"You didn't tell me."

I tried to ignore the hurt in his voice. "What was I supposed to say?"

"How about, 'Hey, Dad, something strange happened on the beach today'?" His eyes sparked with an unfamiliar fury.

"Like it's that easy."

"Why wouldn't it be? I thought we could talk about anything."

I looked away. "Not this."

"Why not this? Why not now? I've been trying to talk to you about it for weeks, months."

"Because you're not the one I'm supposed to talk to about this, remember? It's supposed to be *her*. She was supposed to come back for me. She promised to come back for me."

I was yelling now, the rage I'd kept bottled up inside for so long suddenly spewing out in all directions. "She promised to help me through this, no matter what I decided. And after everything she's done, everything that's happened, a part of me was stupid enough to believe that she would keep that promise."

I looked around the room wildly, held my arms up in an all-encompassing shrug. "But she's not here, is she? And I'm weak enough to still be hurt by that. You would've thought I'd have learned by now, but I guess I'm as stupid about her in my own way as you are in yours."

The words echoed in the room, and as soon as I'd said them I wanted to take them back. Would have done anything to take them back. Because my dad had aged ten years in the space of five minutes and that wasn't fair. I shouldn't be taking my anger out on him—he'd lost as much as anyone else in this whole miserable situation. Stood to lose more still, and yet he was behaving so much better than I was.

"I'm sorry."

He shook his head. "Don't be."

"But I am. You didn't deserve that—"

"Maybe I did." He stood up, walked over to the picture window that made up one whole wall of my bedroom. "I'm sorry,

Tempest. Really, really sorry. I know you love Mark and your brothers. I—"

"And you!" The words exploded from me.

"And me, of course. I also know you want to be a famous artist someday. And it stinks, absolutely stinks, that at seventeen you have to make this decision. Stinks even more that your mother might have been wrong and the decision might be taken out of your hands. I wasn't expecting that."

My laugh was sarcastic. "Neither was I."

"But not talking about it, worrying on your own, or worse, ignoring it, isn't going to make it go away."

"But I want it to go away." It was the cry of a little girl, one who wanted her father to fix everything, and it seemed to strike my dad as an arrow might, straight through the heart.

"God, Tempest, so do I. So do I." For the first time he had tears in his eyes and when he opened his arms, I went straight into them.

We stood there for a long time, but still it wasn't long enough. When he pulled away I wanted to grab on to him, to hold tight, and even though the pressure of his arm around my shoulder hurt like hell, I wanted to beg him not to let me go.

But that's what children did and no matter how I'd been acting, I wasn't a child—hadn't been since the day I'd woken up to find my mother had simply swum away from us, and our life together, like we were no more than a passing fancy.

"I don't know why your mother didn't keep her promise to you—or any of the ones she made to me before she left. All I know is that she loved you very much and if she's not here, there has to be a reason. If you don't have a choice in this mermaid thing, there has to be a reason.

"I don't have all the answers—or any answers, for that matter. Everything is more damn complicated than I ever imagined it would be, and you can't know how much I wish I could help you through this. How much I wish I could just fix this. But I can't and that kills me."

"That's why I didn't tell you. It's not your fault—"

"You're my daughter and you're hurting and I can't help you. Of course it's my fault."

"Tempest?"

We both turned at the interruption, to find a sleepy-looking Moku standing outside my doorway, looking in. I'd probably woken him with my shouting.

"Yeah, Mo?" I crossed to him.

"I woke up. Can I have a glass of water?"

"I'll take you, bud." My dad put an arm around him and started down the hall, but stopped before he reached the stairs. "Get some sleep, Tempest. We'll talk more in the morning."

"It won't change anything." Outside my bedroom, the clock in the hall struck one. "I'm running out of time."

"Hey, it's tomorrow," Mo piped up.

"It is," my dad agreed.

"Happy birthday, Tempest."

My throat swelled shut. "Thanks, bud," I choked out.

"What do you want for your birthday?" he asked as my dad steered him down the stairs.

I didn't answer him. I couldn't. Because I wanted too much and was deathly afraid that I didn't have a chance of getting any of it.

Chapter 9

After my dad left with Mo, I flopped on my bed and tried to block out his words. Tried to block out everything but the sound of the ocean. It didn't work. I listened as the two made their way back up a few minutes later. I heard my dad get Mo into bed, then tensed when his footfalls hesitated outside my room.

But he didn't knock this time, didn't come in, and I figured he was giving me a break. I was grateful; I knew that anything more would send me into emotional overload.

I had no idea how long I lay there, minutes ticking into hours while I watched the stars through the skylight in my bedroom ceiling. I counted them again and again, as I had any number of times in my life when I couldn't sleep.

Looked for constellations.

Made my own pictures.

Did anything and everything but think about the fact that my time was slowly winding down.

When I couldn't count the same stars one more time, I climbed out of bed. I glanced at my clock—it was almost four a.m. and the house was quiet. I thought about painting, but for the first time in my life couldn't work up the energy to put brush to canvas.

As I let myself into the hallway, the only sound was the ticking of my mother's grandfather clock. The rhythmic clicking grated on my nerves as I walked past it, and not for the first time I thought about how good it would feel to smash something into it. To break the glass and the gong and everything else—until there was nothing left of it.

Maybe then, my dad could move on.

Maybe then, we all could.

For years, the stupid clock had gonged at fifteen-minute intervals, ticking off the time my mom had been gone until I'd given up counting it in minutes or hours or days—eventually even weeks and months became too short to measure by.

Six years. My mother had walked out six years ago today and now things were coming full circle. Now I might end up just like her after all—no matter what choice I wanted to make.

I thought about raiding my father's medicine cabinet—and his supply of Ambien—but the idea of climbing back into bed and staring at the same stars for another three hours literally made me sick.

Instead, I took the stairs two at a time, grabbed a sweatshirt from the coat closet near the front door. Then I slipped out of the house and into the night.

Crossing the grass on bare feet, I absorbed the utter silence of my street. It was too early for the lawyers and doctors to be heading into the office, too early even for their spouses to be out for their three-mile jogs. Instead, the houses were locked up tight—heaters blaring and security systems engaged.

102

Up in the sky a full moon the color of a pure, sweet tropical pearl cast a glow over the trees, the only light besides the lone streetlamp at the end of the cul-de-sac. For a moment, I felt like the only person on earth.

Crossing the street, I ignored the gravel and small rocks that bit into my toes and heels until I could sink my feet into the blessed relief of cold winter sand.

I walked along the beach for a long time—right where the tide met the sand—unaware of time passing as the water tickled my toes. I played tag with the waves, tried to avoid the never-ending cycle of tides as they rolled in. I lost more times than I won.

I didn't have any firm destination in mind as I walked, but when I ended up a mile or so down the beach at my thinking rock, I wasn't surprised. I'd been coming here for six years, whenever life got to be too much for me and, jeez, did this week ever qualify as too much.

I climbed the craggy rock swiftly, my hands and feet finding familiar footholds in the rough crevices. Though I was fast, I was also careful—my legs and hips, even the back of my right hand bore numerous scars from the mistakes I'd made while climbing here in the past.

As I settled myself at the top of the rock, the ocean rumbled in a crazed cacophony, a perfect reflection of my mood. I looked out over the water I both loved and despised, praying for just a little bit of the peace I usually got when I was out here alone.

But there was no peace tonight. How could there be? The ocean throbbed and pulsed while the very air itself crackled with electricity.

I gazed out over the waves as I searched my very limited

knowledge base, trying to figure out how the hell to get out of the mess I was currently in. Things were happening so quickly that I couldn't find a way to stop them.

I didn't know how to stop them.

"No!" I screamed so loudly that my throat hurt. "No, no, no!" Again and again until my voice was hoarse and my throat raw.

The ocean seemed to pulse in and out in time with my screams, and I watched, fascinated, as wave after wave pounded the shore, each one bigger and harder than the one before.

It was great surfing weather. Dangerous, sure, if you didn't know what you were doing, but good nonetheless. For a minute, I longed for my board, the call of the ocean so strong that it was painful.

You don't need a board. The thought slipped in slyly. *You're a strong swimmer. Go on out there and see what you're really made of.*

Overhead, lightning crackled, followed closely by a burst of thunder that shook my rock and the ground beneath it.

Go ahead, the little voice at the back of my head whispered again. *You know you want to.*

And I did want to, so badly that I could almost taste it. That was the kicker in all of this—a part of me longed to give myself over to the violent water, a part that was getting harder and harder to deny.

What would it hurt? the voice urged. *A midnight swim, a chance to—*

I was off the rock before I knew what I was doing, heading toward the ocean with a single-minded purpose I couldn't imagine denying.

My gills ached. My lungs burned, blistered. My skin stung, itched, like a thousand wasps had gotten to me.

104

Yes, go. The voice was louder now, more insistent. Triumphant even. And I gave myself to it. Let it pull me to where I wanted to be anyway.

I walked a few steps closer to the water, the sand squishing beneath my toes.

You belong there. You need to be in the water, to feel it around you. Beneath you.

The water lapped at my ankles, my calves. I took another step, then another. Felt it on my knees, my thighs. The cold sting of it penetrated my near-trancelike state and I stopped, confused.

Just a little more, a few more steps. The voice was clearer now—ringing in my head, in my ears. Flowing through me until it was a drumbeat in my blood. Until it was all I could think about. All I could feel.

I took another step. Then another and another and another. The water was around my chest now and I was only going deep enough to—

"No!" Another voice, fainter and more frantic than the first. "Tempest, stop!"

Ignore him, said the first voice. *You've wasted enough time. Come to me. Come to your home.*

"Damn it, Tempest! I said stop!"

This time the voice was much closer and definitely masculine. Young, sexy, pissed off, and maybe even a little scared. I stopped, for the first time uncertain of my course.

What are you doing? screeched the first voice. *You can't stop now. You're almost there.*

Loud splashing came from behind me, and then strong hands were grabbing on to my shoulders, pulling me back against a warm, rock-hard chest.

"Damn it, Tempest." The voice was softer now, in my ear instead of my mind. "What are you doing out here?"

Shivers went down my back and every cell in my body went on red alert. I swear I could feel them knocking against each other in excitement as his arms locked even more tightly around me.

Kona. How could I not have recognized him sooner? Yet, even in the middle of all this, it was a shock to realize that Kona had been speaking inside my head, now and in the water the other day. Compared to the woman's voice, he sounded so normal, so human, that I had a hard time comprehending that he really might be something more.

"Tempest?" he prompted.

"I was walking." The words were stupid and only partially true, but my brain couldn't function with him so close and my new understanding echoing in my head.

"In the ocean?" he whispered against my ear. He was so close I could feel his breath—hot and cinnamon scented—against my neck and shoulder. He was breathing hard, his chest rising and falling rapidly as if he'd been running for a long time.

I looked down at the water we were both standing in, was shocked at how deep it was—and how turbulent. It had kicked up much more since I had first entered it, until it was thrashing and snapping around me like the hungriest of sea animals.

And it was cold, so cold that it seeped into my bones when I was normally impervious to its temperature.

I had the strange, disorienting feeling that if Kona hadn't been holding me I would be sucked under, washed away.

"I guess. I didn't think about it."

"Let's go back to shore."

I nodded. "Okay."

He kept a firm grip on me as he backed toward land. I glanced up at his face, was surprised at how angry he looked, at how his eyes constantly scanned the dark water.

My hands tightened on his arms and for the first time I realized how intimately we were connected—his arms firm bands around me as he pressed me, back to front, against him from shoulder to knee, as if he was afraid to let any space come between us.

Thunder boomed overhead; lightning lit up the sky, hitting around us like a particularly aggressive military strike. My heart started racing, my breath coming in quick, shallow pants that had nothing to do with exertion and everything to do with fear.

"What's going on?" I shouted to be heard over the storm's sudden escalation.

"Can't you feel it?"

"Feel what?"

But I didn't need him to answer, because just that suddenly, I *could* feel it. Fingers wrapping themselves around my ankles, waves pressing against us, forcing us out to sea when all we wanted was to find our way back to shore. An aura of doom—of hopelessness and helplessness—surrounded us, pressing in from every side.

What is the point? I wondered wildly. *What am I fighting to hang on to? Maybe I should just—*

Tempest! It was a harsh reprimand in my mind, delivered in Kona's voice as his arm tightened around me. *She's doing it. She wants you. Don't give in to her.*

107

"Who's doing what?" But I knew. It was a replay of that night six years ago, an almost exact replica of what had happened to me once before. Only this time I wouldn't escape as easily. I could feel her determination, and I had nearly walked straight into it—like a lamb to slaughter.

How could I have been so utterly moronic? She wasn't a nightmare, wasn't a voice in my head. She was real and I had almost fallen right into her trap.

Stop it! Again Kona's voice was in my head, slicing like broken glass. *Just trust me. Hang on for a few more minutes.*

He pulled me another couple of feet toward the sand. I tried to help, but my body was like lead, my feet incapable of moving on their own.

Not again! my frantic brain shouted. I couldn't be turning mermaid now when I so desperately needed to be human.

"Relax." This time he spoke the words aloud, instead of straight into my head. "That's the least of your troubles right now."

Kona moved back yet another foot, his grip on me never wavering. Only my chest moved with him. My feet stayed planted where they were.

"Come on, Tempest! You need to fight!"

"Fight what?" I screamed as I kicked out against invisible bonds. Alarm raked sharp claws down my spine, had me sobbing and bucking and twisting without even knowing what I was doing. "There's nothing to fight!"

"I told you—she wants you."

"*Who* wants me? For what?" They were the same questions I had asked years before, only to be told by my mother that I had gotten tangled in seaweed and imagined the rest.

I'd tried to believe her—for six long years, I'd tried to ignore what I knew was true. But I couldn't do that anymore. Not when I could feel the water witch's evil presence, seething just below the surface as she waited for me. I didn't know who she was or why I was important, but I did know that Kona was right. She wanted me.

Like my mother before him, Kona didn't answer my semi-hysterical inquiries. Instead, I could hear him chanting in some language I didn't understand. It was beautiful, rhythmic, and somehow brought the agitation I was feeling to a manageable level. Even better, it calmed the violent water. Not a lot, but enough for me to pull my legs free of the strange locks that bound me.

Kona seemed to sense my newfound freedom because he broke off chanting long enough to yell, "Run!"

And then we were thrashing through the water, him half carrying, half dragging me as I struggled to keep up with the crazy, breakneck speed he was setting.

It occurred to me, randomly, as we staggered onto the shore that it was inhuman for anyone to move as fast as he had in the water. But I didn't fight him as he pulled me all the way to the shelter of my rock, his body covering mine as the heavens bombarded us in a full-blown tantrum.

I lay there beneath the shelter of him for long minutes, panting up at the sky as I tried to piece together everything that had happened. But as it all hit me—the strange voice, the fact that Kona had spoken to me in my mind now for the second time, the greedy hands that had anchored me in the sea—I stiffened and yanked away from him.

Oblivious to the storm still blasting away at us, I leaped to my feet and asked the question that had been haunting me for over a week now, since that day in the rain when Kona had disappeared right in front of me. Since the day I had my first inkling that he was something more than human.

"Who the hell are you and what do you want from me?"

His eyes were steady and dark as magic as he stared back at me. "Are you sure you're ready for me to answer that?"

Chapter 10

His question hung in the air between us, a loaded gun ready to go off. Suddenly I *wasn't* sure I wanted the answers.

I wasn't sure of anything.

In less than two weeks my entire life had turned upside down, until normal was a world away and every day was just a little more messed up than the one that had come before it.

I stared at Kona and he looked so calm, so *composed* in the shadowy moonlight that for a second I doubted what I knew. Away from the water's frightening and alluring grip, I couldn't be certain I hadn't imagined the last few, panic-filled minutes. And yet, it had to have happened. Right? Otherwise I was just going nuts, a thought I couldn't bear to contemplate on top of everything else.

She wants you.

Kona's words echoed in my head. *Don't give in to her. She wants you.*

No, I hadn't imagined anything—not six years ago and not now. Something *had* been in that water and Kona knew exactly what it was. "Don't give in to what?" I demanded.

Kona's eyes grew wary, his face more closed off than it had ever been. "Let it go, Tempest."

"Don't do that." The words were loud, disjointed, but I couldn't help that. Violent shudders had begun racking my body, making my teeth clatter together and my body jerk. "Something was trying to drag me under. I know you felt it too."

He came forward, wrapped an arm around my shoulders, and pulled me into the shelter of his arms. He was big and broad and toasty warm—an electric blanket of heat seeping through the cold that had invaded every part of me. A small section of my brain wondered how he could feel so hot when the water and air were both frigid, but most of me was just grateful for the heat. For the comfort. It felt so right to be standing here, leaning against him as I absorbed his strength.

But how could that be? I barely knew Kona, no matter what it felt like. I had to remember that.

"The ocean around here is pretty unpredictable at night. The undertow—"

"I said, *don't!*" I shoved away from him, though it cost me. Devoid of his warmth, I suddenly felt twice as cold, twice as lost.

"I've been swimming in this ocean since I was a little girl. I know it better than anything else, and that was *not* an undertow."

"So what was it then?" He watched me curiously, as if waiting for me to figure things out on my own.

But I couldn't. Everything was too messed up and I didn't have enough of the puzzle pieces to be able to make a picture. "That's what I'm asking you! You come here, all dark and mysterious, acting like you have all the answers. But you won't tell me anything. I'm not an idiot, you know."

"I never said you were."

"Give me a break. You tried to convince me that what I felt out there was just the ocean."

"It's happened to you before."

His words cleaved through the air between us, reminding me of what I'd come out here to forget. I wanted to whine that he wasn't being fair, but figured that would make me sound like the idiot I'd just sworn I wasn't. Or even worse, a baby. Besides, he was right. I had nearly bought it—

"Hey, wait a minute. How do you know about that? I met you *after* I nearly drowned that day."

His eyebrows drew together and he was silent for a long time, as if searching for a believable answer. Finally, when the tension between us was as taut as a circus high wire, he muttered, "Mark must have told—"

"Stop lying to me!" I started down the beach, away from him.

"Tempest, wait!"

I ignored him, kept walking. I was too furious to listen—or to pay any attention to where I was going.

"Stop!" I heard his footsteps pounding up the beach behind me, but was totally unprepared for the hand that wrapped around my wrist and jerked me to a standstill.

My temper flared even more brightly as I struggled to free my arm from his inexorable but strangely painless grip. "You're going to want to let go of me."

"You're going in the wrong direction." He cast an uneasy glance down the beach. "Let me walk you home."

"I don't need a babysitter."

"I'm glad, because that's not the relationship I want with you."

For long seconds I couldn't think, my heart suddenly beating so fast I thought it just might take flight. I told myself it was stupid to get worked up over those words—especially since I was still so angry that I wanted to lay him out on the cold, waterlogged beach. But the warning didn't work. Hearing him admit that the strange feelings between us weren't all from my side did something to me.

I tried to take a breath, to swallow, but the inside of my mouth felt like I'd been sucking on cotton, and a barbell had taken up residence in my stomach. Finally, somehow, I forced myself to ask, "What kind of relationship do you want?"

His silver eyes were reproachful as he bent until his face was only inches from mine. "Come on, Tempest. I don't want to play those games."

The barbell grew heavier as my stomach clenched, but everything else about my body felt light, as if I would float away at any second. In the tension of the moment, and the closeness of his body to mine, I forgot about the strange force in the water. Forgot about my birthday. Forgot, even, about Mark.

"So what do you want?" I whispered, again.

His hands came up and tenderly cupped my face. And then he was so close I could feel the feathering of those impossibly long eyelashes against my cheek. My heart beat even faster and there was a roaring in my ears that had nothing to do with the ocean and everything to do with the riot of emotions twisting within me.

"You," he breathed tenderly, and the word brushed against

my parted lips. I sucked it inside me with my next inhalation, held it there in my mouth, in my lungs, as I waited for him to close the scant distance between his mouth and mine.

But he didn't move, didn't bridge that last inch that separated us. As I stood there waiting—trembling with anticipation and curiosity and more need than I would have imagined possible—it suddenly occurred to me that Kona wanted *me* to kiss *him*. He too was waiting.

I didn't think about all the reasons kissing him was a bad idea, didn't think about all the extra problems it would bring into my life. I couldn't. Not when every cell in my body strained toward him.

I kept my eyes open as I melted into Kona, letting my hands slide up his bare arms to circle his neck. And then I did it, leaned forward that last inch and brushed my lips against his.

For a moment, everything seemed to freeze—the wind, the rain, my heart. Even the ocean with its never-ending cycle of waves seemed to hold its breath as it watched us.

It obviously wasn't my first kiss, but it was so different from anything I'd ever experienced before that it might as well have been.

Kona's hands slid from my face into my hair, his fingers fisting in my wet curls as he kissed me again and again. Emotions rioted through me—joy, desire, fear, confusion—so many that I could barely process them as his mouth moved against mine. All I knew was that I was warm, hot even, and that kissing him was like swallowing the sun.

Then, just as suddenly as it had come, all that heat was gone. Kona wrenched himself away from me and stumbled several feet down the beach. We stared at each other, lips swelling, chests rising and falling rapidly, bodies yearning toward each other.

But now that he wasn't touching me, I remembered everything I had so conveniently forgotten. As Mark's face floated in front of my eyes, guilt ripped through me like a chain saw.

How could I have kissed Kona when I was with Mark?

How could I face Mark tomorrow, knowing that I had betrayed him?

More immediate, how could I face Kona now? Or myself?

The questions bombarded me—held my attention for precious seconds as I tried to swallow my guilt and embarrassment—so that I missed whatever it was that had Kona cupping a hand around my elbow and propelling me back up the beach toward home.

"I'm sorry." He ground out the words without looking at me.

I wanted to let him take the blame, but I couldn't. He'd given me the chance to say no, had given me an out, and I hadn't taken it. Instead, *I'd* kissed *him*.

"It's not your fault." I could feel my cheeks turning pink.

"Sure it is." We kept walking, his long legs eating up the sand so that I was forced to nearly run to keep up. More than once I would have stumbled if he hadn't been right there to hold me steady.

The storm kicked up another notch and behind me, the ocean thrashed and churned. Waves hit the sand with long, angry slaps that seemed to grow closer with each second that passed.

Kona's pace grew even faster and more than once, I started to say something. But a glance at the ocean had me stumbling along behind him. Suddenly putting distance between me and the Pacific didn't seem like such a bad thing.

As we walked, the sand clung to my toes and calves, its wet graininess like sandpaper chafing my too-sensitive skin. I didn't complain—the clenched fist of Kona's free hand spoke volumes—just went along with him until we were at the top of my driveway.

The storm died as suddenly as it had started.

In the glow of the lone streetlight, we faced each other. A part of me was horrified by what had just happened on the beach, but another part wanted nothing more than for Kona to kiss me again. No matter what I'd told myself this last week, I knew now that I'd been waiting for him to make a move from the first time I'd met him. Anticipating it, even.

I'd wondered what he would taste like, what his lips would feel like against mine. Now that I knew, it didn't make things easier between us—just more complicated.

"Don't go in the ocean at night, okay?"

Locked deep in thought, I took a minute to register his words. When I did, the annoyance came roaring back. One kiss didn't give him the right to tell me what to do. "Why not?"

"Tempest." He started to say something else, then shook his head regretfully. "Just trust me, okay?"

"How can I trust you when you won't be honest with me?"

"I'm being as honest as I can be."

"That's bull. You're being as honest as you want to be. It's not the same thing."

His eyes grew sad. "Maybe you're right." He turned to go.

"Why can't you just tell me?" It was my turn to reach out for him, to grab his hand.

"Because you're not ready for the answers yet."

"I'm not ready for a lot of things, but it doesn't seem like I'm

117

getting a choice here. When we were out there, you said 'she.' Told me not to give in to 'her.' What did you mean?"

"I misspoke." His voice was low, with a dangerous edge I had never heard from him before, but I was too pissed off to heed the warning.

"Yeah, right." I dropped the hand I was holding, stumbled up the walk toward my house. Was this what Mark felt like when I put him off without answering his questions? I hoped not, because it totally sucked. "Go away, Kona."

"Don't go into the ocean in the dark, Tempest. I mean it."

I whirled to face him. "Don't tell me what to do. If you won't be honest with me, you don't have the right to expect *anything* from me."

He made an exasperated sound, shoved a hand through his too-long hair, started to speak, then changed his mind as he glared at me. His jaw was clenched, the muscles of his shoulders and arms tight and well defined. Good—let him be frustrated for a while. It bugged the hell out of me that I felt so connected to him, felt so much for him, when he obviously didn't feel the same way about me.

He didn't say another word for long seconds and neither did I. Instead, I climbed the steps leading up to my front porch, sat on the top one, and waited for him to calm down.

It didn't take as long as I thought it would, and then he was sitting next to me, his thigh grazing mine with each throbbing beat of his heart. Electricity shot through me with each innocent brush of his skin against my own, and I told myself to scoot away, to put some distance between us, but I couldn't. The connection—when I was so adrift—felt too good.

"When I was young, my mother used to tell me fantastic stories, filled with faraway places and the most amazing magic." His voice was hushed, his eyes focused straight ahead as he continued. "There were always strange creatures and awe-inspiring bravery. Always weird things happening and ferocious battles between good and evil."

My whole body, my entire being, yearned toward him like a puppet on a string, dangling helplessly. Waiting for his next words and whatever truth they would bring.

"There was always a brave warrior who fought valiantly, suffering terrible wounds to save his people—and, of course"—he shot me a grin—"the beautiful maiden who depended on him. There was blood and swordplay, spells and magic wands. Destruction and salvation." The smile faded and he turned to me. "And there was always the evil sea witch and the creatures who followed her—creatures who would do anything for her, *kill* anyone for her."

"Are you telling me that's what I felt out there? A sea witch?" I tried to tell myself I was crazy for even thinking about believing him, but everything that had happened tonight seemed to prove that he was telling the truth.

"She's powerful, Tempest, and she wants you. She needs you. But you can't give in to her."

"Of course I won't give in to her—I don't even know who she is or what she wants!" Yet the insidious voice was still there in the back of my head, hissing at me, demanding that I find my way back to her.

"In my mother's stories, the warrior always won. He rescued the princess and they lived happily ever after."

"Like a fairy tale."

"Exactly. But, like fairy tales, her stories were just make-believe, Tempest. Just made-up things to delight a young boy. The truth is—" He paused, and the look in his eyes was so vulnerable, so filled with sorrow and regret that it had my breath hitching in my throat. I found myself reaching for his hand and squeezing, wanting to chase away the demons that seemed to lurk right below his surface.

"The truth is," he repeated, "that sometimes—most of the time—evil wins. The warrior dies and the beautiful maiden ends up suffering a fate worse than any she ever imagined."

He blinked, and it was as if a shutter came down and blacked out his thoughts. He focused on me again as he ran his hand gently down the side of my face. His fingers were rough with calluses, and my heart, which had jumped to my throat at his words, fluttered like the wings of a captured bird.

"What are you, Kona? Are you a mer—" I paused. What were male mermaids called, anyway?

He laughed, but it wasn't a happy sound. "Do I look like a merman to you?"

I was glad it was dark, so he couldn't see me blush. "I don't know what mermen look like."

"They don't look like me." He paused. "You know, mermaids aren't the only half-human creatures under the sea, Tempest. There are all kinds of other beings down there. I'm one of those."

"So, what—"

"I think I've spilled enough secrets tonight, seeing as how I'm forbidden to talk to you about most of this anyway—at least until you make a decision one way or the other."

"That's not fair!"

"Wow, that's original," he teased, though his levity quickly faded into seriousness. "You need to stay away from the ocean at night, Tempest. I mean it. It isn't safe—not for you."

He leaned over and brushed his lips across my cheek in a kiss that was somehow sweeter and a million times more powerful than what had happened between us on the beach.

And then he was standing, bounding down the steps two at a time. "I'll see you around," he called over his shoulder as he headed down the driveway.

"Kona!" I clambered to my feet, everything he'd said—and hadn't said—whirling around in my brain. It combined with the strange, new emotions for him that were unfolding within me. Emotions that went a lot deeper than I had originally wanted to give them credit for.

He stopped, but didn't turn around. "What?"

"My dad's throwing me a birthday party tomorrow night. You want to come?" I issued the invitation impulsively, knowing only that I wanted to see him again.

He paused, seemed to consider the invite. "Yeah. I do."

"Eight o'clock. Here."

"Sounds good."

I almost let him leave, but there was one more thing I needed to say. It had been burning inside of me since he'd told me about his mother's stories.

"Warriors aren't the only ones who can kick a little ass, you know. Some maidens can more than hold their own."

"That's what I'm counting on, Tempest. That's what we're all counting on." And then he was gone, blending into the night

121

beyond my driveway no matter how hard I strained to keep him in view. But he had disappeared again, like he had twice before, leaving nothing behind save the tingling of my cheek where his rough fingers had tenderly stroked me.

Chapter 11

❧

I sat on the porch for a long time, Kona's words playing and replaying in my mind like a track from my favorite playlist. Eventually night lifted and fingers of pink and purple began streaking their way across the sky.

It was officially my birthday—I was seventeen.

I didn't feel any different than I had before, and as I bounded into the house to check my reflection in the entryway mirror, I was excited to realize I didn't look any different either. I hadn't grown a long tail overnight or anything else that would make me stand out in a crowd.

Feeling suddenly optimistic, I stroked a finger over the delicate skin behind my ears. Maybe, since I'd obviously made my choice, they would have disappeared. No, the gills were still there. Though I tried to keep myself from obsessing, I couldn't help wondering if they were permanent. A reminder of just what I'd turned my back on.

I heard a couple of pots clang together in the kitchen and with a last reassuring glance in the mirror, headed that way to see what my brothers were up to.

But it wasn't the boys making an early-morning raid on the fridge. It was my father. Dressed in yet another pair of board shorts and a surfing T-shirt, his blond hair flopping over his eyes, he looked more like one of my friends than he did a man who was pushing middle age. Unless, of course, you looked past the camouflage and got a good look in those eyes, at the sadness he couldn't hide.

I had just opened my mouth to ask what he was doing when he glanced up and saw me. "Sorry," he muttered sheepishly as he started cracking eggs in a bowl. "I wanted to make you breakfast for your birthday. I didn't mean to wake . . ." His voice trailed off as he got a good look at my wet hair and sand-encrusted clothes.

"Early morning swim?" he asked dryly. "Or late night?"

"I couldn't sleep." I circled the center island, grabbed a loaf of bread out of the pantry, and fed four slices into the toaster.

"Me neither. I'm surprised I didn't hear you go out."

"I was quiet." I watched as he flicked a pat of butter into the hot pan, listened to the familiar sizzle as my stomach growled. *What do mermaids eat?* I wondered absently. It wasn't like they could fire up the stove at a hundred feet below sea level.

"Next time, come get me." He expertly beat the eggs, then slid them into the frying pan. "We'll go out together."

I couldn't stop my quick jerk of surprise. "You would have gone out with me? But you don't like to sur—" I bit my lip to keep from blurting out anything else.

He turned from where he was scrambling the eggs to look at me with a frown. "Is that what you think? That I don't *like* to surf anymore? If so, you couldn't be more wrong."

124

I didn't answer, my head ringing with the conviction behind those words. In the silence that stretched between us, the toaster sounded like a shot as it expelled the bread. Because I couldn't think of what to say—or do—I pulled out the toast and started buttering it, concentrating on the task like it was life or death.

"Tempest? Answer me."

I shrugged, uncomfortable. Navigating the murky waters of my parents' relationship always made me feel like a boat with a slow leak. "You don't go out much anymore."

"You're right, I don't." He glanced at the Pacific. "I should probably fix that."

"I didn't mean—"

"I know." He remembered the eggs just in time and gave them a final stir before dividing them onto two plates. He carried them to the table, then gestured for me to sit.

"You're right. For a while, I didn't like the water."

"Because it took Mom. I know, I get it."

His eyes were bottomless as they met mine across the breakfast table. "No, Tempest. Not because it took your mom from me—how could it? The ocean, as powerful and beautiful as it is, is still just an inanimate object. It couldn't take her even if it wanted to. It was her choice. She left—it didn't take her."

The toast was sawdust in my mouth and I struggled to swallow past the lump in my throat. We were finally going to do it, finally going to talk about my mother. I couldn't get enough moisture in my mouth to choke down the bread and had to rush to the fridge for a glass of water.

When I could finally speak, I asked, "Then why? Why did you stop surfing? Why did you change so much when she left?

It was like one day you were this super-cool dad who showed me a new trick every week and then suddenly you were just gone. I mean, you were here, but you weren't the same."

It hurt to say the words, hurt more to see them rain down on my father like blows. But now that I'd started, I couldn't stop. It was like a giant floodgate had opened and everything inside of me was just rushing out.

"You went from living in the ocean to barely looking at it, unless the boys and I begged you to take us out. Even now, I see you glancing out at it and you look so angry, so full of hate."

"Not hate, Tempest. Sadness. Because I understand why your mother left. I didn't like it. I wanted her to stay as much, if not more, than I want you to stay. Hell, I was even willing to share her—she could spend half her time out there and half her time here."

It was the first I'd heard of it, the first time I realized something like that might be possible. Frissons of electricity ran down my spine at the thought, my brain adjusting to the idea that being a mermaid wasn't all or nothing.

"Is that possible?" I demanded. "And if so, why didn't she do that? Why didn't she decide to stay with us at least part of the time?" I held my breath, my whole being waiting for his answer. Not just as an answer to my own predicament, but also as an answer to why my mother had abandoned us. Why she'd turned her back on the four of us, like we were a mistake she couldn't wait to get away from.

"I don't know, baby. I guess it's more complicated than that. I mean, for a while that's what I really thought she was going to do. Before she left, she told me she'd be back if she could. I believed her, spent years waiting for her." He shoved away from the table, went to stand next to the same window I liked to look out of and brood. "A part of me is still waiting for her to keep that promise."

It was back, that sense of betrayal that welled up inside of me whenever I spent too much time thinking about my mother. She'd promised me she'd come back too, promised that she'd see me through the change—or the rejection of it. But here it was, my seventeenth birthday, and she was nowhere in sight. It hurt to realize, even after everything she'd done, that I'd been waiting for her as much as my father had.

But enough was enough. No more waiting. No more wondering. No more mermaid stuff. I'd made my choice and I was done with it—no matter what Kona said or didn't say. I wasn't going to waste one more minute thinking of it—or my mother.

Still, the idea of turning mermaid not being all or nothing—it was hard to wrap my mind around it after all this time. Harder still to ignore it.

Blocking it out for a while, I said, "I've decided what I want for my birthday, Dad."

He turned to me absently, his eyes a million miles away. "What, Tempe?"

"I want you to come surfing with me, like you used to. Just you and me and the water."

"Right now?"

I glanced out at the ocean, thought of Kona's warning and the weird force I'd felt out there only a few hours before. But it was daylight now and my dad looked like he was considering my request. I wasn't going to let anything get in the way of a chance to surf with my father again, especially not something as stupid as fear.

"Yeah. Right now."

My father grinned, and for the first time in a long time it reached his eyes. "First one changed and in the garage picks the ice cream." It was an old ritual, so old I'd nearly forgotten it. I bolted for the door, my father hot on my heels.

Maybe turning seventeen was going to be all right after all.

Word spread quickly that Bobby Maguire was out and about, and soon the beach was crowded with early morning surfers wanting a glimpse of their hero. Even Brianne and Mickey made it down and mingled with the guys as they watched my father surf.

I didn't blame any of them, even as it bugged me that my time with my father was being encroached on. Watching him, even after all this time, was like watching poetry in motion. He was born to ride the waves—even the ocean seemed to know this.

"You ready, baby?" he asked as we paddled out for the fifth time, Mark, Logan, and Bach hot on our tails.

"You bet." We'd already ridden the perfect tube, not to mention two bombs that had felled every other surfer who'd tried them. The morning was perfect.

I was happy for the first time in a long time—and from the looks of it, so was my dad. I could keep this up all day.

As I took off, a couple of seconds behind my father, I felt a powerful burning across my shoulders, as if the salt water had leaked into an open, aching wound. Pain flashed up my neck and down my back, its intensity catching me off guard. I bobbled, nearly fell off my board—a behavior that was becoming irritatingly habitual—but at the last minute managed to right myself.

Still, I'd lost the sweet spot and spent the rest of the time following my father—who'd nailed it like the pro he was—back to shore. As soon as we hit the beach, he was surrounded by a bunch of hopefuls, including some of my friends. He looked uncomfortable but not unwilling as he answered question after question.

Shaking my head in amused disbelief, I headed up the beach for my towel. My back was still on fire and I wanted to dry off—then get to a mirror and see if I'd somehow brushed up against something in the water that had cut or stung me.

Mark grabbed me before I got to my stuff, his arms going around my waist as he lifted me off the ground in an exuberant bear hug. I squealed and laughed, hanging on to his shoulders for dear life as he shook me like a rag doll.

"Put me down!" I demanded, but I was laughing so hard even I couldn't understand the words coming out of my mouth. "Mark!"

With a grin, he did as I asked, but took his time sliding my body down his own. As he wrapped his arms around me and held me close, I pressed my ear to his chest and hung on tight. Guilt nearly suffocated me when I realized that I'd been kissing Kona less than four hours before. I told myself to let Mark go, that I didn't deserve his affection.

Yet he felt so good, so *normal*, that I held on anyway. The beat of his heart beneath my ear soothed me like nothing else could.

I knew I should tell him about what had happened, but I couldn't. Too many things were changing too fast. I couldn't give up Mark too, and with his jealousy, I knew he'd never be able to get past it if he knew.

"Happy birthday, Tempest," he whispered to me as his lips brushed over my hair and down my cheek.

"Thanks." I held on tighter, afraid he would pull away.

He didn't, seemingly as content to hold me as I was to be held. And as the salt water dried, the burning in my back weakened to a dull throb that was easy to ignore. At least until Brianne yelled "Get a room" to us.

I pulled away from Mark, then froze as I saw Kona chatting smoothly with my father about ten yards away.

What is he doing here? I felt panicked. He should be at home, asleep. Or at least out in Del Mar, riding the monster waves up there. Anywhere but down here on *my* beach, reminding me of all my crazy, mixed-up feelings.

When he and my father started ambling up the beach toward Mark and me, I turned away. I didn't know what to say to Kona, didn't know how to hide all the emotions rattling around inside of me after our late-night kiss and conversation. I knew he would be hurt and angry at the way I was ignoring him, but I couldn't help it. I didn't want the next time I spoke to him to be in front of Mark, not when I knew my confusion would be written all over my face. As I already mentioned, my boyfriend had a tendency to see too much.

I turned away, headed toward my towel, but stopped when Mark grabbed my hand. "Whoa, Tempest. What is that?"

"What's what?"

"Like you don't know?" He traced a light finger over my upper back. "That's a frickin' gorgeous tattoo. And it's huge!" His hand skimmed down to the center of my back. "How long did it take you to get it inked?"

The throbbing in my back finally made sense. I stared at him, mutely, for as long as I dared, then muttered, "Not all that long actually."

"No way! It looks like it should have taken hours."

If he only knew.

It had taken seventeen years, but I wasn't about to tell him that.

Chapter 12

My birthday party was in full swing the next time someone commented on my new tattoo. I was hiding out on the family room balcony, trying to ignore the crowd that had invaded my house. I hadn't wanted the party to begin with; when my dad had broached the subject a few weeks ago, I had turned him down flat. After all, the last thing I wanted my friends to see was me suddenly sprouting a six-foot tail.

But he had insisted, and what had started out as a small gathering of my closest friends had somehow turned into a party of more than fifty people. As the doorbell rang again, I hunched my shoulders against the cold and prepared for an excruciatingly long night.

"Tempest, what are you doing hiding out here?" I turned to see Mickey lounging in the doorway. She was wearing a pair of ripped, faded boyfriend jeans and a lacy white top that showed off her mocha-colored skin to its best advantage.

"I'm not hiding," I lied. "I just needed to take a break for a second."

"What for?" She crossed the balcony, handed me a Diet Coke.

"There are some seriously fine guys in there—including yours—and you'd rather be out here, brooding into the ocean?"

"Mark will find me if he wants me." I still felt guilty about kissing Kona, and right now the idea of facing my boyfriend was less than appealing.

"Of course he wants to see you—everyone does. This is your birthday party, after all." She laid a hand on my shoulder, then drew it away quickly when I winced.

"Is it still tender?" she asked, pulling back to look at the crazy mixture of purple and magenta swirls that now decorated much of my back.

"Not really. I'm just not used to it yet."

"I bet. But it's gorgeous—really. I've never seen anything like it." She pouted for a second. "I just wish you'd let me come with you when you got it done. Maybe I would have worked up the nerve to get one of my own."

I didn't know how to answer her, so I settled for a nod and a "sorry."

"I really like the colors—this magenta is wicked hot." She bent down a little, got closer to the part of my back exposed by my halter top, and I could almost see her squinting in that way she had when she was trying to figure something out.

"You know, it reminds me of the ocean."

"What?" I whirled to face her. "How?" I'd studied the tattoo in my mirror for nearly an hour after I'd gotten back to the house today—had listened as my father told me of similar tattoos my mother had, although hers were emerald green. Neither of us had made the connection to the ocean—beyond, of course, the mermaid thing.

Which was bad enough. Yet somehow it felt even worse to

133

know the changes were continuing after I'd had those few bliss-ful, worry-free hours this morning, thinking the worst was behind me.

"They're not waves."

"No," she agreed, tracing a light finger over one of the swirls. "I don't mean literally like the water. Just—I don't know. It's more of an impression, you know? Like that painting you did a few months ago."

I froze at her words, my mind jumping back to the painting she was referring to. It had made no sense to me at the time, the swirls and curlicues that had come pouring out of me without conscious thought. I had almost trashed it—I'm not normally what you would call an abstract painter—but in the end I had decided against it. Something appealed to me about the way the cacophony of colors shouted out from the canvas.

It was still in my room, buried in the corner behind a bunch of other canvases, some that were prepped and some that I had already used. I hadn't thought of it in months, but now that Mickey had made the connection I could do nothing but think of its wild purples.

"We should probably go back in," I said awkwardly, keeping my eyes from Mickey's. Not only was she a good friend, but she was also a human lie detector—which made this whole mer-maid thing just a little more difficult to pull off.

"That's what I've been saying." At that moment, someone put Beyoncé on the stereo and Mickey squealed.

"Come on, girl. You've got to dance to this one." She grabbed my wrist and started dragging me toward the makeshift dance floor in the middle of my living room.

Dancing was the last thing on my mind, but she wouldn't take no for an answer, and soon I found myself in the center of the floor, bumping and grinding with her and Bri and Scooter and Logan. Eventually Beyoncé shifted into Kings of Leon, and Mark joined me, his long, lean body pressing against mine from the back as his arms wrapped around my stomach.

"You look amazing," he whispered in my ear, his peppermint-scented breath hot against my neck.

"It's the necklace." I touched his present awkwardly—it had taken me half an hour to work up the nerve to actually wear it, but the look in Mark's eyes when he'd seen it around my neck had made the stress worthwhile.

"It's you. You're beautiful."

I laughed. "Did someone spike the punch?"

"I wish you could see yourself the way I see you."

My mouth went desert dry. I swallowed convulsively, trying to find the words to say what needed to be said.

But in the end, I couldn't, instead choking out, "What do you see?" as I turned my head so I could look at his face. His eyes were a lush, warm chocolate that reminded me of all the little things I would give up if I became mermaid.

Walks through the nearby park with its rich vegetation and nearly overwhelming smell of jasmine.

Hand-in-hand excursions with Mark through Balboa Park with its abundant flowers and awe-inspiring museums.

Fast rides on his motorcycle.

Hot kisses stretched across his bed.

Rolling in the grass in the summertime.

Football on the front lawn in the fall.

Christmas trees.

The way he looked at me first thing in the morning, on our surf runs at dawn.

"Everything." His lips brushed over my temple, down my cheek to the dimple at the corner of my mouth that I've always hated but that he loved to play with. "I see the whole world when I look at you, Tempest."

His mouth skimmed down my jaw, nibbled at the sensitive skin of my neck. "I see the future. My future."

His words were an open, aching wound inside me, yet I immersed myself in them anyway. Immersed myself in the husky rasp of his voice as he continued to whisper to me. Immersed myself in the fresh, clean scent of him as he surrounded me from all sides.

Was it selfish? Yes. Hurtful? I hoped not. As necessary to me as breathing? Absolutely. I wanted this moment, needed it, with a desperation that bordered on the insane.

Closing my eyes, I cuddled back against him and gave myself to the music. To him—even if it was just for a little while.

Song after song played, from Nickelback to Muse to Coldplay, and still I stayed in Mark's arms. He was everything real and familiar and comfortable, but sexy too, and I found myself wishing these moments could go on forever. His arms just felt right around me. *He* felt right and as he held me the fact and fantasy of my life had never seemed so far from each other.

At least until there was a break in the music.

Opening my eyes slowly, reluctantly, my gaze collided with *his*. As it did, I could swear I felt the ground tremble beneath my feet.

My knees buckled and I probably would have fallen if Mark hadn't been holding me. But I could no longer feel his arms around me, no longer feel his breath against my neck.

All I knew was Kona's burning stare, his eyes dark as the stormy sea where I had first seen him as he glared at me in Mark's arms. I don't know if he was still mad at how I'd ignored him that morning, or if he didn't like the way I was currently wrapped around Mark. Either way, it was obvious he was angry. My already shaky confidence plummeted to my toes as my heart skipped a beat. Two.

Kona's jaw was tight, his fists clenched, and for a moment I thought, maybe . . .

I don't know what I thought, what I was thinking, as my world crashed down around my head. Only that in those moments, everything vanished. The house, the party, my friends, my father. Even Mark. They were all gone and then it was just Kona and me and the crazy, mixed-up emotions that throbbed between us. There was certainly nothing comfortable about him—or what I felt for him. Not like it was with Mark.

I don't know how long we stayed like that—how long we *would* have stayed like that—but reality crept in with a new song on the stereo. The murmur of voices. A high-pitched giggle from Bri.

I knew the exact moment Mark noticed Kona—and realized that he was staring at me with a mixture of rage and longing. Mark's body tensed against mine, his biceps turning hard and tight where they rested outside my own. His hands, which had been holding mine so gently, tightened to the point of pain.

Normally I would call him on his jealousy, tell him how

ridiculous he was being. But this time I couldn't, not after I'd betrayed him by kissing Kona. I couldn't help wondering how I was stupid enough to invite Kona to my party. It didn't take a genius to figure out this would probably happen.

I winced at the thought, then regretted the involuntary action as I saw Kona react to it. His eyes, already stormy, turned the molten platinum of a hurricane-tossed sea as he started across the room toward us.

He was spoiling for a fight, and as Mark shifted in front of me, I was terrified that Kona was going to get it.

I'm not this girl, I thought frantically, attempting to put myself between them. I wasn't a tease who played two guys against each other just to see how far they would go.

"Stop it, Mark," I hissed, wrapping my hands around his arm and trying to tug him out of the path of Hurricane Kona. But Mark was suddenly as immovable as an island. I flashed back to every ocean storm I'd ever heard about on the news, remembering how hurricanes devastated the land masses that got in their way.

Against anyone else, Mark could more than hold his own—he hadn't gotten his bad-boy reputation for nothing. But with Kona . . . I just didn't know. And I didn't want to find out—I couldn't stand the idea of either being hurt because of me.

"Mark, don't ruin my party. Come on, just ignore him."

"How can I ignore him when he's coming straight at us?"

"You're the one who introduced the two of us. He probably just wants to say hello."

"Yeah, well, when I introduced you, I didn't expect him to make a play for you." If possible, Mark's stance grew even more aggressive.

138

I glanced around for help, figuring the entire party was watching, waiting for the fireworks to explode in the middle of my living room. But to my shock, no one was paying attention. They were all too busy talking and dancing and laughing to notice that the two sides of my world were about to collide.

What should I do, what should I do, what should I do? The words spun through my brain in a mantra of distress as Kona finally succeeded in negotiating his way through the crush of bodies.

"What are you doing here?" Mark demanded in the most abrasive tone I had ever heard him use.

"Tempest invited me."

Mark's fist clenched at Kona's words and I held on to his arm as tightly as I could, ignoring Mark's attempts to pull away from me. Though Kona was talking to him, Kona was still looking at me, which I knew was sending Mark's anger soaring into the stratosphere.

"Yeah, well, I'm uninviting you. Leave."

The arrogance in Mark's statement got my back up—this was my party and he didn't have the right to uninvite anyone. Part of me wanted to tell him to lay off the macho-man act, but I couldn't—not then. Not without giving Mark, and Kona, the excuse for the fight both looked ready to throw down.

Kona leisurely shifted his gaze from my face to Mark's and the change that came over him astounded me. And scared me, a little. Gone was any trace of warmth, and in its place was a shocking iciness. Days before, on the beach—before Mark had "introduced" us—they'd seemed like friends. But looking at them now, it was as if the ease of their earlier relationship had never existed.

139

"I don't think you get to make that choice."

Mark bristled. "That's where you're wrong."

"Am I?" Kona raised one sardonic brow as he turned to me. "Tempest?"

I knew what he was asking, but what was I supposed to say? Anything that came out of my mouth was going to sound like I was taking sides. If I let him stay, Mark would be furious enough to take a swing at him. If I asked him to go, I might never see him again. How many rejections could a guy be expected to take, after all?

Pain radiated through me at the thought of either occurrence—not my first clue that I was in serious trouble, but definitely my most powerful one. Which left me in even more of a quandary: what was I supposed to do when it was becoming abundantly clear that I cared for both of them?

"Don't talk to her." Mark shoved him, hard, but Kona didn't so much as flinch. "Talk to me."

Even with violence looming, the chauvinism in that remark was too much for me to let pass. "Excuse me?"

"Not now, Tempest."

"Definitely now, Mark." I knew I was only making things worse, but I couldn't help it. No way was I going to stand here and be dismissed—especially not when they were making me the rope in their little game of tug-of-war. "You don't get to decide who talks to me."

He turned incredulous brown eyes to me. "You want to hang out with this guy?"

"That's not the point."

"I'd say that was exactly the point," Kona interjected helpfully.

"You stay out of this." I turned on him, suddenly furious with both of them.

"I'm not sure I can do that, Tempest," he answered, leaning closer to me in a deliberate attempt to provoke Mark.

"Stop it." I reached out, slapped a palm on his chest to push him back. But as soon as I touched him I felt a jolt of electricity race up my arm, and under my horrified stare, Kona stumbled back a good five or six feet.

For a minute I couldn't register what had happened. I was too busy paying attention to the sizzle of power winding its way through my bloodstream. It was an adrenaline cocktail to my nervous system, a shock of energy straight to my heart and every muscle in my body.

I could feel it inside me, a turmoil of current reshaping who I was into what I would become.

At first I was too astounded to do anything but stare, but eventually one thought registered above all others: Mark had shoved Kona as hard as he could and he hadn't moved him so much as an inch. All I'd done was touch him and he was halfway across my living room.

"Kona?" I called his name in a trembling whisper that sounded more like a scared little girl's than a self-assured woman's, but at the moment it was the best I could do.

"It's okay, Tempest," he answered, walking back toward me.

But it wasn't okay—I could see it in the way Mark was looking at me, as if I had, indeed, just grown that tail I'd been so worried about earlier. And when I followed his horrified gaze, I could see why. This time I was the one who was glowing.

And not just that wimpy, is-he-or-isn't-he kind of glow Kona

141

had emitted that day at the beach. No, nothing that sedate for me. I was sending out enough wattage to light up a small village—or a nuclear power plant.

As Kona reached for me and Mark stumbled out of range, I did the only thing I could think of doing. I fled.

PART THREE

Hitting the Tip

❧

The voice of the sea speaks to the soul.
KATE CHOPIN

Chapter 13

I ran until my calves ached.

Until my lungs shuddered.

Until my heart felt like it was going to explode.

And then I ran some more, kicking up sand with every footfall as I wound my way down the long stretch of empty beach.

Finally, when my vision had blurred and my pulse was pounding in my head, I collapsed onto the soft, loose sand and tried to get control of my emotions—and my unruly body.

At least I wasn't glowing anymore. That had to be a plus, right?

Still, I had fled from my own birthday party. Not that I'd had much of a choice—I mean, what was I supposed to say when people noticed my little problem? That I'd fallen into a vat of toxic waste earlier in the day and this was just a fun little side effect? Myth was one thing, but this whole mermaid experience, and me along with it, was beginning to fall into comic-book realm. I didn't like it. At all.

The wind picked up, whipping around me, playing with my

hair and making me shiver. I ignored it, concentrating instead on trying to figure out what to do.

How could you have left me like this, Mom? How could you be somewhere else when I need you so badly?

It was stupid, but I concentrated on the question really hard, hoping against all logic and reason that she would somehow hear it. That she would somehow feel my distress and come home, like she'd promised to do so long ago.

How could you just leave me alone to deal with this? I demanded. *It's not like your letter was a freaking instruction manual.*

I need you, Mom. I need you.

I waited, eyes squeezed shut for what seemed like forever. But there was no answer.

Big surprise.

When had she ever been there when I needed her? When had she ever thought of anyone but herself? If that's what being mermaid meant, then I wanted no part of it. They could take all these crazy, messed-up changes back to the deep, where they'd come from.

You don't really want that. Think of what you can do with all that power.

The voice was crafty, cunning as it slipped inside of me, and quiet—so quiet that I barely noticed it as I pulled my knees into my chest and brooded.

You need to accept the gift, accept yourself. Being mermaid is not a curse but a wonderful, incomparable gift.

Yeah, right. Some gift.

Don't mock me. The wind slammed into me with much more force than it had before and too late I remembered Kona's warning. *Don't go down to the beach at night, Tempest.*

146

A sly, sharp laugh sounded in my head and that's when I finally realized something wasn't right—just a little too late.

I started to climb to my feet, but the wind slapped against me, hard, until I was flat on my back in the cold, wet sand.

Spread-eagled.

Helpless.

I struggled to sit up, but I couldn't. Something was holding me down, pressing me deeper into the sand despite the incredible strength I felt coursing through my body. Suddenly the vicious rivalry between Mark and Kona didn't feel so bad. Even the glowing was okay.

Anything had to be better than this.

The wind kicked up another notch, or twelve. It wound itself around my wrists and ankles, manacling me in place even as I told myself it wasn't possible. Wind was intangible—it couldn't touch me, couldn't hold me down. This had to be some kind of hallucination—maybe someone had spiked the party punch.

I mean, this couldn't really be happening.

Only it was.

I strained against the invisible bonds, yanked and pulled and cursed as I tried to get free. Nothing worked.

Forcing myself to be calm when everything inside of me wanted to freak out, I attempted to reason with myself. Whatever this was, whoever was doing it, couldn't keep it up forever. Eventually daylight—and people—would come. While the idea of being trapped on the beach for the rest of the night wasn't a pleasant one, it wasn't the first time I'd spent a night next to the water.

Of course, judging from the way things had been going lately, it might very well be my last.

Taking a few deep breaths, I tried to relax. To stop fighting. To just go with the flow. I could do this. I could lie here, for hours if I had to. Eventually I would be free again and when I was . . . When I was, there would be hell to pay. I would find a way to make sure of it. The thought cheered me up for a second as I imagined my revenge against whatever was doing this to me.

And then I felt the water tickle my toes.

It was such a normal feeling, one I was so intimately acquainted with that it took me a second to realize what was happening. When I did, alarm slammed through me—so intense it made everything I'd felt before seem like a small child's fit. Instinctively I tried to sit up and once again the invisible restraints kept me in place.

The water was around my ankles now, lapping at me. Toying with me. High tide had been hours ago, so whatever was making the water rise had to be coming from her.

But how far up the beach would it get? How deep would it be?

Craning my head, I narrowed my eyes and strained to see what was going on. To understand what was happening, even though deep inside, I already knew.

That one look confirmed my worst fears and had alarm turning to terror so deep that for a minute I couldn't think. Couldn't feel. Couldn't do anything but ineffectually thrash against my bonds in an animal's headlong struggle for flight. For the first time I understood why a wolf would chew off its own foot rather than stay captive. If I could have reached mine, I might very well have done the same thing.

The water was rising—quickly—and I was trussed up like

Andromeda, waiting for Poseidon's sea monster to devour me. Only in this case, the ocean itself was my monster.

The water was around my waist now, licking at me in a nightmarish parody of a caress, and my heart was pounding so hard I was afraid it would burst right out of my chest.

With every breath I took, the water crept higher, and I knew that if I didn't think of something soon I was going to get a chance to try out my new gills in the most miserable way possible. Seeing as how none of this whole mermaid thing was turning out the way I'd thought it would—the way I'd been told that it should—I wasn't exactly counting on the stupid things to do what they were supposed to. Which meant I might drown if I didn't figure a way out of this—and quickly.

There's only one way out. It was that damn voice again, echoing from the deepest, darkest corners of my mind. *Come to us. Come to me. We will save you.*

Yeah, and if I believed that, she probably also had some nice beachfront property in Colorado to sell me.

Choose me, Tempest. Choose the beauty of the darkness. Keep resisting and you'll die.

Maybe she meant to sway me with her threats, but all they did was piss me off. She could stop this anytime she wanted. She was torturing me, pinning me down like an animal for slaughter, all in an effort to break me. But I would rather drown than listen to her, rather die than become whatever it was she wanted me to be.

Anger burned through me, not erasing the horror and dismay, but definitely overtaking them. It cleared my head, let me think past the imminent threat of oncoming death. As the rage crackled down my nerve endings, growing and expanding with

149

each breath I took, I focused on it. Used it. Let it—and the power that came with it—fill up every part of me.

It was a fire burning inside me, a blaze that threatened to consume all of me if I kept it inside. I didn't know what I was doing, didn't know how to do what my instincts told me I could. I knew only that I would not die, not here. Not now. Not like this, at the mercy of some madwoman with a God complex.

Taking a deep breath, I unclenched my fingers one by one and sent the heat inside of me outward in one fast, quick strike.

I didn't know what I was doing—or even if I was doing anything at all—but whatever it was must have worked because her scream ripped through me, tearing at me until I felt like I was bleeding.

But the wind was gone. My bonds were gone. Then I was up and running straight back from the ocean, desperate to get away from the sea witch Kona had warned me against.

Desperate to find safety, somewhere.

I didn't realize the wind had come back, stronger than ever, until it slapped me in the back so hard that I stumbled, nearly fell. Would have fallen, if I hadn't known what was waiting for me if I gave in.

You didn't think it would be that easy, did you, little girl? The voice was a high-pitched cackle now, a supernatural sieve that drained the power from me as quickly as it had come.

No, but I had hoped. The wind came up, formed a wall in front of me that made it almost impossible for me to move forward. I dug deep, tried to find more of that same, strange electric current, but it was gone. Used up. There was nothing left and I was trapped out here in this maelstrom, unable to defend myself against a monster who wanted every part of me.

Give up. Give in. The voice was everywhere now.

You can't fight me. I slipped, fell to my knees. Tried to crawl forward but I couldn't do it. The wind was just too strong.

You can't resist me. I was determined to do just that, clawing at the sand until my fingers bled. But still I couldn't hang on.

You belong to me. An inexorable force was dragging me back, dragging me down.

I WILL NOT BE DENIED! Lightning rent the sky above me, cleaving it in two before ripping through the night straight at the ground in front of me.

"No!" I screamed out my opposition just as a new but unmalicious force hit me, sent me rolling through the sand at a crazy speed. And then it was rolling with me, straight across the sand to a large pile of rocks just feet from the shoreline.

We didn't stop until we'd crashed right up against the stones. I lay there for a moment, stunned, as the earth around us bucked and roiled. Between the impact of hitting the rocks and the strong, hard male body above mine, it took me a minute to drag breath into my tortured lungs.

But eventually they started working again, and as my oxygen-starved brain finally got what it needed to function, I became aware of just who was resting above me. "You!" I said, shoving at Kona as hard as I could.

"Stop!" he hissed at me, pressing me deeper into the sand.

I cried out in pain as something dug into my back, and I reached beneath me, yanking out a child's bucket and shovel that had been left behind by someone who had had better luck than I on this stretch of beach.

"Stop moving! You're making yourself a target."

"I'm sorry." I shrank into myself, tried to make my body as

151

small as possible as he tucked himself around me, ensuring that no part was exposed. Which was a really good thing for me as lightning popped and sizzled all around us, striking the rocks and the sand.

But it wasn't so good for Kona, I realized with a detached kind of dread as lightning arced straight at us. Kona tensed against me then, his entire body arching into one taut line.

And then he began to convulse.

Chapter 14

⑥

"Kona!" I screamed, rolling him over as his body wigged out in about a hundred different directions.

Forget him. He can't help you. No one can. Another bolt of lightning shot down, struck him straight in the chest. At the impact, his body literally came off the ground, then slammed back again, hard.

The convulsions stopped when he hit, but as I stared at him I was terrified to see that his breathing had stopped as well.

His shirt was in tatters and there was a huge, black, oval-shaped burn in the center of his chest, directly over his breastbone. Over his heart. I ripped the rest of his shirt away, laid a trembling hand on his stomach—too scared to touch the wound—and waited for the inhalation of breath that signified he was still alive.

Nothing happened.

Ohmygod, ohmygod, ohmygod. The words circled in my brain as I stared at Kona's lifeless body. This wasn't supposed to happen.

This wasn't supposed to happen!

Around me the world was exploding, claps of thunder booming across the sky, one right after the other. Frenzied streaks of lightning blasted the sand around us repeatedly, gouging huge holes in the normally pristine beach, hitting and breaking rocks all around me. There was no rain, no water, just the most freaked-out electric storm I had ever seen, and I knew then that whatever battle I was locked in was far from over.

She—whoever she was—was still looking for me. Would drag me straight out to sea if she had half a chance.

Every instinct I had told me to run, to duck down low and put as much distance between me and the thrashing sea as I could. But Kona had sacrificed everything to save me and I couldn't just run away. Not until I at least tried to save him.

With my ninth-grade CPR instructions rusty in my head, I knelt on the ground next to him. Again I searched for a sign that he was breathing and found none. I searched for a pulse, to the same effect.

Tilting his head back, I sucked in a huge gulp of air, then leaned forward and covered his lips with mine. I breathed the air into his mouth, before moving to his chest to start the compressions. Except the spot I was supposed to press was exactly where the burn was. Would it hurt him more if I touched it? Would I do more damage?

He's dead, Tempest, I told myself as pain like nothing I'd ever felt before ripped through my soul. *Dead. There's no worse damage you can do, so stop being an idiot and try. Just try.*

I gingerly pressed around until I found the bottom of his sternum. Put two fingers below it like Ms. Johnson had taught us in health class, and then pressed thirty times in rapid succession, doing my best to ignore the fact that my hand was in the center of the burn. Lightning had struck him almost directly in the heart.

I tilted his chin up again, breathed for him two more times.

Did more compressions.

Breathed.

Did more compressions.

Breathed.

Did more compressions.

Checked for a pulse.

Nothing.

Breathed.

Did more compressions.

Again and again, I breathed for him. Again and again, I tried to start his heart even though common sense told me that he was gone.

That no one could survive being struck like that.

That I was trying to do the impossible.

But still I didn't stop. I couldn't, not when everything inside of me was screaming for him to live.

Not Kona, I silently pleaded, tears streaming down my face as I compressed his chest thirty more times. Not Kona, when I'd already lost my mother. Not Kona, when I still might lose my dad and brothers and Mark.

Not Kona, when all he'd ever done was try to help me.

Not Kona. Not Kona. Not Kona. The words were a rhythm in my head while I worked, repeating the same motions again and again. But eventually I grew lightheaded and my arms began to ache, my muscles trembling under the strain.

"No!" It was a cry from deep inside of me, from a place I was just beginning to recognize. "Damn it, no!" There had to be a way.

I leaned over him, preparing to press my mouth over his yet again. My tears slid unchecked and unheeded down my cheeks and onto his face, then rolled over his cheek as well. It was at that moment that I felt the soft exhalation of his breath on my face.

It was such a shock that at first I could do nothing but stare, breath held, as I waited—much longer than should have been necessary—for him to do it again. But he didn't.

Had I imagined it, then, that soft pulse of air against my cheek? I had been so certain . . .

Suddenly an idea came to me—so wild, so outlandish, that I did everything I could to ignore it. But once it had taken root, I couldn't pretend that it wasn't there.

He needed water. Not air. Not chest compressions. Water. His only response since being hit by the lightning was when my tears had touched his face.

I lifted my head for the first time since I'd started CPR, stared at the water that was just beyond the rocks. It might as well have been a hundred miles away. The earth was still trembling around me, the sky still split with bolts of lightning. How was I supposed to get his massive body down to the water when the world around me had gone utterly insane?

I couldn't, at least not without risking his being hurt worse. Which meant—I glanced around, looked for something, anything, that I might use . . . My gaze fell on the small, red bucket I had pushed aside earlier and I wondered just how much water he needed.

Before I could think better of my completely suicidal plan, I scooped up the bucket and dashed straight back toward the ocean. As I ran, the sand fell away from beneath my feet and each step I took was across rockier, more uneven ground.

The voice I had heard earlier was strangely absent, the low, compelling demand of it finally silent. *Is she gone, then?* I wondered warily.

But the storm was stronger than ever.

When I was only a few feet from the ocean, I tripped over the roiling ground. Fell. Climbed back to my feet as the world exploded around me and then ran some more. I had only minutes before Kona would slip away forever—I didn't know how I knew that, but the same instinct that had told me he needed water also told me this, and I believed it.

I finally made it to the water's edge and scooped up a bucketful of the churning, agitated water. As I did so, I looked directly into the waves and nearly screamed at what I saw.

A dark, eerie face stared back at me, just below the wild surface of the ocean. I screamed, stumbled back, yet couldn't resist looking for it again.

But it was gone. Just another crazy trick of my imagination, I figured, as I turned back toward the rocks and started running. Or was something there, waiting for me? Waiting for Kona?

This whole thing was getting creepier by the second. And my father wondered why I didn't want to turn mermaid? After tonight, I wasn't sure I'd ever want to set foot in the ocean again—even to surf. God only knew what was out there.

Of course, I had to survive until tomorrow, which was seeming more and more unlikely as a crack opened up in front of me and I nearly pitched face-first into it. I stopped in time, but negotiating around it was slow going—especially since I was terrified the stupid crack would grow large enough to swallow me at any moment. It was a fear I would have laughed off at any other time, but in that moment, on that beach, the threat seemed all too real.

Don't do it. The voice was back. *You'll kill him if you do.*

I paused, fear a wild thing beating against my ribs. Was I making the biggest mistake yet? Would the water end any hope—

Yes! That's it. Let the water go. Pour it out onto the beach. Forget about—

No! I pushed back at the voice, tried to get it out of my head. I was right. I had to be because there were no other choices. It was this or Kona would be gone forever—simply because he'd cared enough to follow me. Cared enough to stand between me and whatever hell was waiting out there when I didn't know how to fight for myself.

A strange compulsion came over me then, one that had me suddenly needing to dive into the ocean, despite my dark feelings about it. Needing it more than I wanted to take my next breath—more than I wanted to save Kona or see my family again. Ignoring the impulse, I dragged myself up the beach one slow, halting step at a time.

With each foot that I moved up the beach, the wind grew harsher. Sand flew through the air, along with shells and kelp—strange but effective marine missiles, transformed from simple detritus to painful weapons with a stroke of the wind.

The shells slammed into me, razor sharp against my too-sensitive skin, but still I didn't stop. I couldn't. To do so meant death, my instincts screamed. Death to Kona and death to me.

I stumbled onward and finally—finally—made it back to the shoddy protection of the rocks. Kona was still lying where I'd left him. With a quick prayer that I was doing the right thing, I flung the water directly onto his wound.

The second the water hit him, the lesion began to sizzle. Kona gasped, his body jerking spasmodically on the cold, hard sand.

Relief swept through me and I fell to my knees beside him. "Kona. Can you hear me?" There was no answer. "Kona?"

He groaned so low I barely heard it over the rumbling thunder and crack of lightning. But it was there, and it gave me hope when I had just about given up. He didn't awaken, though. And before my horrified eyes, the ugly black burn on his chest changed, opened up, became a jagged-edged laceration—as if he'd been cut with a serrated knife.

Blood began to gush from the opening.

For long seconds I did nothing but stare at it, then raised my head and instinctively glanced around for help. But, of course, no one had suddenly appeared in the last five minutes. When I had fled the party, I'd run far and fast up the beach until I was in a secluded area, with no houses or hotels in sight. No one lived near here and the storm was keeping any visitors away. I was completely on my own.

Muttering one of Logan's favorite—and most vile—curses, I whipped off my halter top and pressed it to the wound, trying desperately to stanch the flow of blood.

This was good, I tried to convince myself as I fought off hysteria for the second time that night. It was better. Kona was jerking around as if in pain, but that was a huge improvement from where he'd been. At least it was proof that he was still alive.

Which was much better than being dead. But as blood soaked through the yellow fabric and coated my fingers, I wondered how long I could keep him alive when he was bleeding this copiously.

I pressed harder, but my halter top was saturated—unable to take any more blood at all. Why hadn't I worn a turtleneck? It was February—who wore a halter top in February?

Use the sand.

The thought came to me in the same way the one about the water had—from a place deep inside me that I hadn't known existed before tonight.

Without giving myself a chance to think, I scooped up handfuls of sand and packed them into the gaping hole in the center of Kona's chest. Wincing, I tried to ignore everything I knew about bacteria and open wounds and focus instead on covering the entire cut with sand.

The bleeding slowed to an angry ooze, but Kona was getting paler by the second, the involuntary movements of his body becoming smaller, harder to distinguish.

It wasn't enough. Nothing I was doing was enough. Kona was slipping away, my grand idea of using water to help him causing him only pain instead.

What had I been thinking? Following my instincts? What instincts? The same ones that had had me running from my own party? The same ones that had caused this entire mess?

For a second I contemplated running back to the house. My father could help—but I was too far away. The way Kona was bleeding, there was no way he would make it long enough for me to run home and back again. Besides, I wasn't sure how I would make it through the lightning and pitching earth when I'd barely made it the distance to the water and back.

That was it. The thought ripped through me. Kona was a water creature. He needed more water—a lot more water than that stupid bucket could carry. It wasn't that the water I'd gotten earlier hadn't helped him—it was that it hadn't been enough.

He needed to be immersed in the sea if he had any chance of healing at all.

Which meant his only chance was for me to get him into the water. I poked my head out from the rocks, nearly got it sliced off when a lightning bolt struck inches from where I was. How the hell was I supposed to get him down there, when I had barely managed to do it on my own?

I glanced back at Kona and knew I didn't have a choice. While he was breathing on his own, each inhalation was shallow and rattling. It was either this—a last-ditch attempt to save him—or sitting there watching him die, for good this time.

Cursing my mother, my gifts, and whatever else was responsible for landing us in the middle of this whole freakish nightmare, I crouched behind Kona and grabbed him under his arms. Then I began to pull—and nearly fell over with the first tug.

He was a lot heavier than he looked—and he looked pretty heavy. Still, it wasn't like there were so many other options floating around. So I tugged and pulled, yanked and wiggled him slowly down the sand as the world around us went completely insane.

I'd thought it was bad before, but what happened next really was the stuff nightmares were made of. The sand came alive around us, tried to grab on to my ankles, tried to anchor Kona to it with talons of steel. I ignored it, told myself it was just more mind games from the hideous sea witch thing that liked to lurk inside my head. It wasn't nearly as easy to ignore the rawness in my ankles, from where I yanked and pulled against the abrasive sand. But I couldn't let Kona die for me, I just couldn't.

I took a few more steps and nearly sobbed with relief when I realized the water was closer than I had expected. Once again it had come up the shore to meet me, only this time it brought salvation instead of certain death. I didn't pause to think about how strange it was that the water seemed to sense my desperation.

I dragged Kona the last few feet to the oddly high tide, heard the witch—or whatever it was—screaming and uttering vile threats inside my head. I ignored it like I had the clutching sand. There was no other choice.

I took my first step into the roiling sea, and pain exploded through me as the salt water licked at my bleeding ankles. I bit my lip to keep from screaming—or worse, whimpering. Then I moved deeper to ensure that Kona was submerged up to his neck.

But the second I got him all the way in, the second the ocean touched his wound, wrinkled black hands reached up from the water and grabbed his arms and legs, pulling him straight down below the surface.

Chapter 15

❻

I did scream then, Kona's name—over and over again.

Then I plunged into the ocean, searching for him in the storm-tossed waves. I dove under the water until my lungs ached and my eyes burned, looking for some sign—any sign—of him. But he had vanished, and with him the frightening creatures that had pulled him under.

I surfaced close to shore, sucked huge breaths of air into my starving lungs, and realized with a start that the storm had vanished. The sky was clear and the ocean calm.

Had they gotten what they'd come for, then? Was Kona their objective all along, with me only a pawn?

But I remembered the voice, remembered the urgency as she'd demanded that I come to her. No, Kona hadn't been her objective. I had—he had sacrificed himself to save me. The guilt was nearly overwhelming, the desperate need to find him and save him even more so.

I couldn't leave him with those hideous things, not without at least trying to get him back. He deserved better than that.

And every second I was sitting here, treading water, they were getting farther and farther away.

Taking a deep breath, I dove under the water once again. I knew I didn't stand a chance of catching them as a human, but I was completely unsure of how to be mermaid. Just the thought of turning made me sick, but Kona was out there, and he needed me.

For a moment, I saw him the way he'd looked the night before—his eyes naked with his emotions for me. My feelings for him welled up inside of me and I knew I'd do anything— even this—if it meant saving Kona from the sea witch's clutches.

There was only one problem. I'd spent so long fighting the transformation that now that I temporarily welcomed it—now that I needed it—I had no idea what to do.

I shot through the water, swimming straight out into the blackness of the ocean at night. My heart was beating like a metronome at top speed and I could feel myself shaking. I tried to pretend it was from the cold, but the truth was that I was warmer than I had been in a very long time. Still, adrenaline was coursing through me, making every stroke of my arms choppy and unsteady as I refused to think about the disaster I was suddenly courting.

Mermaid, I thought, even as I trembled at the magnitude of what I was doing. The magnitude of now seeking what I had so long tried to avoid.

But I couldn't let them take Kona, not when the only reason he'd been on that beach was to save me.

I need to be mermaid, I thought again, concentrating as hard as I could. I swam some more, waited for the tail to come, for the gills to work. But nothing happened.

Why should I be surprised? I wondered bitterly. Nothing about this change, this choice, had been convenient so far. Everything had happened at the worst possible moment—why, then, would it happen now, when it was most necessary?

Still, I kept swimming, refusing to glance back at the shore to see how far away the lights were. It didn't matter. Kona was under there somewhere, at the mercy of God only knew what, and I had to get him back.

The waves were getting choppier, the water colder, and I knew I was farther out than I had ever been before. I tried not to think of my numerous cuts and scrapes, of how they were bleeding into the water with each stroke and kick. Tried not to think of all the night predators that were out hunting for food. If I did, I'd panic. And that would get me absolutely nowhere.

Instead, I concentrated on the feel of the water against my body. The effort of putting one arm in front of the other. The rhythm of turning my head to breathe.

It was feeling more and more like I was on a suicide mission, one I would have no way of returning from. I was swimming straight out from shore, into utter and complete darkness. Exhausting myself, pushing myself to the limits, and if this didn't work, I really didn't think I'd have enough strength to make it back to the beach.

Part of me wanted to stop. More than once, I almost did. But Kona's pale, drawn face flashed behind my closed eyelids and for a moment, I swore I felt his lips brush against mine as they had twice before.

Resolve tightened my stomach and I plunged onward. I blocked everything from my mind but the next stroke, the next kick, the next breath, until I was utterly mindless—just a machine

165

concentrating on the next movement. And the next. And the next.

Which is why when it finally happened, I almost missed it.

It started as a burning in my chest, a breathlessness that left me weak and gasping for oxygen. I struggled to draw air into my aching lungs, but nothing happened. I wheezed and panted, wondered if I'd finally pushed myself too far.

Was my body too exhausted to continue?

Was I finally going to drown?

My dad's face—along with Rio's and Moku's and Mark's and Bri's and Mickey's and Logan's—fluttered through my brain as I clutched at my throat. Clawed at it. Tried to get it to work, to deliver air to my now-starving lungs.

They wouldn't know what had happened to me, would think I had just disappeared. Dad and my brothers would assume I had done what my mother had—turned mermaid and gone under without another thought of them. As for my friends, I couldn't imagine what horrors they would think had befallen me.

Everything around me was going blacker—although I didn't know how that was possible. Already I was out in the middle of night. Blind to all but the darkness. Deaf to all but the crashing of the waves. I couldn't help but wonder if maybe this was what had happened to my mother. Had she suffered like this, died like this? Was that why she'd never come back?

I sank under the water before the thought had a chance to really register, then forced myself to claw my way back up.

Sank again. Again tried to find the surface.

But it didn't work. I was dying. And Kona, Kona would be lost forever. We both would.

I sank deeper, the water pulling me down, down, down. The fear was gone; in its place was a weariness that told me to just give up, to just give in. I couldn't fight it anymore. It was over.

I closed my eyes, opened my mouth. Swallowed a mouthful of water and prayed.

Moments passed, long, excruciating seconds while I waited for death to claim me. One minute, then two before it finally occurred to me that my lungs no longer hurt. That the fuzziness—and the exhaustion—were gone.

Was I already dead? Had I missed the whole thing? But how could that be? Did death really feel so much like life?

That's when I felt it, the flare of something unfamiliar behind my ears. The opening and closing of those little slits that had made me so distressed for the last few days.

My gills were working. I was breathing—*in* the water.

Holy crap! Did that mean the change had finally kicked in? Was I mermaid?

I opened my eyes cautiously, expecting the burn of the water and more blackness. Instead, the whole underwater world around me was lit up like Horton Plaza at Christmastime. I could see for miles, in phosphorescent shades of blue and green and red and yellow.

Fish were everywhere, darting around me, bumping into me, checking out this strange creature who was suddenly caught, spellbound, in their midst.

Using my hands, I somersaulted, tried to see if I had a tail. But no, my legs were still there. My jeans were ripped and torn, and in between my toes was a strange webbing that hadn't been there before. But I definitely still had legs.

Weird.

Maybe it wasn't my gills helping me breathe after all. Maybe I really was dead.

I gave an experimental kick and shot forward a good three or four feet. Gave another one and moved even farther and faster.

My mind scrambled for an explanation. I'd had a tail once before, for those few seconds after I'd fallen off my surfboard. Besides, I knew mermaids had tails. But now I had legs. What did that mean?

What did any of this mean?

A small fish darted up to my face, swam through a few strands of my hair, which was billowing out behind me like a weird, blond curtain. Another fish came up, did the same thing, and I laughed. Then clamped my mouth shut, terrified of swallowing more water.

But this time it didn't go into my lungs, just slipped harmlessly into my mouth and back out again. I thought, randomly, of all the sea water that had burned down my throat as I surfed over the years and wondered if maybe there was more to this mermaid thing than I had ever imagined.

I swam a little, shocked at how much distance I could cover with a single stroke. My jeans were slowing me down, annoying me, so I dragged them off, let them float away. As I did, the sheer wonder of my surroundings faded away and I remembered Kona.

Kona was down here somewhere, and I now had the means of catching up to him. Maybe. It was a big ocean and those things had gotten a big head start as I'd floundered around up there, above the ocean. Still, I had to try.

A long silver line stretched in front of me, the exact color of Kona's eyes at midnight. Figuring I had almost no other options, I followed it, hoping that I was heading toward him instead of away. But the truth was I was at a total loss as to what else to do. I was trapped somewhere between human and mermaid—an oddity, now, in both worlds—and there was no going back.

I started to swim in earnest then, following the wavery silver line as if the fate of the world depended on it. And in a strange way, it did. Not the whole world, maybe, but certainly my little corner of it.

I zipped through the water, the feel of it cool and refreshing and oh so welcome against my skin. For the first time that I could remember, my reaction to the ocean wasn't mixed. Gone was the fear and anger and distrust; in its place was sheer joy at finally being where I belonged—even if it was without a tail.

The line stretched for miles and I followed it, growing more and more anxious as I did. Kona had been in bad shape, close to death, when they'd grabbed him.

Had he survived being stolen by those things?

Had the ocean healed him?

Or had they taken advantage of his weakened state to kill him?

Of course, I didn't even know if he could breathe under the sea. I suspected that he was something other than human, something more, but I didn't know for sure. And if he wasn't, then surely he was already gone.

Something brushed against me as I swam and I turned my head, expecting to see another fish. Instead it was the arm of an octopus, its tentacles brushing against the bare skin of my belly while its opaque eyes stared right through me.

I shuddered, forced myself not to jerk away as I reminded myself that the poison in its tentacles wouldn't hurt me—not like that of the small, blue-ringed octopuses that my dad and I had run into a few years before when we'd visited Australia.

Still, it creeped me out. The thing wasn't huge, but it was at least half my size and as I looked beyond it I realized there were more of them. A lot more. I must have swum into a garden of the ugly things.

Kicking harder and faster, I propelled myself through the water, determined not to pay too much attention to what was around me. It was weird enough that I was swimming under the water without having to come up for air. Focusing on all the sea life, most of which I had only ever seen before in aquariums, would totally trip me out.

I had no idea how far or how long I had been swimming—I was completely thrown off by the speed and agility I suddenly had. My fingers had grown the same slight webbing as my toes had, just at the base where each finger met my palm. Combined with the gills and the semiwebbed toes and the huge increase in strength, it made me feel like I was flying, especially since the water felt as light as air.

The silver line was growing stronger, heavier, easier to see, and I wondered if I was getting closer. To Kona, I hoped. Or to those strange creatures who had grabbed him? I couldn't help worrying that I was on the trail of something else entirely.

No. I shoved the thought away. I refused to think that I had done all this for nothing. That I was on a wild-goose chase and Kona was halfway across the ocean in another direction.

More time passed—maybe half an hour, maybe an hour. It was hard to tell down here, where everything was so foreign and ambiguous and reality seemed just beyond the reach of my fingertips.

I curved up and around, made a sharp right, and then stopped abruptly as I realized the trail had suddenly plunged straight down. Already I was deep under the ocean, deeper, I knew, than I had ever been, despite the numerous times my father had taken me scuba diving this past summer. I had enjoyed diving at the time, but even then I remember looking up at the surface of the water and wondering what would happen if I suddenly ran out of air. The boat had been a long way up.

I didn't have to worry about the air thing anymore, but the surface was already too far up for me to see. Going deeper, now, was sheer lunacy.

An old movie flashed through my head, one where a submarine had to dive down deeper than usual to avoid an enemy's radar and the water started pressing in on it. Leaks sprang in every compartment and the ship creaked and shuddered as the weight of the water slowly smashed it from every side.

I didn't want to be that ship, my body imploding as the water literally crushed my organs and liquefied my brain.

Of course, in the movie everything had turned out fine. The enemy ship had finally moved on and the crew had been able to lift back up to a safe depth before the ship was compressed into a thin sheet of metal. Still, their submarine had been severely crippled, and that was with them staying down for only a few minutes.

But this wasn't the movies. A happily ever after wasn't

guaranteed, and if I followed the trail, who knew how deep I'd have to go—and for how long.

In that moment of indecision, I was more aware of the role fate played in my life than I had ever been before. As far as I could tell, I had two choices. I could turn around, try to retrace my path back home, and hope that everything would be all right. Or I could continue down after Kona, and hope that everything would be all right.

It was a fifty-fifty shot either way.

Through it all, there was a tug in my stomach. A pressure in my spine. A nearly irresistible urge to go deep, no matter what the consequences were.

I closed my eyes, counted to ten. And then dove straight down, telling myself as I did that I had finally and completely lost my mind.

Chapter 16

It felt like what I figured falling off a skyscraper would feel like.

Fast.

Scary.

And in some small part of my brain whose existence I didn't like to acknowledge, completely exhilarating.

I'm not sure if it was gravity or terror or a combination of both that had me moving so quickly, but I was spiraling down like a runaway locomotive. Deep, deep, deeper, until the water pushed in on me from every side. It no longer felt light, but so heavy that I could barely think. So heavy I could barely feel past the pressure in my head and chest and limbs.

I started to freak out, to put on the brakes, but some inner compulsion kept me moving. Some feeling that this was what I needed to do. Where I needed to go. For a split second I feared that this had all been a trap, that she had used the promise of Kona to get me to her.

But then even that thought was gone as the ocean floor appeared a few feet in front of me, glowing with an odd phosphorescence. I tried to stop, tried to slow my incredible momentum, but it was too late. I hit hard, skidded across the sand, then tumbled, head over heels, for what felt like a mile.

When I finally came to a stop I was bruised and scraped and dizzy as hell, but at least I was alive. And relatively unhurt. I sat there for a minute, flat on my butt, and tried to get my bearings while the watery world whirled around me.

Colors were so much brighter down here—electric pinks and greens and purples spun around me in kaleidoscopic images I couldn't quite bring into focus.

When my head finally quit spinning, however, I realized that I was in the middle of what I supposed passed for an underground city. There were caves everywhere and huge structures made of stones and coral and shells. Strange black creatures that looked like long, slim sea lions swam from one structure to another. And swimming with them were people who looked just like I did. Or more accurately, just like Kona with his long black hair and strange, silvery eyes.

Mermaids, I thought dazedly as a few swam by. Or rather, mermen, as they were male. But they didn't have tails, which made what I was seeing nearly impossible. People couldn't breathe under the ocean.

Of course, I didn't have a tail either. My brain, which was finally starting to work, struggled to put the pieces together.

Was the whole tail thing a myth?

Did mermaids not have tails after all?

But how could that be possible? I remembered seeing my mother's tail a few times when I was young and we were in the water, far from land. It was a deep, vibrant emerald green. Surely I hadn't imagined it.

Kona had told me that there were a lot more half-human

174

creatures under the sea than just mermaids. Were these people what he'd been talking about?

One of them swam up to me, smiled. I smiled back, unsure of what she wanted. When she didn't move away, I started to go around her, but she shifted so she was once again directly in my path.

She obviously had something she wanted to say to me, but I didn't have a clue what it was. It was just as obvious that she wouldn't let me move on until I figured it out.

For the longest time, we simply stared at each other. Her eyes were wide and expressive and followed my every movement, almost as if she expected me to have some idea as to what she wanted. But I didn't and the longer we stood there, the more uncomfortable I became.

To begin with, her eyes were too direct, the look in them saying that she saw way too much of me. I'd spent such a large part of my life trying to hide who I was that her ability to look inside me was freakish in the extreme.

Add to that the fact that she was gorgeous—as everyone down here seemed to be—and dressed like some underwater queen in a scarlet robe made of a light, diaphanous material. Standing on the ocean floor next to her in my simple white underwear, I'd never been more acutely aware of how plain I looked—it wasn't a good feeling.

Finally, she seemed to realize that I wasn't getting whatever it was she was trying to tell me, because she gestured for me to follow her. I didn't move. Everything that had happened since I left my birthday party caught up to me all at once, and suddenly I was more than a little stressed out. I needed to find Kona—if he was even at this strange underwater city.

175

And if he wasn't—if he wasn't then I was completely screwed. I had nowhere else to look for him. I would have to head back toward home and hope that I could somehow find my way.

But the mermaid—or whatever she was—wouldn't take no for an answer. Instead of leaving me to look for Kona in peace, she reached for my hand. I yanked it away, but still she didn't turn away—just reached for me again and started to tug me toward one of the caves I had noticed after my less-than-graceful entrance.

I wanted to resist, wanted to flee, but the part of my brain that was still functioning figured that following the one person or thing down here that actually acknowledged my existence might not be a bad thing. It wasn't like I had such a great alternative plan going on.

Besides, I figured if she'd wanted to hurt me she probably would have done it already.

She led me over to what looked like the smallest of the caves. I have to admit when she started to tug me inside I almost lost it. After that last, harrowing descent into total and complete blindness, the idea of trading in the strange and beautiful lights of the city for another blackout did not appeal to me. At all.

But her grip had turned to iron around my wrist. Not going was obviously not an option, which annoyed me all over again. This whole lack-of-choice thing in my life was really starting to get on my nerves.

In the end, I went along without making too much of a fuss, unsure at that point of what else I could do. She led me through a dark and winding cave—room after room of low ceilings and narrow passageways. I'd never been claustrophobic, but after today I might very well have a number of phobias if I ever made it out of the ocean. Absently I wondered if the fear of turning mermaid had an official name, like agoraphobia or hydrophobia. Somehow mermaidaphobia didn't quite cut it.

When we finally stopped, it was in a room with just enough light for me to distinguish that I was standing underneath a small, narrow, vertical passage. A very small, very narrow, *very* vertical passage.

"No," I tried to say, backing away. But of course, all that came out was an odd gurgling sound as I swallowed a huge glug of sea water that left me gagging. The salt content was even higher down here than at the surface, something I might have found interesting if I wasn't on the verge of completely and totally wigging out.

She smiled, tugged on my arm. I shook my head vehemently. There was no way I was going up that tiny little death trap. No way in hell.

Her eyes were kind and she nodded like she understood. I knew, deep inside, that she didn't want to hurt me, but still I couldn't. I just couldn't.

Stop being such a wimp, Tempest, and get your butt up here. Kona's voice—rich and deliberately snotty—slipped into my thoughts like it had always been there.

For a moment everything inside of me shut down as I worried that I was finally losing it. That the events of the past two weeks had become too much for me.

Even so, his name was a question at the back of my mind. *Kona?*

Who else would it be? he demanded. His voice was weaker than it usually was, but it was definitely him.

177

Oh, I don't know. How about a sadistic sea monster who seems to be doing her best to kill us both? I couldn't help the sarcasm that leaked through.

Oh, right. He paused. *Tiamat won't hurt you here.*

Is that her name? Tiamat? I racked my brain, trying to figure out if I had ever heard it before.

Come up and I'll tell you all about her.

I stared at the narrow passageway with extreme consternation. *Are you up there?*

I am. His voice turned impatient. And tired—so tired. *Come on, Tempest. Trust me.*

Said the spider to the fly, I thought to myself, only to hear echoes of his laughter in the back of my mind.

I take exception to being referred to as an eight-legged, bloodsucking bug.

Yeah, well, spiders are insects, not true bugs. And if you don't like it, then stay out of my brain.

But I was already inching forward, my gaze on the hole that was now almost directly above me. I wasn't even sure how to get up there . . .

If I do this, I told him in the most hard-ass voice I could manage, *you are going to owe me so huge.*

There was another pause, this one longer than the first. Then, *I already owe you huge. I can't believe you came after me.*

My cheeks grew warm despite the nearly frigid temperature of the water. Nice to know I could still blush twenty thousand leagues under the sea. *Doesn't this mermaid gig have any advantages to it at all?* I wondered as I put my arms above my head and grabbed on to two narrow handholds on either side of the passageway's interior.

Don't be embarrassed.

Stay out of my head! I slapped the words at him as I pulled myself up.

There was just enough room for me to wiggle into the tube-like structure—and maybe enough for me to kick my feet shallowly. But my arms weren't much use. They were still stretched above my head and there wasn't room to pull them down to my sides.

I looked straight up, could see nothing but blackness above me, and felt my already shaky resolve weaken even more. That plunge downward I'd taken earlier had really messed with my head, and the idea of going back up in the same darkness scared me to death. Especially since I couldn't figure out how I was supposed to swim with such limited use of my limbs.

It'll be okay. Kona's voice was a soft, warm caress to my frazzled nerves. *Do you trust me?*

Do I trust you? I echoed the question incredulously. I had plunged into the icy Pacific after him, had followed him for what felt like days without having a clue where I was going. Had actually tried to become mermaid to get to him. I would have done none of those things if I hadn't trusted him implicitly.

So do this, he said. *This one last thing. I promise you, when you make it to the top you won't be scared anymore.*

Yeah, I'll probably be catatonic. But I reluctantly shoved off. Just keep your eyes on the prize, I told myself as I made my way slowly through the odd tunnel. Or at least your brain on it, since it's too dark in here to keep your eyes on much of anything.

I kicked a little, used my hands to scoop water, but it was slow going—at least until I was about seventy feet up the passage. Then I heard a strange, roaring sound—like the crash of waves on the surface—and a wicked, whirling current caught me and shot me straight up. Like an elevator at the Empire State Building, I climbed hundreds of feet—thousands maybe—in mere seconds.

The apprentice scuba diver in me was horrified, worried about surfacing too quickly without plateauing numerous times. All of my father's warnings of the bends or nitrogen embolisms bombarded me.

You're not breathing oxygen—or nitrogen. You don't have to worry about that.

Right. Of course. I had gills. There was nothing to worry about, except whatever was waiting for me at the other end of this very kick-ass ride.

I'm *waiting for you.*

Right.

I tried to enjoy the experience, told myself it was just like one of the roller coasters at Six Flags. Except dark and closed-in and scary as hell.

Tilting my head up, I realized that there was finally light above me—real light, not artificial. I really was climbing back to the surface. *Why, then, had I been forced to go so deep to begin with?* I wondered as resentment began to simmer.

It's the only way to get here. Kona again, eavesdropping on my thoughts.

Stop that. I tried to shove him out of my head.

He only laughed. *Sorry. You make it too easy.*

Well, excuse me. I've never had to worry about someone getting in my mind and reading my thoughts before. I paused, then asked curiously, *Is there a way to block it?*

Of course there is. I'll teach you.

When?

Soon. Get ready, because you're almost—

And then I was breaking through the surface of the water, the sun so bright I had to squeeze my eyes shut in self-defense. I tried to take a deep breath, but gagged instead.

Give it a second, Kona cautioned. *You've been breathing water for hours and now you're gulping down air like it's about to disappear. Don't panic and your body will adjust.*

Will it? I answered sarcastically, finally understanding what it meant to be a fish out of water. I felt like someone was holding a pillow over my face and waiting for me to give up the fight.

It'll get a little easier every time you change. It just takes some getting used to.

I was too busy trying to get my lungs to work like a human's again to answer. But that didn't mean I wasn't wondering—what was he that he knew so much about the change?

For once he must not have been reading my thoughts, because no answer popped into my head.

When I was reasonably certain I wasn't going to suffocate above water, I focused on my surroundings for the first time. My eyes were still sensitive to light after being under the water for so long, and everything I looked at had that weird, golden halo that came when too much salt water mixed with too much sun, and your retinas felt like they were being burned out.

Still, I could see enough to know that I was in the shallows off an island with beautiful white sand. Palm trees billowed in the distance and in front of me was a gigantic structure that could only be called a castle.

It wasn't any ordinary castle either. In fact, it put me in mind of the ornate sand creations of my childhood—the wild, soaring imaginings of my mother as she sat with me and helped me build the best fortress on six beaches. We would sit in the sand for hours, crafting soaring structures with minute attention to detail and pining for the beautiful princess who needed to be rescued from the evil witch's locked tower.

But this wasn't my mom's imagination, I realized dazedly as I waded to shore. The pointy turrets, the intricately carved bridges, the long, high windows, were all right in front of me.

My stomach twisted and flopped, knotted and plunged to somewhere in the vicinity of my knees. Was this it, then? Was this her home? Was my *mother* inside of there, right now, waiting for me?

Chapter 17

❧

I'd barely had a chance to formulate the idea when Kona cut into my frantic imaginings. *No, Tempest. I'm sorry, but your mother isn't here. This is my home.*

The hope growing inside of me—hope I hadn't even been aware of harboring—quickly died. Who had I been kidding, I told myself roughly. My mother? Why would she be sticking around waiting for me now, when she never had before?

Please don't do that. Kona again. *Come up to the house. I'd come down to meet you, but I'm supposed to stay in this stupid bed, per doctor's orders.* Disgust crept into his tone. *I'm completely fine, but no one wants to take chances with the heir to—*

He stopped abruptly. *Heir to what?* I asked as I made my way up the silvery sands of what I supposed was his own personal beach. Which was kind of a shock, since I'd gotten used to thinking of him as some nomadic surfer dude, his board his only possession.

I squinted at the castle. Boy, had I ever gotten that wrong.

I glanced around as I walked, wondered just how far from

home I'd come. The sun was bright here, golden. The ocean a perfect blue that was as clear as glass. It reminded me of the islands we'd visited last summer and I suddenly remembered Kona's unwillingness to be pinned down when I'd asked about his name. Had my headlong flight last night led me all the way to the Pacific Islands?

Not exactly.

Ugh. He was in my brain again. *Are none of my thoughts sacred?*

I don't know. Are they?

How had I forgotten how perverse Kona was? Once again, he was taking great delight in tormenting me.

So, if I'm not in Tahiti, where exactly am I? I demanded.

Don't rack your brain trying to figure out that stuff. We're not on any map—any human map, that is.

What's that supposed to mean? The more agitated I grew, the faster I walked. I was almost at the castle.

Don't worry about it.

I gritted my teeth. *I'm not an imbecile, you know. You don't get to pat me on the head and tell me to be a good girl. You promised me answers and you* will *give them to me.*

He laughed. *You're a real hard-ass, you know that?* The way he said it made it seem like a compliment.

I've had to be.

That's one of the things I like best about you. One of the things you'll need when . . .

Keep breaking off like that in midsentence and you're a dead man when I finally get my hands on you.

Ooh, I'm shaking.

You should be.

184

Nah, you worked too hard to save me to kill me now.

Don't bet on it. I approached the door, reached for it. *I faced down a garden of octopuses for you, but that doesn't mean I'm a pushover. In fact—*

The door swung open before I could turn the handle. A man, about fifty, stood on the other side of the threshold. Despite being dressed in a pair of baggy shorts and one of my father's surfing tees, he was a dead ringer for Alfred, Batman's very formal butler dude. And I should know—Rio and Moku watched the stupid movie about ten times a week.

The look he gave me was so full of disapproval that I started to take offense—I'd come too long a way to have to deal with attitude. But then I remembered. Most of my body was bruised or bleeding, and I had shown up at the door in nothing but my bra and panties.

The realization had me glancing down, mortified, but one look made me wish I hadn't. Make that my completely *translucent* bra and panties. Ugh.

I crossed my arms awkwardly over my breasts, waited for him to invite me in—or tell me to get lost. He did neither, just continued to stare until I was squirming where I stood. When I couldn't take the tense silence any longer, I finally muttered, "I'm Tempest. I need to see Kona."

His eyes widened at my name, the tight purse of his lips relaxing slightly. "Certainly. Come in." He stepped away from the door, ushered me inside, then eyed my sandy feet with complete repugnance. "Let me get you something to dry off." And clean up—he didn't say it, but the words were definitely implied.

"That'd be great." Part of me wanted to tell him what he

could do with his obvious disgust, but I wasn't exactly coming from a position of strength. After all, it wasn't like I could meet Kona in my underwear.

Why not? It wouldn't bother me. I could almost see his smile.

Yeah, I just bet.

"This should help, madam." The odd surfer-turned-butler held out a brightly patterned towel and navy blue robe. I reached for the towel first, tried to brush off as much sand as I possibly could under his eagle eye. Then wrapped the robe around me, shocked at how soft and plush it was. When I rubbed my nose against the collar, I realized that it smelled like Kona.

I was wearing Kona's robe. The idea made me tingle all over, but I kept my tone casual as I thought, *Thanks.*

My pleasure. Although you really don't have to cover up on my account.

Already been there, dude. And it so isn't happening.

Is that a dare? His voice was lower, huskier, than it had been a few moments before. Chills shot up my spine, but they weren't the bad kind. Of course, with Kona, they almost never were. That was the problem.

Doesn't sound like a problem to me.

Kona!

All right, all right. My room's on the fourth floor. It's the last door on your right.

Are you sure Alfred won't mind me heading up unescorted?

Alfred? He seemed confused—obviously not a Batman fan. But then he didn't have to be. He was living his own secret life.

I almost explained the reference to him, but kind of liked the fact that I knew something he didn't for once—even if it was only a stupid superhero allusion.

Come on up. I've been waiting for you.

Interesting, since I've been imagining you dead, your body devoured by hungry sea animals.

Yeah. He had the grace to sound uncomfortable. *I'm really sorry about that.*

I refused to say the patented *it's okay*, because obviously it wasn't. I had swum all night—into the very depths of the frickin' Pacific Ocean. My dad was probably frantic, or at least devastated, and I was on some alternate-reality island that didn't exist in the real world.

No, things were definitely *not* okay.

I headed up the staircase, yanking on the robe as I did so I wouldn't trip on the stupid thing. It was way too long for me and I had visions of tumbling down the stairs to my death—or at least one heck of a concussion.

Still, I felt totally girly all wrapped up in it. At almost six feet tall, I hadn't felt dainty since kindergarten, but Kona was about five inches taller than me and really well muscled. Next to him, I actually looked like something besides a throwback to the Amazons.

I got to the third-floor landing and headed up one more flight of stairs to Kona's room. As I climbed, I became aware of the tapestry that ran the length of the second staircase. It was huge, its colors muted—by time or design, I didn't know. But if I'd had to guess, I would say that it was time. The thing looked really old.

A little curl of excitement unwound inside of me as I realized that even in this alternate world, people created art. Maybe I wouldn't have to give up my painting after all . . .

I cut off the thought, nowhere close to considering being a mermaid for life. Then I started to rush past the tapestry, figuring I could check it out later. I wanted to see Kona with my own eyes, to make sure he was as okay as he sounded.

And I wanted answers. A lot of answers. I had more questions than I could count.

But slowly the story on the tapestry seeped into my consciousness and I paused to get a better look at the thing. It was an underwater scene, though in the distance stood Kona's castle, rising out of the water and into the clouds. In the forefront was a major battle. I stared at it as a sick kind of fascination unwound inside of me.

In the center of the tapestry was a great, ugly sea monster— slimy and gray and multitentacled. In each of its—I paused to count—twenty-three tentacles, the thing held a mermaid or a human or one of these black, sea lion–type creatures I'd seen near the ocean's bottom.

One of the tentacles was halfway to its huge gaping mouth and I realized that in it he held a headless mermaid with an emerald tail and green tattoos across her shoulders.

Gross.

In the water around the monster were thirty or forty of the same human and semihuman creatures locked in battle with other humanlike creatures with gray skin and pointy features, as well as ones that were half octopus. I thought with distaste of the huge garden of octopuses I had swum through earlier and wondered if they'd had the ability to morph into the things I was presently looking at.

One woman—or mermaid, really—stood out from the rest. She was bearing down on the disgusting sea monster, a jeweled sword in one hand and a lightning bolt in the other. Her long hair was streaming behind her and purple tattoos covered her back and ran down her arms.

She seemed familiar and I squinted, trying to get a better look at her face. But it wasn't well defined, despite the clarity of the rest of the tapestry. As I studied her, I couldn't help wondering if she had won the battle being depicted—or if she had fallen to the creature like so many of her people. Their bodies littered the water and ocean floor around the terrible beast.

"So, you like the Lusca?"

I jumped at the voice so close to me, nearly fell down after trying so hard to avoid it. Probably would have, if Kona hadn't reached out and grabbed me, pulling me against his warm bare chest.

"Whoa, sorry."

"I thought you were in bed." I pushed against him, trying to get free. It felt entirely too good to be standing so close.

"You were taking so long I wondered if you'd gotten lost." His wild silver eyes gleamed down at me.

"Yeah, well, I wasn't expecting you to be skulking around the hallways." I shoved at his shoulders again and this time he let me go. I looked at him for a minute, shocked at how relieved I was to see him. He looked good—really good, especially considering the fact that I'd spent part of the previous night giving him CPR. The wound on his chest had closed up, a long, pinkish scar the only evidence that he had nearly died less than twenty-four hours before. Amazing.

He caught me looking. "My people heal quickly."

"Obviously." I wanted to ask who his people were, *what* they were. If he wasn't a mermaid like me, then what was he?

But I didn't know how to start, so I settled for, "You look different. Kind of—" I stopped myself before I could say glowy, but that definitely was what I was thinking. He was giving off a silvery light so bright that it looked like he had swallowed the moon.

He grinned like he knew exactly what I meant. "It's the water."

"Right. The water." I paused. "What does that mean?"

"It's dark under the sea, so after we've been in the water for a while we give off light, so we can see each other."

"So, you glow."

He winced. "That isn't exactly how I would describe it. More like a phosphorescent reaction to—"

"You glow."

"All right. Yes. We glow. But don't get too cocky—you look different too."

"Yeah, like a drowned rat."

"More like a flower about to open." He paused. "I'm sorry. That was totally lame."

"No. It was . . ." I burst out laughing. "Yeah, pretty lame." But sweet too, especially coming from a guy like Kona. I'd been around him long enough to know he didn't just say things like that—ever. Plus, the faint blush on his cheeks was kind of endearing.

"So, what's a Lusca?" I asked, searching for a way to change the subject.

"That is." He nodded to the tapestry. "He's one of Tiamat's enforcers. A giant octopus-type creature that lives underground. He comes out every once in a while, gorges himself on our blood and causes as much trouble as he can, then heads back underground until she needs him again."

Tiamat. There was that name again. "She needs enforcers?" After what she'd done to us on the beach, I had trouble believing that she needed help with anything.

"I wouldn't say she *needs* them so much as she *wants* them. They make her job easier."

I studied the creature with distaste, even more disgusted by it now that I knew it lived off human—or semihuman—blood. "I'm still not clear on how a giant, vampiric octopus could make anyone's life easier."

"That's because you don't know enough about Tiamat."

"That's true. I don't." I gave him a pointed look. "Is that ever going to change?"

"Absolutely. But—" He turned serious. "Are you sure, Tempest? I didn't tell you before, because once you know . . ."

At his words, butterflies trembled inside me but I tried to laugh them off. "What? Is this one of those if-you-tell-me-you'll-have-to-kill-me things?"

He looked startled for a second, then laughed. "Are you always so dramatic?"

"Actually, no. But swimming all night after being confronted by an evil sea witch brings out my inner drama queen. Besides, you can't diss *Top Gun* like that."

"*Top Gun*?" He looked even more confused.

"Yeah, you know. Tom Cruise, Kelly McGillis. Fast airplanes. San Diego?" He shook his head and I pretended to be dismayed. "How could you *not* know that movie? It's where the whole tell me/kill me line originated."

"Oh. Right. I must have missed that one."

Of course he had. Did they even get movies over here? Everything else seemed so normal, so *human* that it was easy to forget that some things just didn't translate.

"Just tell me," I finally said. "I saved your life, after all. You owe me."

"Nothing like using your altruism as a bargaining chip. Maybe you should have asked before you saved me—dangled the carrot of life over my head."

"I would have, but you were unconscious."

"Oh, yeah. It's coming back to me now."

"Glad to hear it. So spill."

He leaned toward me, eyes sparkling, and I felt a little hitch in my breathing. Was he going to kiss me again? Was I going to let him?

In the end, all he did was reach forward and grab a lock of my hair. He tweaked it softly. "So, what do you want to know?"

It was an effort to stay focused with him so close, but I'd been waiting to hear those words for too long to let the opportunity pass. "Well, to begin with, you said it makes her job easier. What kind of job does she have that she needs creatures like that to make it easier?"

"Okay, maybe job was the wrong word. I guess I would have said her ambitions."

"Which are?"

"To rule the Pacific Ocean and everything in it."

His words set off a weird, low-grade buzz inside of me, one that made me feel like I was shaking apart. Yet another strike against this mermaid thing—I was completely sick of my body

192

wigging out with absolutely no warning. I mean, was it too much to ask to have a simple conversation without vibrating like a giant tuning fork?

Kona didn't seem to notice my discomfort and I wasn't going to clue him in to it. Now that he was actually talking, I wasn't going to do anything to get him off track.

I reached out, traced a finger over the decapitated mermaid in the tapestry. Her tail was bright green like my mother's. "Just the Pacific Ocean, huh?"

"For now. I'm sure her plan includes conquering all seven of the seas eventually."

"But she's starting here."

"Yes."

"What is she?"

"I'm not exactly sure how to explain that to you."

"Try hard."

"Okay, okay. No need to get testy."

"Says the guy with so many secrets he needs a chart to keep them straight."

"Oh, there aren't enough for a chart. A graph maybe."

I shot him a look that showed him just how unamused I was.

"Sorry. I'm trying to figure out how best to describe her. Part sea witch, part dragon, part Loch Ness Monster, I guess. And one hundred percent evil."

I closed my eyes, trying to form a picture of what Tiamat looked like, but all that came to mind was a strange dinosaur/dragon–looking thing with a human face. As it was kind of cute in a cartoonish way, I figured it wasn't quite the image Kona had been going for.

But he seemed to understand my dilemma, because he draped an arm over my shoulder and started pulling me up the stairs. "Come on. Let's get some of those cuts cleaned up before they get infected. I'll tell you all about her after you take a shower, *and* I'll even try to see if there's a picture of her lying around somewhere."

He was saying all the right things, but still I wasn't convinced. "Are you trying to distract me?" I asked as I followed him up the stairs to his room.

"Would it work, if I did?"

"No."

"Then maybe I'm just trying to take care of you. I don't always have to have ulterior motives, you know."

"Just most of the time."

He grinned. "You know me too well."

That was the thing—part of me felt like I'd known him forever, like I could look inside of him and see all the way to his soul. But another part of me—the skeptical one—felt sure I didn't know him at all.

As we climbed the stairs, I looked down below us and realized his house was built very much like mine. Most of the walls were actually windows facing out toward the ocean. They provided a ton of light and a feeling of freedom even when inside.

Of course, that's where the similarities ended. Everything in this house screamed money and prestige, from the ornate furniture to the jeweled sculptures to the incredible paintings and tapestries hanging on every nonwindowed wall. We passed a bunch as we climbed to the fourth floor and headed down the hall.

The artist in me was dying to get close to them, to study each brushstroke and woven thread, but Kona was moving too fast, as if he wanted to shuffle me down the hall as quickly as possible.

We finally reached his bedroom and for a second, all I could do was stand at the door and gape. It was gigantic, probably half as big as my entire house—which was saying something. And yet every available surface was covered with huge bookshelves loaded with leather-bound volumes, a state-of-the-art entertainment center that included a PlayStation 3 and an Xbox, and piles of CDs, DVDs, and video games. In the corner sat two surfboards complete with stands.

In other words, it looked a lot like every other guy's room I'd ever seen, just on a much grander scale. Weird. He had all this and he'd never heard of *Top Gun*?

I perused the titles, wondering what kind of movies he *did* like, then shuddered at what I found. It looked like he had every horror movie ever made. If I stuck around, we were seriously going to have to work on his taste.

"So," I said, searching for a way to get our discussion back on track. "What are you the heir to?"

Kona whipped his head around to stare at me. "What did you say?"

"Earlier, you mentioned that they didn't want to take chances with the heir. What are you the heir to?" I paused for a moment, then decided to go ahead and push his buttons. God knew, he'd pushed enough of mine in the short time we'd known each other. "Are you king of the mermaids or something?"

"I already told you, I am not a *mermaid*." He said the word like it tasted bad.

195

"Merman, then?" I teased.

"No." He looked so insulted that I almost took offense myself—but since I wasn't overly happy about that part of my heritage either, I thought it might be hypocritical to call him on his obvious distaste for the things.

"So are we going to play twenty questions all morning or are you just going to tell me?"

"Tell you what?"

I rolled my eyes. "Come on, Kona. Spill it. If you're not a mermaid, then what exactly are you?"

Chapter 18

My question hung in the air between us as Kona studied me, almost as if he was trying to assess how I'd react to his answer. I have to admit I was getting a little nervous—the way he was acting, I was afraid he would admit to being a bloodsucking octopus himself. So when he finally shrugged and said simply, "I'm a selkie," I didn't know whether to be relieved or confused.

I spent the better half of the next minute racking my brain, trying to remember exactly what a selkie was. I had heard the word before, but the definition danced just out of reach. Admittedly, I wasn't exactly up on my mythical, or in this case not-so-mythical, water creatures, but I was pretty sure I remembered reading something about them at some point.

A picture of the creatures I'd seen earlier formed in my head and everything suddenly clicked into place. Before I could think better of it, I blurted out, "You're a sea lion?"

"I'm a *selkie*." This time the words came out through gritted teeth. "It's an entirely different thing."

"Okay. Right. Yeah. Of course." My mind was whirling. "But

still, you're a shape-shifter. You change from human to . . ." I trailed off, not wanting to use the dreaded "sea lion" words again.

"Seal."

"Right." It was coming back to me now. There'd been a story about selkies in a book of sea tales my mother had read to me when I was little. "And you have a pelt, don't you, that you slip off when you're on land?"

"I do."

A horrible thought occurred to me. "Did you leave it in San Diego, near my house? Is that why you're still . . ." I gestured to his human form.

"No. I'm in human form because I was expecting you." He grinned. "And because I prefer it. I always have my pelt with me." He gestured to his necklace.

"That's what's in the pouch?" I asked, amazed. I stepped closer to get a better look at the thing.

"It is."

"But how does it fit? I mean, you're huge and that thing is . . ."

"Not?"

"Exactly."

"Shrinking the pelt is an easy spell. Not all selkies can do it, but my family's pretty gifted with magic—not to mention paranoid about keeping our pelts with us at all times."

I thought of the story my mother had told me, about the woman who had bound a selkie to her by holding on to his seal skin. "If somebody finds it, you're under their control, right? You can't shift back and you can't leave them, ever."

"That's right." The smile had faded from his face.

"No wonder you keep it with you." I shuddered at the thought of being held against my will. The whole mermaid thing was bad enough, but jeez. The selkies had it so much worse. "I'd never let it out of my sight."

He laughed then, and I watched in amazement as everything about him relaxed. Strange that I hadn't realized how tense he was until he'd loosened up.

"What's so funny?"

"You are."

I faked a scowl. "I'm pretty sure I should take offense at that."

"You shouldn't. It's just crazy that I spent so much time worrying about how you would react when you found out I was . . ."

"What?"

"Different."

I started to ask him why he'd worried about my reaction, but the look in his eyes said it all. Dark, intense, and so hot I could barely breathe, it told me all I needed to know about Kona's feelings for me.

He inched closer and my heartbeat kicked up until it could keep time with the drums in an eighties heavy-metal song. My palms grew damp and my tongue twisted around itself. There was so much I wanted to say to him, but I didn't have a clue how to start.

And in the end, I didn't have to. He broke the silence first. "By the way, I wanted to thank you in person. You kept me alive until my brothers could find me. I appreciate it."

I remembered the wrinkly black hands that had pulled him from my arms. "Those guys who took you—they were your brothers?"

"My three younger brothers, yes."

"How did they know you were in trouble?"

He shrugged. "It just works that way. How did I know you were below, looking for me?"

It just works that way. Great. Too bad it hadn't worked like that for me—I could have saved myself a completely useless swim. I shook my head, not believing how idiotic I must look. He'd been completely safe, yet I'd plunged into the ocean after him, thinking that he needed to be rescued. What a joke.

"Don't do that." Kona grabbed my hand, held it tight.

"Do what?"

"Coming after me was the nicest thing anyone's ever done for me—don't feel stupid about it."

I could feel the red stain creeping over my neck and up my cheeks. "I told you to stay out of my head."

"This time I wasn't in your head, I promise. I'm just getting to know your expressions."

"Lucky me."

"Come on, Tempest. I swear, there's nothing to be embarrassed about." Kona's breath quickened and he moved even closer. So close that I could see the rise and fall of his chest. So close that I could feel his warm breath as it fanned against my cheek.

In that moment, I finally understood the meaning of the phrase "cut the tension with a knife." If the air around us got any thicker, I swear we'd be able to spoon it up like ice cream.

Heat bloomed inside of me, chased away the last of the chill that had dogged me since I stepped out of the ocean. It embarrassed me, scared me, so I ducked my head and let my still-damp hair fall over my face.

He reached out, pushed the hair back. Stroked the palm of

his hand down my cheek and tilted my face up to meet his. For a minute, as our eyes locked, my brain stopped working. Just utterly and completely short-circuited as I remembered what his lips had felt like against my own.

"I—" My throat closed up from sheer nervousness, which was probably a good thing because I wasn't sure what I wanted to say anyway. Certainly not that I cared about Kona or that I was attracted to him or that when I closed my eyes and thought about the future, more often than not it was *his* face that I saw. I wasn't ready to say that—wasn't sure I was even ready to feel it, not when I still had such complicated feelings for Mark too.

Kona must have sensed my confusion because he pulled away before I did something stupid, like melted right into him and forgot all about Mark and my family and the crazy sea witch who seemed to be carrying the mother of all grudges against me.

"You're a shape-shifter too, you know."

It took a minute for his words to register. "I'm human."

"You're mermaid, you just aren't ready to acknowledge it yet."

Anger whipped through me, burning me with its meteoric rise. "You only see what you want to see. I have a choice—I can be human. I *will* be human."

"You *want* to be human. That's not the same thing. Besides, I know you, Tempest. I know you won't turn your back on us."

His words were confusing, too confusing to deal with when my emotions were a maelstrom inside of me, so I did what I did best—I ignored them. The last few weeks had made me an expert at thinking about only what was right under my feet.

"So, can I take that shower you promised me?" I changed the subject abruptly.

"Of course. My bathroom's through there." He pointed toward a door in the left wall of his bedroom.

"Thanks."

"No problem. I'll go ask around, see if one of my sisters has something you can wear."

"You have sisters too?"

"Five of them."

I stared at him, aghast. "There are *nine* of you?"

"Yep."

"And none of you were twins?"

"Nope."

"What, was your mother insane?" Maybe I shouldn't have asked that, but really? Nine?

He laughed. "No. Just determined to contribute to the selkie population. There are a lot less of us than there used to be."

"So you're an endangered species?"

"I wouldn't call us a species. More like an endangered people."

"Oh. Right." Was I ever going to stop putting my foot in my mouth around him? *Doubtful, Tempest,* I told myself. *Very doubtful.*

Not to mention the fact that Kona's lips were twisted once again into that sexy grin of his, the one that got my hormones all tied into a knot. I needed to escape, quickly. Before I did something that I probably wouldn't regret. "I'm going to go take that shower now. Tell your sister thanks for the clothes."

"I will." But he didn't move, just kept watching me with those enigmatic eyes until I closed the bathroom door behind me.

Whew. I leaned against the door for a second, tried to get my brain back together. That guy should come complete with a warning label—or three.

I had planned on taking a quick shower, but once I got

beneath the hot spray I couldn't make myself leave. It felt too good, especially as the water hit the knotted muscles in my shoulders and upper back.

As I let the shower wash over me, I wondered, again, just how far I'd traveled. I'd spent my life paddling out to catch the next wave—my shoulder muscles were some of the strongest on my body. If my late-night swim had worn them out to the point of soreness, I must have been in the water a very long time.

But even worse than the soreness were the jagged cuts all over my body. Some were minuscule—from flying shells and debris—and some were huge, like the long, painful slice on the outside of my left thigh. And after being submerged in ocean water for hours, I could only imagine what bacteria had gotten into them.

I did my best to wash them out with soap. But it burned like hell—especially my ankles. They looked like someone really had clawed the skin off them. Raw and oozing, they were completely disgusting. Just one more thing I had to thank the sea witch for . . .

Eventually, the soap and hot water and shampoo made me feel almost human again. Plus I figured I'd been in there so long that Kona would be wondering if I'd jumped out a window.

With a sigh of regret, I shut off the water and reached for one of the thick blue towels that were hanging on the towel rack next to the shower. The pain had done a good job of keeping my mind blank while I was cleaning up, but as I dried off, I couldn't help thinking about Kona's last words.

"I've got some clothes out here for you, Tempest." Kona's voice came through the wall as if he'd been standing around, waiting for the shower to turn off.

"Great." I opened the door just enough to take them from

him, then rushed to pull on the jean shorts and tank top. It took me longer than expected, since I had to fight to get the stupid shorts buttoned. All I can say is his sister must be a lot smaller than Kona. I mean, even the shirt was a little too tight—and a little too low-cut—for my comfort. But it wasn't like I had so many better options: Kona's robe now smelled like drowned mermaid, and not in a good way.

By the time I got out to Kona, I was in a crappy mood. The shorts I was wearing were so tight that I swore they were cutting off circulation to my butt, I was starving, and I still hadn't had most of my questions answered. In fact, everything he'd told me had only given me more things to think about and more questions to ask.

Kona's eyes nearly bugged out of his head when he saw me. "Wow. You look—"

"Don't even. One word and I swear to God I'm going to hit you. Hard."

He was silent for a second, but I guess the temptation proved too much, because he gave me a huge smirk as he said, "It's a good thing you didn't say 'kick me.' I don't think those shorts could take it. They'd probably split right down the—"

I nudged his shoulder, not superhard as he *was* injured, but definitely with enough force to let him know I was serious. He must have gotten the message, because he shut up. Fast.

He sat on the bed, gestured for me to join him. But I wasn't sure the jeans—or my hormones—could handle the extra pressure, so I stayed near the window, looking at the ocean and the setting sun.

My dad must be freaking out. And Moku—who had made

him pancakes this morning? Or helped him put together his new puzzle? "Has it really been almost twenty-four hours since I took off after you?"

"Not exactly."

I shot him a look over my shoulder—I was sick to death of his cryptic answers. "What is that supposed to mean?"

"Time passes differently here than it does on your side."

"My *side*? What are we, in the middle of a Greek epic or something? Are you a siren, holding me captive on Circe's island?"

"Sirens are mermaids, not selkies."

"I know that." I shoved a hand through my hair in frustration, tugging at the ends so hard it was amazing I didn't make myself bald. "But what did you mean? If it's Sunday night here—"

"It's probably Tuesday morning in San Diego."

"Tuesday *morning*? But I left when it was still Saturday night. Are you saying I've lost two days?"

"In the human world? Yes."

God. My father was probably going nuts and Mark—I didn't even want to imagine what Mark was thinking. Seeing as how the last time I'd seen him I'd been glowing purple and ogling Kona . . . I shook my head. Yeah, in his mind I was probably up for the worst-girlfriend-of-all-time award. Not that I exactly blamed him.

"How are your cuts?" Kona crossed to the dresser, holding out a bottle of hydrogen peroxide and some bandages with the air of a captive waving the white flag. I smiled despite myself.

"They're fine."

"You know, it's going to be okay, Tempest."

"I *don't* know that. And neither can you."

205

"Sure I can. The power of positive thinking and all."

At that exact moment, the only thing I was positive about was that my life was completely, totally, 100 percent screwed up—all because I'd dived into the water after a guy who hadn't even needed me.

Typical. Just typical.

I leaned down, started dabbing peroxide on my injuries.

"Here, let me do that. You're being way too rough."

"It doesn't hurt."

"Liar." Kona took the brown bottle from my hands, grabbed some cotton, and started cleaning my ankles so gently I barely felt it. He didn't talk for the longest time, and neither did I. But as he finished with one leg and moved on to the second, I couldn't keep the questions at bay any longer.

"My mom said I had a choice—that at seventeen I could choose what I wanted to become. Are you saying that isn't true?"

"No, it's true."

"So I *can* still be human."

"Strictly speaking, yes. But—"

"Good. I want to go home." I hadn't been able to get Moku, or Mark, out of my mind since I realized it had been over two days since my party.

"*But*," he continued as if I hadn't interrupted him, "I don't think that's the choice you'll make. Not when you hear everything that's at stake."

"Sure, I will. It's not like I'm a real mermaid anyway."

I noticed with satisfaction that this slowed him down a little bit. He squatted back on his haunches and stared at me. "What's that supposed to mean?"

"When I came after you, when I tried to shift—I couldn't."

"Of course you could. You got here, didn't you? You wouldn't be able to do that if you were still human."

"Yes, but—" I paused, strangely humiliated by what I was about to say. Which was insane, right? Because it's not like I wanted to be a stupid mermaid anyway. "I didn't grow a tail. I tried to—I mean, I wanted to shift so that I could follow you, and my gills started working, but . . ."

"That's it?" he asked incredulously. "That's all you've got? 'I'm not a mermaid because I didn't get my tail'?"

"You make it sound like a little thing. I kind of thought having a tail was the defining factor in being a mermaid."

"It is. But every merperson gets his or her tail at a different time. You can't just wish it to happen—God knows, tens of thousands have tried, but it doesn't work."

He recapped the peroxide, put it aside. "Tempest, your tail is the last thing you get and it doesn't happen until you've proven yourself."

"Proven myself to whom?"

He shrugged. "That, I don't know—the ocean gods, the universe, *fate*? It's not like I ever had to go through it. With selkies, things are way different."

Part of me wanted to explore the differences he was talking about, but another part was completely hung up on what he'd said about mermaids. "Are you sure? My mother never told me that—"

"Yeah, but from what I can tell, your mom never told you much of anything, right?"

I hadn't anticipated the attack and his words hit me like a runaway train. I wanted to protest, to tell him to leave my mother out of this, but the fact of the matter was, he was right.

My mother *hadn't* told me what to expect, hadn't kept any of her promises to me, hadn't done anything to make my transition—or lack thereof—any easier. Which made the fact that I was down here all the more absurd.

My thoughts must have shown on my face again, because Kona murmured, "You know, just because your mom didn't tell you things doesn't mean she doesn't care about you."

"Yeah, but it doesn't mean she does, either."

It was his turn to look out the window, his turn to stare at the ocean instead of at me. He sounded so tired when he said, "It's not that easy, Tempest. Things are all mixed up down here right now and—"

"Yeah, and things are really mixed up with me too. She promised me she'd come back and instead she's left me to deal with all this whacked-out stuff on my own. That's not love."

"Maybe she's got her own stuff to deal with."

"What does that mean?" I demanded, determined to keep at him until he looked me in the eye.

"It means that the whole world doesn't revolve around you."

"That's a crappy thing to say. I've never thought that it did."

"No. But you sure feel that way about your mother, and her world."

Was he being deliberately obtuse, or was he just crazy? "She's my *mother*," I repeated. What about that fact was he missing? One day she'd been the most important person in my life and the next she'd been gone. One pathetic letter didn't make up for that and it sure as hell didn't count as maternal support. How could Kona not see that?

"I'm sure, if she'd been able, your mother would have come to you, Tempest. But sometimes what you *want* to do is very

208

different from what you *have* to do. Believe me, if being a member of my clan's royal family has taught me anything, it's definitely taught me that."

His words were razor-sharp talons scraping across my already-raw emotions. I felt exposed, as if everything I was inside was just hanging out for his own personal amusement.

Of course, the ridiculous clothes I was wearing didn't help. I flopped on the bed and pulled my knees up to my chest for more coverage, all the while praying the shorts didn't do what Kona had predicted and split right down the middle.

But then again, that was the least of my problems right now. I couldn't believe he was talking to me like this. I'd spent years listening to my dad defend her and couldn't stand that Kona was doing the same thing. He was supposed to be on my side, damn it. Not hers. *Somebody* was supposed to be on my side, right?

I wanted to call him on it, but settled instead on simply asking, "What do you know about it anyway?"

Kona finally turned to me. Sighed. "Look, it's complicated."

The anger came roaring back, stoked hotter by the hurt that lay just under the surface. "Don't you tell me that!" I yelled. "Don't you tell me that it's complicated like I'm some kind of child who can't understand. Tell me the truth, lie to me. I don't care. But don't tell me that."

My mother had told me in her letter that things were complicated. My father had told me the same thing over and over again, every time I asked him anything about why she had walked out on us. Nothing else, just that it was complicated and that I wouldn't understand. I'd taken it from them because I hadn't had a choice, but there was no way I was taking it from Kona too. Not after everything I'd been through.

"For most of my life someone has patted me on the head and told me they'd explain things to me when I was older. That there were things in this world that were beyond comprehension—" I was shouting, but couldn't seem to stop.

"They are beyond comprehension."

"You could at least try. I'm not an idiot. I can understand basic English!"

"I never said you were an idiot. But that doesn't mean I can explain to you what's going on. It doesn't mean that you'll understand it when you know nothing of our rules or our lives."

"If you can't tell me, then show me. But do something! I—"

"What is all the commotion about in here?" The regal-sounding voice sliced through the room like a switchblade and had me pausing midcomplaint.

Turning toward the interruption I saw a tall woman standing at Kona's bedroom door. She wore a beautiful black suit, four-inch heels, and more diamonds than I had ever seen on one person. She also bore a striking resemblance to Kona, though her black hair was pulled into a bun at the top of her head instead of flowing loose around her shoulders. Behind her was a man with Kona's silver eyes and an even more massive build. He too wore an expensively tailored suit.

"Mom. Dad." Kona's grin was relaxed, but there was something in his eyes that alarmed me. "I thought you weren't going to be back until late."

"Obviously," his mother bit out. "When are you going to remember your responsibilities?"

Kona's expression turned stormy. "I am well aware of my responsibilities, Mother."

"Really?" She arched one eyebrow and in that moment looked very much the queen I was just realizing she was. "You're supposed to be in bed, resting, not standing around half naked with this—" Her eyes swept over me in a look that said I should be paid by the hour, and minimum wage at that. I tried not to grimace—there was nothing quite like making a good first impression.

"Tempest." Kona's teeth were clamped together so tightly the word was almost indistinguishable. I wasn't sure what he wanted to say to me, but whatever it was, I was for it—especially if it got me out of the middle of this.

"What, Kona?"

But he merely shook his head at me, instead focusing his attention on his mother. "This is *Tempest*, Mom. She wanted to make sure I was okay after the accident, so she followed me."

I wasn't sure why he'd referred to Tiamat's attack as an accident, any more than I was sure that telling her I'd followed her son home like a stray dog was the way to diffuse the tension.

But he must have been right, because his mother, who had been so full of argument just a minute before, was struck completely speechless. Instead of continuing on with her rampage, she just stared at me, eyes wide, while her mouth opened and shut like a guppy's.

Even Kona's father, who had shown an amazing amount of equanimity up until that point, seemed at a loss for words.

Just when I was beginning to think they'd been struck dumb by the horror of their son being involved with a mermaid—or worse, a human—Kona's mother extended a hand and murmured, "It's so nice to finally meet you, Tempest."

"Yes." His father—the king, as it was just occurring to me with dawning horror—enveloped me in a huge bear hug. "It's about time you found your way down here."

"It is?"

"Absolutely. We've been waiting a long time for you." His smile was as open and welcoming as his hug had been.

What did that mean? Had Kona told them about me? But we'd only known each other a few days—far from the long time his father was describing.

"But she was worth the wait." The queen studied me with shrewd eyes, then turned to her husband. "It looks like the prophecy was right on, doesn't it?"

"What prophecy?" I asked, wondering how Kona's parents could be even more confusing and mysterious than he was. Obviously the apple hadn't fallen far from the tree.

"Oh, don't you worry about that right now," she all but cooed at me. "We'll talk about it later, after you have a chance to rest."

Her smile was blinding—or maybe that was the diamond pendant that hung around her neck. Either way, I tried to respond in kind, but could barely get my lips to tip up at the corners.

The walls were closing in and I suddenly felt, all too clearly, like Alice *after* she'd fallen down the rabbit hole.

PART FOUR

Getting Axed

When beholding the tranquil beauty and brilliancy
of the ocean's skin, one forgets the tiger heart
that pants beneath it.
HERMAN MELVILLE

Chapter 19

❧

Early the next morning, Kona and I walked down to the ocean in silence. A small table had been set up on the edge of the surf and it was covered with fresh fruit and sweet rolls. A carafe of some kind of tropical juice was nestled into a gold ice bucket with jewels the size of a baby's fist inlaid around the rim. Next to it was a big bouquet of the most beautiful and exotic-looking flowers I had ever seen.

If I didn't know better, I really would think this was paradise.

Last night, Kona's parents had all but fawned over me. His mother had ordered some clothes—in my size, this time—to be delivered, and Vernon (his name wasn't Alfred after all) was instructed to kill the fatted calf—or swordfish, as had been the case. Dinner was a formal affair, as far removed from what usually happened at my house as it could possibly get and still be considered a family meal.

The king had sat at one end of a long polished table and the queen at the other. Kona, his sister Alana—who had loaned me the too-tight clothes—and I had sat spread out, between them. None of the rest of his siblings had been home.

Conversation ebbed and flowed around me, and though none of the words spoken had been about me, I had sensed an electricity in the air, an excitement that had everyone at the table glowing. Everyone but me, who was still on the outside looking in. It was a position I was rapidly getting sick of.

Now, as we sat down at the breakfast table, Kona glanced over and caught me grimacing. "What's wrong?" he asked.

"Why should anything be wrong? Your family is treating me like I'm a cross between a magician and a messiah, but I have no idea why. I ask questions that go unanswered, am caught in some kind of odd time warp, and haven't slept in over thirty-six hours because I've been too busy trying to figure out what the hell is going on."

Kona's smile was sympathetic, but then he ruined it by gesturing to the food. "Are you hungry?"

"Are you serious? That's the best you've got?" I shook my head, stood up, and stormed past him as I went to the water's edge and looked out across the vast ocean. It went on forever and I despaired of ever finding my way back home.

An awkward silence stretched between us, not because there was nothing to say, but because there was too much. I had a million questions and Kona had all the answers, yet he would give me almost none of them. It was incredibly frustrating, and fury burned in my gut. But I wasn't going to ask again. I wasn't going to beg him to tell me something I should already know.

I would find a way home without his help and when I did . . . When I did, there was no way I would ever come back here again. My mom and Kona could take this world and the whole mermaid gig and go drown with it.

216

I was finished.

"You know I'm on your side, don't you?" Kona broke first.

"I didn't know there were sides."

"Sure you did. That's why you're so mad."

"I'm mad because I don't know what the rules are. Every time I think I have something figured out, you come along and change it."

"That's why I told you it was complicated. But you didn't want to hear me."

"That's bull and you know it. It's not that I won't listen, it's that I'm sick of half truths and evasions. At dinner last night, even your parents dodged every question I asked. Everybody seems to know more about my life than I do. Can't you see how frustrating that is?"

"We're just trying to protect you, Tempest."

"I'm not some child who needs to be protected from the truth."

"You're seventeen. And that's all your mother was trying to do by keeping you in the dark, you know. Protect you."

"Yeah. Her way's worked out real well for me, so far." I glanced pointedly at the scrapes and cuts that covered me, ignoring his wince of sympathy. "Why do you keep bringing her up, anyway? You act like you know her."

He paused for long seconds, then finally said, "I do know her."

Shock reverberated through me, kept me motionless when part of me wanted nothing more than to throw myself at him and plead for details. Was she okay? What was she like? Why had she left me alone for so long? Only the fact that it would

217

make me look completely pathetic kept me where I was. That and the fact that even though she knew Kona's family, she'd made no effort to contact me since I'd gotten here.

"You know, most of the time life down here isn't like this." Again he motioned for me to sit and this time I did, sensing that I had finally gotten through to him and he was ready to talk.

"Like what?" There was an urgency inside of me, a need to know that had every cell in my body vibrating with excitement—and trepidation.

"Dangerous. Crazy. Usually we all manage to coexist without letting all this crap get in the way." He reached for the juice, poured two glasses, and handed me one.

"So what's different now?" I grabbed a muffin, tore off a chunk, and popped it in my mouth. Despite ignoring Kona's earlier offer of food, I was starving—and had been since I'd shown up here the day before. "What has Tiamat on the warpath after all those years of peace?"

"*You*. She's convinced you're the one she's been waiting for. The one who can give her everything she wants."

It took the words a second to register and when they did, my appetite deserted me, the muffin turning to sawdust in my mouth. I forced myself to keep chewing when what I really wanted to do was spit out the whole mouthful.

It took me a few tries, but I finally managed to get the food past the lump in my throat. "You're saying I'm causing all of this?"

"Not you. Her perception of you—well, that and your seventeenth birthday."

"But that's insane. All I want is to be left alone to paint. I

218

want to surf and study in Paris and take care of my little brothers. *I want to be human.*"

"Yeah, well, we don't always get what we want. Isn't that what you told me a few days ago?"

I ignored him. "If I'm responsible for getting Tiamat all pissed off, why did you draw her attention to me? Why did you even come ashore? I mean, I'm assuming you weren't on that beach in Del Mar by accident."

Kona reached for a pomegranate, broke it open with his bare hands, and handed me half. "You're the unknown factor. The one person who has the ability to tip the scales after a millennium of peace. I wanted to get a look at you."

"You wanted a look—" I thought of the way he kissed me, of how the whole world faded when Kona pulled me into his arms. Of how his eyes followed me whenever he was near me. Had that all just been a game? A chance for him to see what I was made of?

Then I thought of Mark, of the way he'd looked at me that last night, as if he couldn't believe that I was interested in Kona. Suddenly I couldn't believe it either.

"I don't think I like where your brain is going." Kona leaned forward and grabbed my hand.

I jerked it away. "Are you in my head again?"

"I wish. But you're not projecting, so I'm stuck guessing what you're thinking. Whatever it is, though, I can tell it's not good."

What did he mean by projecting? I filed away the question— and my hurt over the fact that I had just been a curiosity to Kona—to be dealt with later. I had more important things to worry about right now than how Kona managed to read my mind. Or how he felt about me.

"You know, this whole conversation is ridiculous. One mermaid can't make that much of a difference. I saw the tapestry—there are hundreds of my kind."

"More like hundreds of thousands. There are mermaids in every ocean on earth."

"But doesn't that just prove my point? How can I shift the balance when I don't even know what life down here is like? I don't have a clue about all these secrets you all seem to be keeping."

Kona didn't answer, just kept prying seeds from within the pomegranate's shell, almost as if he was waiting for me to make a connection.

I'm not sure how long I sat there waiting for the light to dawn. When it did, it came along with a feeling of dread so oppressive I could barely speak. "You're talking about that prophecy again?" My voice was little more than a whisper.

"I am."

"But you don't really believe in those things, do you?"

"It's hard not to, when I've seen so many come true."

My fingers were curled into fists, my nails digging sharply into my palms though the pain barely registered. "What does it say?"

For the longest time, he didn't answer and when he did, his words were so low I had to strain to hear them.

"Bathed in shades of violet, she comes in the dark.
Power unrecognized, half human, half mar.

Born in lightning, anointed in tears,
Magic abounds, while its painful heat sears.
The battle draws ever closer and one side will fall.
Good and evil collide, once and for all,
The victor uncertain, as fate evens the scales.
A winter storm's coming, a dark night's tale—
A Tempest rising, without fail."

When he finished, he just looked at me, waiting for my reaction. Since I had about a billion different ones, ranging from disbelief to amusement—my mother had repeated that rhyme to me so often when I was a child that I could have recited it with him—I said the first stupid thing that came to mind. "That's it? That's your big prophecy? It's a child's poem."

He laughed. "A certain kind of child, maybe."

"Give me a break. That rhyme's been around forever."

"Maybe. But why do you think your mom told it to you so often?"

"Because it's got my name in it." I rolled my eyes. "I always asked for it because it made me feel like I was famous to hear my name in a nursery rhyme."

"You *are* famous."

"What are you saying?" I demanded, food forgotten as I leaned across the table at him. "You people really believe that stupid thing?"

"We do. The last few years have been unpleasant—this is what gives our people hope."

"And you think all that stuff in there is about me?"

"I know it is."

"Why? Because my name is Tempest? Because my tattoos are purple? The whole thing doesn't make any sense."

"Because you're the daughter of the most powerful priestess in existence. Because you have more magic inside of you than anyone I've ever met. Because I look at you and I just *know*."

Shock wound its way up my spine, down my arms. Curled inside of me until I could no longer feel the heat from the slowly rising sun. "I think you're all confused. My mother's a mermaid. Just a mermaid. And I don't have any power—"

"Really? How do you think you moved me halfway across the room at your party? No one else could have done that—not even your mother. How do you think you followed me through the ocean?"

"You left a trail."

"No, I didn't. You *saw* a trail. You created it from sheer will. Anyone else would have been lost, but you followed me. You found me because you wanted to, even though my brothers went to great pains to hide my presence—and my injuries."

His words lit a fire that burned through the cold of disbelief and denial. Because I knew he was right? Or because I wanted him to be wrong?

"The trail was there," I insisted. "It was the same color as your eyes—clear as day. You didn't see it because you were bleeding to death."

"I didn't see it because it was *not* there—at least not for anyone but you."

I didn't know how to argue with his certainty, so I let it go, though the memory of that shining silver path stayed with me—at least until his other words registered. "You said my mother is a priestess?"

"She is—an incredibly powerful one. Five hundred years ago she imprisoned Tiamat in a cage at the bottom of the Mariana Trench. It was so strong it's taken her half a millennium to break free."

"Do you really believe what you're saying?" I asked, incredulous.

"I do."

"But it's ridiculous. The whole thing is crazy. My mother is thirty-nine."

He laughed. "Your mother is well over six hundred years old."

"That's absurd!"

"Is it?"

"Of course it is! Nobody lives that long."

"Sure they do." He smiled grimly. "I'm two hundred and twenty-four."

I gaped at him, sure that this time I was the one whose mouth was moving like a fish's. "Now I know you're messing with me. You look like you're nineteen. Maybe twenty. But two hundred? No way."

He shook his head. "Selkies live a long time—we age normally until we become adults and then some kind of switch gets flipped and we start to age very slowly."

"How slowly?"

"My parents are nearly five hundred years old and they're in their prime. They won't hit old age for another three hundred years or so."

"And mermaids?" I asked faintly.

"Much the same."

"So you're telling me I'm going to live to be eight hundred?"

His expression turned serious. "Honestly, Tempest? I'm not

223

sure you'll make it to eighteen, let alone eight hundred. Not with the way Tiamat is gunning for you."

I shoved back from the table, knocking over my chair as I tried to get away from him. Maybe I wasn't ready for what he had to tell me, no matter how much I'd protested that I was.

Confused and more than a little freaked out, I made my way down the beach, his words spinning in my head. What he was suggesting was ridiculous, nonsensical. Not to mention completely bizarre.

And yet it fit. The way Kona always seemed so much more mature than Mark and the other guys I knew. The way he was so patient with me, despite the intensity I could feel inside of him. The way he kissed, with so much more finesse than any teenager should have.

The last thought stuck with me, though I did my best to banish it. With everything going on right now, kissing Kona should be the absolute last thing on my mind.

Be careful what you ask for. The old cliché came to me as I looked out at the ocean. *You just might get it.*

I'd wanted answers and I was getting them. But Kona had been right after all. Things *were* more complicated than I ever could have imagined and getting more so with each piece of the puzzle he gave me.

My mother was a priestess. I was—I didn't know what I was, but it didn't sound good. Tiamat was after me because of some stupid "prophecy" and the guy I'd been falling for was two hundred and seven years older than I was. Not to mention hoping to use me to save the entire freakin' Pacific.

Around me the ocean seethed and thrashed, the waves growing bigger with each breath I took.

"Relax, Tempest."

"I don't want to relax!" I whirled on him. "How can I?"

He didn't respond, just stared at me with eyes the same color as the clouds that were slowly rolling in above us. A fine mist of rain fell like a curtain, covering me with drops of water that sparkled like diamonds.

"Why does it always rain when I'm around you, anyway?"

Kona did respond then, with a laugh that was both harsh and sympathetic. "I think you have that backward."

"Excuse me?"

He shrugged. "I'm not doing this. You are."

"What are you talking about? No one's doing it—except maybe Mother Nature."

"Are you so sure about that? Really? Look around, Tempest, and then tell me it isn't you."

"Of course it isn't me. How could I possibly be responsible for all of this?"

But even as I denied it, I could feel the truth of his words deep inside me.

Could see all the times the ocean had clouded over and poured in the last couple of years when my emotions got to be too much for me.

Could hear the echoes of magic words in the unexplored corners of my soul.

A wave of denial rolled through me so fast and so hard that it nearly brought me to my knees. Lightning split the sky, slammed into the beach about ten feet from where Kona was sitting as thunder crackled directly above us.

"Control it, Tempest." Kona's voice was steady, unafraid. His eyes calm despite the sudden furor raging around us.

225

Another bolt of lightning hit, this one even closer to him than the first one had been. "Oh my God." I did fall then, as an ugly truth started to dawn.

"It's okay, Tempest."

"How can it be okay?" I screamed to be heard over the suddenly raging storm. "I nearly killed you. I *did* kill you!"

"You saved me." He crouched next to me in the sand, grabbed on to my hands and brought them to rest against his chest. "I'm fine now, because of you."

"No!" I wrenched away from him as the sand beneath us trembled. "If I'm doing this now, that means I did it then. I hit you with lightning. Not Tiamat. *Me!*"

Chapter 20

The rain was coming down heavier now, as if the sky had simply opened up and poured the entire weight of the Pacific onto us. Kona reached for me but I stumbled just out of his grasp, almost certain that I was going to be sick.

"Let me go!" I screamed as he walked toward me, a wealth of purpose in every step he took. "Just let me go!"

"I can't. Don't you think I would if I could?"

The rain had plastered his long, ebony hair to his skull and shoulders, had made his chest gleam and his tattoos shimmer until he looked more like an avenging god than a man. More like the fallen angel I had first compared him to than the mortal I had fallen half in love with over these last few days.

"Don't you think I see how this whole change is tearing you apart?" He grabbed me, his huge, calloused hands closing around my biceps as he forced me to hold my ground. "I need you, Tempest. I need you!"

His words moved through me, had me staring at him as I tried to figure out the truth of his feelings for me. Was it possible he was as confused, as mixed up, as I was? But—"How can you? I'm nothing." I tried to wrench myself away, but he held tight.

"You're everything."

"Come on, Kona. Look around you! I'm a disaster—from the moment you first met me, I've done nothing but try to destroy you." Images of the first time I saw him bombarded me, of him riding those monster waves. Waves I had caused. Waves that could have crushed him as surely as the storm that was swirling around us now.

"You're young, unschooled. That doesn't make you a disaster." His voice was hoarse, his eyes wild slashes of silver against the suddenly harsh planes of his face.

"What does it make me then?" It was a rhetorical question, one I really didn't expect an answer to. He gave me one anyway, though his words were so soft I had to strain to hear them.

"Our salvation."

I tried to close my eyes, to block out his words and the look in his eyes as he stared down at me. But I was spellbound, mesmerized, as wrapped up in him in that moment as I had been the first time I'd laid eyes on him.

Kona's grip loosened and he smoothed his hands up my arms to my shoulders. His long fingers stroked my collarbone and the hollows of my throat before sliding up to cup my face. His fingers were rough, and the feel of them set off mini-explosions inside of me as they brushed over my eyebrows and down my cheeks.

I shuddered, my body humming like I was hooked up to my own personal generator. As his thumb glanced across my mouth, I darted my tongue out, licked him. He tasted of pomegranates and salt water and deep, dark chocolate.

And then he was bending his head, his lips brushing against mine, once, twice, and so much heat roared through me that I couldn't imagine ever being cold again.

"I need you, Tempest." He whispered the words against my mouth and I drew them inside of me, tasted them. They were sweet, sweeter than I could ever have imagined.

Around us the storm quieted, the lightning sizzling into nothingness even as the sweet silkiness of the rain continued to fall. I reached up, covered his hands with my own, and gave myself up to him and this kiss that I wanted more than I wanted my next breath.

His lips were soft and warm and they lit me up from the inside. I was glowing—I could feel it—but this time it had nothing to do with the water, with my so-called power, and everything to do with Kona. I closed my eyes and colors exploded against the darkness of my eyelids. It was like the finale at a Fourth of July celebration, like riding a roller coaster in the rain, like floating through meadows of beautiful, blooming things.

His hands slid over my face, tangled in my hair, tilted my head back until I was completely open to him. His tongue glanced over mine, then swept inside to explore the very essence of me. I let him do it—begged him to do it, with the press of my body against his and the tug of my own fingers in his wicked, wonderful hair.

I couldn't have stopped, even if I wanted to. The taste—the feel—of him was addictive. Like surfing. Like flying. Like a thousand shooting stars streaking across the inky blackness of midnight over the Pacific, and in that moment, I swear I could feel him deep inside myself.

Time passed in a maelstrom of need and emotion—seconds, minutes, hours. I didn't know how long we stood there, locked together, and I didn't care. All I knew was that for the first moment in a very long time, I felt like things were going to be okay.

Kona pulled away too soon and I clutched at him, determined to hold him to me. But I didn't need to worry; he wasn't going anywhere. His arms were locked around me like a vice, his cheek resting against the top of my head as I listened to the pounding of his heart.

We stayed like that for a while, our breathing harsh and our bodies trembling. But eventually the real world crept in and with it all my fears and self-recrimination.

"How could I have hurt you like that?" I asked, stroking my fingers down the long, thin scar that sliced across the center of his chest.

He grabbed my hand, brought it to his lips, where he licked delicately across my palm. If another guy had done that I might have been totally weirded out, but with Kona it was okay. More than okay, as sparks shot through every part of me.

"It's not your fault."

"How could it not be? If I really can bring on storms—"

"There's no *if* about it." Kona held out his hand, palm up, and collected a few of the cool, sweet raindrops that were still falling. "But what makes you think you should be able to control it when no one has ever taught you how?"

"Is that what you're supposed to be doing? Teaching me how to use my *powers*?" The word felt strange in my mouth.

He laughed. "How can I, when you have magic inside of you

that I can only dream of? Tempest, I wasn't kidding when I said you were special."

The idea that I was special in the way he was describing was so far outside my realm of thought that I couldn't touch it. Instead I focused on the mundane details—if there were such things with magic. "Still, how am I supposed to control it if nobody tells me anything? I don't want to hurt you again. I don't want to hurt anybody."

"Shh." He leaned forward so that his lips brushed against my temple. "You won't hurt anyone."

"How can you say that? I almost killed you."

"But you didn't. And no offense, but have you looked in a mirror lately?" He skimmed his fingers over a particularly deep gouge on my shoulder. "You're in much worse shape than I am."

Strangely, it was true. "Why is that, by the way? If water heals us—"

"It doesn't. Just me. I keep telling you, selkies and mermaids are very different creatures."

"Well, that doesn't seem fair. You get hit by lightning and water heals you right away. I get scratched by a seashell and I'm stuck with it for days?"

"Most of these are a lot deeper than your average scratch. And I wouldn't have healed so quickly if the wound had been inflicted with dark magic—only untainted wounds heal in the water. Besides, mermaids have other gifts."

I snorted. "Yeah, like being able to kill people with lightning bolts. Whoop-de-do."

"Hey, that'll come in handy more often than you think."

"That's what I'm afraid of."

"Don't be. I told you, Tempest, it's usually really calm around here. You just came at a bad time."

"That's the understatement of the year." I looked out at the ocean as it slowly settled down. "But if I can't control this thing, how can I keep from striking someone else?"

"You'll learn. It just takes practice. And if you do hurt someone in the meantime, we'll fix it."

"What if whoever I hurt isn't a selkie? What if we can't heal him or her?" I asked fiercely. "I want you to explain things to me. To teach me everything my mother should have, so that *this* never happens again." I held out my hands, gesturing to the rain that was continuing to fall.

He pulled away then, his arms dropping from around me as he put space between us. "Are you sure? Because once you start down this path, you can't just go back. It doesn't work that way."

I stared at him incredulously. "I thought you were the one who wanted me here."

"I did. I do. But if you get in any deeper, if Tiamat figures out that you're here, training against her—"

"I wouldn't exactly call it training."

"I would. And that's not the point. If she knows you're down here but not with her, she won't let you leave. She'll kill you first."

His words seeped inside of me, mixed with the emotions and fears I already had. For the first time since I'd gotten that letter from my mother—for the first time since I realized she'd left me—I began to wonder if it had been more than the call of the sea that had pulled her away from us. More than selfishness. More than greed.

Because if the prophecy was as real as Kona said—if Tiamat

was real—then I couldn't help wondering about that night six years before. Had I gotten tangled in seaweed, as my mother had tried to convince me, or had Tiamat come for me, even then?

I turned back to Kona. "Well, don't pull your punches. Tell me how you really feel."

"You said you wanted to know."

"Yeah, but hearing you talk about my death so casually—"

"It's not casual. Believe me."

"Whatever. But you really think Tiamat believes that stupid prophecy? That she's afraid I'm going to kill her?"

"Or save her. There's a chance—or at least she believes there is—that she can bring you over to her side."

"So that I can live off the blood of mermaids? Eeew. No thank you."

He rolled his eyes. "Trust you to get caught up in that one small fact."

"I don't really consider drinking blood a small thing."

"Glad to hear it. But you *are* a mermaid. I don't think the whole drink-blood-to-stay-young-and-beautiful rule applies to you."

"Yeah, but if she's got me, doesn't that mean she's got her own built-in blood supply?" I shuddered at the thought of being some sea monster's midnight snack, again and again and again.

"You're smarter than you look."

I sneered at him. "Too bad I can't say the same about you."

He laughed and the arm he had draped around my shoulder tightened a little bit. Suddenly, the feeling of comfort was gone. In its place was a warmth that was decidedly uncomfortable.

233

"So what do we do now?" I asked, shocked at how husky my voice had turned.

He brushed his thumb down my cheek and over my jaw. I closed my eyes, shivered as he stroked my upper lip, then my lower one. He lingered for a moment, toyed with the deep *v* in the center of my top lip.

I wanted him to kiss me again. How crazy was that? Here I was, locked in a battle for my life and my sanity—maybe for the entire Pacific Ocean—and for a moment all I could think about was the feel of his mouth on mine.

"Now, Tempest . . ." His breath was warm against my temple.

"Yes?"

"Now, we swim."

I was so far gone that his words barely registered, at least not until he stood up with me in his arms and tossed me, sputtering, into the surf.

⬦

By the time I surfaced, Kona was already in the water, a good twenty feet in front of me. Annoyed by the unexpected dunking— though it had definitely cooled me off—I kicked hard in an effort to catch up to him.

Three strokes and I was next to him, another two and I was ahead. Finally an advantage to this whole mermaid thing. It had only taken me seventeen years to find it.

Kona kicked hard a couple of times and caught up with me, a huge grin splitting his face. It was a distinctly wicked smile and the wink he added to it had my brain stuttering just a little bit. Still, I couldn't just let him get away with dropping me like that. Reaching out, I grabbed his shoulders and shoved him down hard.

He went under the water instantly, but grabbed on to me as he sank. Before I knew what was happening, I was going down with him, my body plastered to his. I started to pull away, then changed my mind at the last minute. If Kona wanted to hold me like this, who was I to protest?

A minute later I was very glad that I hadn't. His eyes darkened and then he wrapped his arms firmly around me and we took off, spiraling through the water at speeds so fast they made my head spin. But at least my gills had kicked in quickly this time. I was breathing easily, no clawing at my throat required.

Kona zipped us through a huge coral reef and I gaped at the incredible reds and blues and violets. Then we dove under a forest of jellyfish—I looked up over his shoulder and was awed by the sight of all those translucent bodies floating directly above us. Was I ever going to get used to how vivid everything was down here?

I hope not. Kona slowed us a little bit as we came up next to a school of multicolored fish. *I like seeing the world through your eyes.*

I wanted to yell at him for being in my head again, but couldn't work up any indignation—not when the world he was showing me was more beautiful than anything I had ever imagined. My mermaid vision let me see things I never would have been able to as a human.

You need to block the thoughts you don't want me to hear, he said, amusement ripe in his voice as he took me in a deep dive that had me squealing and hanging on to him for dear life.

Why are we going so fast? I was breathless with the new sensations bombarding me.

How else will I get you to hold on to me like that?

I swallowed uneasily, unsure of what to say to that. But my arms tightened even more, until we were pressed so tightly together that I could feel the wild beat of his heart against my own. His eyes went darker and his hands pressed more firmly into my back. He liked being this close as much as I did.

How do I block my thoughts? I asked, shocked at how breathless I sounded, despite the fact that the sounds were coming from my mind and not my voice box.

I must not have been the only one affected by our closeness, however, because I had to ask the question three times before I finally got an answer.

Why do you want to know that right now? he demanded, his voice a rumbly growl in my mind.

Because. I smiled mischievously. *There are some things going through my mind at the moment that I'm not sure I'm ready for you to hear.*

His grin disappeared, was replaced by a look of such intense longing that I shivered despite the water's warmth. At that moment I wanted nothing more than to bury my hands in his hair and pull his mouth to mine. When I was kissing Kona the whole world faded away, and with everything he'd told me rattling around in my brain, I could use some oblivion.

But right before his lips closed over mine, his hand slid up to my throat. Toyed with the necklace that was still resting there—the one Mark had given me. Though it had been a birthday gift, I knew he'd meant it to be more than that. He'd meant it to be a promise, one I'd done a lousy job of keeping so far.

I closed my eyes and thought of him. Smart, strong, protective. Sure, he was a little moody, a little possessive. But he'd been good to me—for a long time he'd been the only one I could talk to. Cheating on him didn't sit well with me.

Until I figured out just what Kona wanted—what I wanted—maybe I should concentrate on learning the rules in this strange underwater world and nothing else.

At the last possible second, I ducked out of Kona's arms and shot through the water, somersaulting every few yards. He lunged for me, but I darted just out of reach, swimming back toward the surface.

I ran into a pod of dolphins that seemed delighted to have me near them. They rubbed up against me, prodded me gently with their pointy noses, spun through the water, and encouraged me to do the same.

I played with them for a while, conscious the whole time of Kona's heated gaze following my every movement. It made me clumsy, had me tumbling over a dolphin more than once, then laughing as they chattered at me—a series of high-pitched clicks I had no hope of understanding.

They like you. Kona swam closer, not touching me, but still near enough that I could feel his heat.

How do you know that?

They just told you so.

I grinned at him. *Are you saying you speak dolphin?* I didn't bother to hide my skepticism.

Selkies speak almost everything, he answered, reaching for me. He pulled me from the loose circle the dolphins had formed around me. *It's one of our gifts.*

What about mermaids?

He shook his head. *Sorry.*

You don't look sorry. I sniffed disparagingly, then ruined the whole thing by snorting up a large swallow of water. This underwater thing was going to take some more getting used to.

Kona stood by, laughing, as I had a huge coughing fit.

When I'd finally emptied my lungs, I returned to the conversation. *That doesn't seem fair. I want to talk to the dolphins too.*

Wave to them. They'll come back to see you soon.

But would I be here? I wondered as I watched the playful animals swim away. Or would I be back home before they returned for me?

This is your home.

Says you.

Says anyone with any sense. Look at yourself, Tempest. You belong down here.

I glanced down, realized for the first time that I was glowing purple again, from head to foot. *We're a matched pair,* I said, nodding to his own silvery glow.

That's what I've been trying to tell you. His smile was intimate.

Yeah, but what happens when we don't fit anymore?

What does that mean?

I don't know. I shrugged, swam a short distance away. *I'm not the only mermaid in the sea.*

No, but you're the only one that I want. He was behind me, his hands on my shoulders, his lips mere inches from my ear.

For now.

For ever. Can't you feel it, Tempest? We're meant to be together.

Because of some stupid prophecy?

Because we fit. He grabbed my arm, spun me around. *From the moment I first saw you I knew that we belonged together.*

That's crazy.

He cupped my face in his hands. *No, it isn't. Tell me it wasn't the same for you. Tell me you didn't recognize me that day.* His lips brushed over my forehead. *Tell me you don't feel something for me that you never felt for Mark.*

I wanted to tell him just that. I even started to, but in the end I couldn't force the words out. When Kona touched me, when he looked at me, something inside me recognized him on a whole different level.

Still, I wasn't sure what it meant. How much of Kona's feelings for me were because he thought I was the one in the prophecy? How much of his interaction with me was just to keep me in the water, where he wanted me?

I wanted to trust him, *needed* to trust him. He was the only person down here I had any attachment to at all—save my mother, and it wasn't like she'd made any effort to find me. But it was hard to believe what he said, knowing that he'd come to shore for the specific purpose of convincing me to become mermaid. How could I be sure this wasn't just an act?

Come on, Tempest. You don't really believe that. Kona's voice tore through the fragile barriers I'd been trying to erect between us, shot straight to my heart despite all the worries I had about him. About us.

I don't know what I believe. Everything's so mixed up.

That's because you're thinking it to death. Just let yourself feel for a while, let yourself enjoy being down here.

Yeah, but while I'm down here playing with dolphins, time is passing in my real life.

This is your real life.

Once again, says you.

239

Yes. Says me. Says the prophecy. Says biology.

I'm really more of a chemistry girl myself.

Kona smiled and, for a moment, the water between us seemed charged with electricity.

You can say that again. He grew serious. *But look at you. You're breathing underwater. Your fingers are webbed. You're talking to me with your mind. Do you really think, after all this, you can just go back to being human again?*

His words hit me like arrows, played on my worst fears until it was all I could do to breathe.

I pushed away from him, started swimming in the opposite direction from where we'd come. It was too much. This was *all* too much and I needed a little time to process.

Kona must have realized that I was on emotional overload, because he didn't say anything else. But he also didn't let me swim away on my own. He let me set the pace, and followed behind me as I swam as fast and as far as I could.

I wanted to outrun myself and the decisions I had to make, wanted to think about nothing more complicated than my next chemistry test. But as I swam, searching for a mindlessness that just wouldn't come, I realized that Kona was right. My life on land had never been further away from me.

I stopped abruptly and Kona nearly careened into my back. *What was that for?* he demanded, his eyes glowing with a combination of anger and understanding. My indecision obviously wasn't any easier on him than it was on me.

I know what I want now.

And?

I closed my eyes, prayed I was doing the right thing. Then

tossed out the request that had been brewing since the moment I'd first seen Kona's home, though I hadn't recognized it until just this minute.

I want you to help me find my mother.

Chapter 21

For a long time Kona didn't say anything at all, and I was sure he was going to tell me it wasn't possible. Eventually, though, he nodded. *Okay.*

I waited for him to say something else, and when he didn't I asked, suspiciously, *That's it?*

What were you expecting?

I don't know. Some kind of major protest, I guess. It's not like you've exactly been forthcoming about her.

Yeah, well. He shrugged. *Things have changed.*

What things?

Do you want to go or not? he demanded.

Of course I want to.

Then stop asking questions and let's move. He turned me around to face the way we'd just come. *And just so you know, if that's where you were headed when you took control, you were going in the wrong direction.*

Well, perhaps if I'd grown up down here I'd have a better sense of where things are. As it is, everything looks the same to me.

We swam in silence for a few minutes, then I asked again,

What things have changed? I wasn't going to let him put me off. Not now, not about this.

When we first met, my loyalty was to Cecily. Now it's to you.

It was a shock hearing my mother's name come so casually from Kona, especially in reference to the word "loyalty." It made it sound like he knew her really well.

I do. She's been a friend of my family's since long before I was born. He shot me a glance out of the corner of his eye. *She's the one who asked me to check on you, to make sure you were okay.*

I didn't know what to say to that, didn't even know how I felt about it, so I didn't say anything. Just swam silently beside Kona as I tried to figure out how this new information about my mom changed my idea of her—or if it changed it at all.

Where is she? I asked abruptly.

I'm not sure. Kona looked calm when he said it, but there was tension in his body that belied the serenity of his face.

I thought you were taking me to her. I tried to stop, but he grabbed my arm, propelled me forward.

I'm taking you to her clan. I'm not sure if she'll be there or not, but it's the best place to start looking for her.

Her clan?

It's made up of about ten thousand mermaids. She's the high priest-ess, which means she's the queen's major adviser. But everyone knows that Cecily's pretty much been running things for the last six years.

The timing wasn't lost on me, and as Kona's grip on my wrist loosened, I wondered if he'd phrased it like that deliber-ately—to show me that when my mom had chosen to leave me six years before, it was because she had something really impor-tant to do down here.

I turned the idea over in my mind, the thought that my

mother had abandoned us not because the lure of the ocean got to be too much, but because her people needed her. Wondered if it would make any difference in how I felt about her.

It turned out it didn't. Maybe that was cruel of me, maybe it showed my self-absorption, but I didn't care. She'd run out on us, left my dad alone with three kids who didn't know where their mother had gone.

It was all well and good that she'd wanted to sacrifice her old life for her clan, but what about everything that came with that decision? No one had ever asked my brothers and me if we were okay with her sacrifice. With our own. Maybe she should have thought about how things were going to end up all those years ago, before she'd crawled out of the ocean and gone looking for a human lover.

If she's so important to her clan, why isn't she there? I finally asked. *Where is she?*

She's looking for Tiamat. Once she realized the sea witch had broken free from her imprisonment when you were ten, Cecily started hunting her. And when she realized Tiamat was after you—she sent me to find you.

That doesn't make any sense. If she thought Tiamat would try for me, why didn't she come herself? Maybe she could have caught her.

Again, he didn't answer, but by then he was so tense that I didn't need him to. I was figuring things out on my own. She *had* been there. My mother had watched as Tiamat had tried to talk me into joining her, had watched as I'd tried to save Kona's life after he'd been struck by lightning.

And she had done nothing. She'd been too busy setting me up as bait.

244

When I thought of how I'd called out to her, how I'd pleaded in my head for her to help me even as she was betraying me, it made me feel like I was breaking apart. Made me scream deep inside of myself. It was worse, so much worse than anything I could ever have imagined.

You wonder why I don't want to be mermaid? I demanded, my voice shaking with rage. *Why on earth would I want to be like her?*

They're not all like her, you know. Cecily is . . . He struggled with how to describe my mother, so I filled in the blank for him.

As big a menace as Tiamat?

No. It's not like that. She's just driven.

Driven enough to use her daughter to trap a monster?

Kona turned on me then, his anger as palpable as mine. *You don't know what it was like. When Tiamat was free last time, no one was safe. Not merpeople, not selkies, not even humans. The carnage was unbelievable.*

And how do you know that? I thought she's been trapped for five centuries. You may be old, but you're not old enough to have lived through that.

Cecily said— He stopped abruptly, figuring, I guess, that any quote he attributed to my mother wasn't going to get him very far with me.

Or maybe he was finally clueing in to the fact that she had used him too. Had sent him to the surface to "help" me when she could have done it herself. Had nearly gotten him killed and then stood by and watched as I fumbled around trying to save him.

Look, it wasn't a lie, Tempest. The history books in school talk about that time, about how nothing was safe when Tiamat was around. She

245

took down ships, caused tidal waves that wiped out whole cities, killing anyone who came near her. She had to be stopped, and your mother stopped her. She's a hero.

Right. A hero. The word tasted bad.

I kicked, hard, suddenly not wanting to be anywhere near Kona. She might have used him, might even have been willing to sit back and watch him die. That was on her.

But for a while there, he'd let her. He'd hung out with me, with my friends, and all along he'd had a secret agenda. He'd kissed me and all along he'd been plotting behind my back with the mother who had abandoned me. He'd told me we were meant to be together, yet hadn't bothered to tell me what I needed to know to make an informed decision.

I turned on him, suddenly. *Which way is San Diego?*

He got it right away. *No. Tempest, come on. Don't do that.*

You don't get to tell me what to do. Either point me toward home, or I swear, I will blunder around this whole damn ocean on my own until I find it.

That's ridiculous. We've come this far—just let me get you to your mother's territory and then we'll try to figure everything out.

What's there to figure out? She used me. You used me.

It wasn't like that.

Oh, really? Then, please, tell me. I'm all ears. What was it like?

She came to me, told me your seventeenth birthday was coming up. She asked me to look in on you, that's all. To keep you safe.

And you just agreed?

Yes.

Why?

Because Cecily asked me to. You don't know what she is to our people. Because she's your mother, you don't see her for what she really is. I couldn't turn her down.

So that's what all this has been about? I demanded. *You trying to keep me safe for your precious Cecily?*

No! He turned around, shoved his hand through his hair in obvious frustration. *Maybe at the beginning, but not after I met you on that beach. Not after I kissed you.*

I stared at him, confused. *I don't know what to believe.*

Then don't you owe it to yourself to find out?

His words calmed me as nothing else could have. Maybe it was because he didn't try to convince me that he was telling the truth. Maybe it was because he wasn't trying to convince me of my mother's innocence, or of his own. For the first time since this whole mess started, I felt like I might actually have some kind of control over how it ended.

All right, I said.

All right?

You win. I'll stay for a while, meet my mother. Try to figure this whole thing out before I make any decisions.

His grin was wide enough to rival the sun and he grabbed me, hugging me tightly, before I could even think to protest.

Then he was letting me go, pushing me behind him, and before I could ask what was going on I realized that I had completely lost his attention. Instead, he was staring, hard, into the distance.

I couldn't see anything—mermaids' eyesight, though good, must not be as acute as selkies'. But within a couple of minutes I realized what he was staring at—five selkies were swimming through the water, straight at us. At least, I thought they were selkies. They were in human form and breathing under the water, exactly like Kona was doing.

Who are they? I whispered, trying to figure out if I should be scared or intrigued.

Kona didn't answer, squinting hard into the darkness. But as they got closer, he smiled. *My two youngest brothers, Ari and Oliwa, and a few of their friends.*

Your brothers? I looked at him, startled. *What are they doing way out here?* Though we'd done a lot of doubling back today, my best guess was that we were probably a couple of hundred miles from Kona's castle.

We're not like humans, Tempest. While the ocean is divided into territories, those territories are vast and we like to roam them. Staying within the same ten or twenty miles every day would drive us nuts.

Are we still in your territory? I asked.

We are, for another five hundred miles at least. Then we'll hit your mother's area.

When the five selkies finally got close to us, they stopped a few feet away and regarded me curiously. I was pretty sure I was looking at them the same way.

Like Kona, they all had dark hair, but their eyes were different. Two of the guys had bright blue eyes—the same color as Kona's mother—and I wondered if they were his brothers, while the others all had dark eyes.

Tempest, these are my brothers, Kona said, pointing at the two with the blue eyes, as I'd suspected. *Ari and Oliwa. And their friends Malu, Jake, and Aaron.*

I watched as they nodded as Kona said their names and it occurred to me—for the first time—that the communication between Kona and me wasn't unusual down here. It was the norm.

Of course. That's how everyone speaks when we're underwater.

Are they saying anything? I asked. Because if they were, I couldn't hear them. I thought of the woman in the red robe, who had stared at me like she'd expected me to answer her when I first arrived in this place. I realized, now, that that was exactly what she'd been expecting.

They are.

I can't hear them, I said again, starting to panic. Was this another failure on my part, like the tail thing? I couldn't speak the way everyone else did.

Kona laughed. *No, Tempest, calm down. There are general paths of communication, ones that everyone knows and speaks on, and then there are individualized ones, like the one you and I use. They're using the general one right now and you don't know how to tap into it yet.*

You have different frequencies *to talk to each other? Seriously?*

I wouldn't exactly call them frequencies, but yeah. It is kind of like that. When I introduced you, I was using the general frequency, but also the one that connects only you and me.

But how could I talk to you so easily, even in the beginning, if I didn't understand how these things work? I asked the question quickly, rushing the words together. The five guys were still staring at me, waiting for me to say something, and I was growing more self-conscious by the minute.

I told you before. We're connected. His hand ran in soothing circles on my back. *I knew it the second I first saw you.*

That's great and all, I said, doing my best to ignore the warmth his words sparked in me. *But how do I talk to these guys now?*

249

Say something to them. It may take a minute, but once they pick up on it they'll be able to project a path for you to follow back to them.

The whole thing sounded a little wonky to me, but if it meant that they would stop staring at me, I'd be willing to try anything. Smiling at them, I said, *Hi. Nice ocean you've got down here.*

Kona's brother Ari was the first to hear me and he laughed. A minute later, his voice—rich and a little deeper than Kona's—answered back. *Nice beach you have up there.*

Once he spoke, it was easy to find what path to answer him on. It was just a little different from the one I normally spoke to Kona on.

Oh, right. I forgot you were up there the other night. I studied him closely. *Were you the one I saw in the water?*

No, that was me, Oliwa said. *I'm sorry about that. We wanted to help you, but we were all in seal form and weren't sure how you would take to the three of us coming out of the water and shifting right in front of you.*

Yeah, none of us wanted to get hit by one of your rogue lightning bolts. Ari nodded at Kona's chest. *Good aim, though.*

Kona punched him in the arm, but I could tell it was a gesture of affection. *Don't embarrass her.*

It's a little late for me to be embarrassed, isn't it? They pretty much saw me at my worst.

If that's your worst, I can't wait to see your best. You were awesome, Oliwa said. *The way you used that storm to keep Tiamat at bay. Seriously awesome.*

I started to tell him that it hadn't been deliberate, but Kona said *Don't!* sharply, his voice coming across the path only the two of us used.

I gave him a weird look, tried to catch his eye, but he wouldn't look at me. And he didn't say anything else to me privately—he was too busy keeping up his end of the conversation with his brothers' friends.

So, where are you guys headed? Aaron asked.

To Cecily's.

Oh, right. Oliwa's eyes grew wide as he looked at me. *Your mom's a real cool lady.*

I didn't know how to respond to that, particularly since at the moment she seemed anything but. In the end, though, I just nodded. It was easier than the alternative.

Mind if we tag along? Malu asked. *Things have been boring as hell around here lately.*

We're not heading to a party, Kona said.

Sure, of course. We won't go all the way to Cecily's with you. Ari's grin was charming and just a little bit wicked. *We just figure the maids should be out and about.*

Right. I should have known this was all about the mermaids.

Not all about it, objected Jake as we set off again. *We want to get to know Tempest too.*

Who is also a mermaid. Kona smirked.

Oh, right. Then I guess it is all about the maids. Jake's grin was so open and relaxed it was impossible to be offended.

So, mermaids are a hot commodity down here too, huh? I asked Kona as we swam.

Oh yeah. They have a tendency to stick to their own territories, so we like to take any chance we can get to head over and explore a little.

We? I asked archly.

They, he corrected himself hastily. *They like to take any excuse.*

That was a pretty pathetic save.

Hey, give a guy a break, will you? At least I tried. He pulled me

251

close, wrapped his arms around me so my back was to his front, and used his powerful legs to propel us through the water. *Besides, I'm crazy about one particular mermaid.*

Yeah, but you don't have to go all the way to my mother's territory to find her.

For which I am very grateful.

I laughed softly and the sound seemed to work its way right through Kona. Pressed together the way we were, I actually felt him shudder.

I'm not sure how long we swam like that, Kona holding me against him while the others cracked jokes. I know we covered a lot of distance, because the ocean changed around us. For a long time we saw only small, brightly colored fish, but eventually we ran into groups of other animals. Another forest of octopuses that repulsed me but made Kona laugh. A pod of dolphins that was nowhere near as friendly as the one we had run into that morning. And then, much to my consternation, a few hammerhead sharks that followed us for a while.

Should I be concerned? I asked, glancing uneasily behind us at the long, gray bodies.

Don't worry about them. We're a little too big for their tastes, said Ari. *Besides, I'm pretty sure they prefer octopus.*

I didn't realize they were so picky. I mean, this is one of the species of sharks that eat their own young.

Yeah, well, they only do that if they're hungry. Kona's arms tightened reassuringly around me.

Oh, right. That makes me feel so much better.

You know, sarcasm really becomes you.

Good to know, since I use it so often.

Though the guys continued to tell me I had nothing to worry

252

about, I realized that after the sharks had started following us the guys had positioned themselves behind me, so that they were between the nasty things and me. I don't know if they did it simply to give me peace of mind or if they viewed the animals as more of a threat than they were letting on.

Either way, it made me uncomfortable that they were putting themselves in harm's way in an effort to make me feel better. But when I said something to Kona, he told me not to worry about it. That it was just how things worked down here.

Eventually we passed another school of fish and the sharks peeled off in search of tastier game. I relaxed as soon as I saw the last of their tails, so it took me a few seconds to realize that Kona and the others hadn't relaxed along with me.

What's wrong? I asked them.

Don't talk. Kona's answer was immediate, and so low and firm that I automatically shut up.

I glanced behind me, saw that the other guys looked just as grim as he did. *What's wrong?* I asked him again, this time on our own private path. I could feel their anxiety creeping into me. *The sharks are gone.*

The sharks were never a problem to begin with.

Then what—

I don't know. His eyes were the color of smoldering ashes as they darted from side to side. *But something is.*

How do you know?

I can feel it. Can't you?

The words were barely out of his mouth before his hands tightened on me to the point of pain. And then we were shooting straight down toward the ocean's bottom like the hounds of hell were nipping at our heels.

Chapter 22

We were going so fast that it made me dizzy, but I didn't protest. I didn't do anything, really, but hang on for dear life. I was too worried about distracting Kona, which seemed like a particularly bad idea, as we were swimming at what I estimated to be close to a hundred miles an hour. As the ocean sped by, I wondered randomly how fast he could go in his seal skin. He'd told me his human form was the slow one.

He swooped to avoid a couple of small whales, both of whom seemed to be booking it out of the area almost as fast as we were, and I closed my eyes. If we were going to hit anything I didn't want to know about it—I could only imagine what a crash at this speed could do to all of us, which meant that whatever had spooked Kona had to be pretty bad.

As we sped through the water like missiles in search of a target, frightening images ran through my head. Pictures of great white sharks and electric eels, mermaid-eating octopuses and Tiamat herself, who wasn't looking nearly as cartoonish this time around.

I opened my eyes again, hoping that the real world would banish the images. It didn't work. Even worse, I was so wrapped up in worrying about what was behind us that I didn't notice the ocean floor looming in front of us until I almost smacked face-first into it.

Stop! I yelled, remembering my last tumble across the bottom. But Kona was obviously a lot better at this than I was. He pulled up at the last second, shot straight across the ocean floor to a large cave I could just make out in the distance. Caves were good, I thought. We could hide there. We could—

Kona turned away from the cave's gaping mouth at the last second, slammed instead into the much smaller opening to its right—at full speed. We passed so close to the bottom of the ocean that I felt my new swimsuit catch on a few of the clamshells that crowded the opening.

We were still going full speed as we zipped through one room after another. I held on to Kona so tightly my fingers cramped, convinced we were going to crash at any moment. Somehow, though I really didn't have a clue how, we managed to avoid disaster until Kona finally slowed down. If I'd counted correctly, we were five rooms away from the cave's opening.

By the time he set me gently on the sand, I was shaking so badly Kona had to pry my trembling hands off his arms. I wasn't normally a coward, but that roller-coaster ride from hell would have shaken up almost anyone—or so I told myself.

He pulled me into his arms, ran a soothing hand over my hair. *It's okay, Tempest. I won't let anything happen to you.*

I looked over his shoulder, realized for the first time that the other guys weren't with us. *Where—*

Malu, Aaron, and Jake are up above. My brothers are outside, waiting for me.

What? No! I grabbed on to his shoulders. *If something's out there, shouldn't you all be in here?*

This isn't the kind of something that goes away if you ignore it, Tempest.

What do you mean? Why did we even bother running then?

I needed to get you someplace safe.

Meaning what, that you're planning on dropping me here and taking off again? When he didn't answer, I realized that was exactly what he planned to do. I narrowed my eyes. *Don't even think about it. I want to go with you.*

Absolutely not. He was already backing away and I tried to follow him.

What if you get hurt? What if whatever is up there does something to you?

Then Ari or Oliwa will come back and get you. I promise, I won't leave you here any longer than necessary.

He was being deliberately obtuse and I wanted to smack him for it. *That's not what I meant and you know it.* I laid my hand over his. *Kona, I don't want anything to happen to you.*

Nothing's going to happen to me. He pulled me into his arms, held me tightly for the length of one heartbeat, two.

You don't know that.

No, but I'm pretty good at this whole fighting thing. Honest. He pushed me a little distance away, leaned down so that we were eye to eye. *Listen to me, Tempest. You are not to leave this cave. Not unless one of the three of us comes for you. Do you understand me?*

What's up there, Kona? And don't try that whole I-don't-know routine again.

256

He was silent for a minute, as if debating how much to tell me. I narrowed my eyes at him—I really had had enough of being kept in the dark. He must have gotten the message, because finally he relented. *It's Tiamat.*

Tiamat?

Yes, she and some of her army are headed this way.

She has an army? I demanded. *Since when does a wicked sea witch have a fighting force to back her up?*

Since she uses magic to give them whatever they want and then fear to control them once they realize that material possessions aren't worth their souls. It was his turn to glare at me. *I want you to promise me that you'll stay here. That you won't even think about leaving this cave.*

Okay, but—

No buts. Someone sold us out, sold you out, and it might very well have been Jake or Aaron or Malu.

You don't really believe that.

He didn't answer right away, but then he didn't have to. The fierce look on his face said it all.

Eventually, he said, *I don't know. Maybe. Someone certainly tipped her off.*

You're crazy. All of the stories he told me flashed through my brain at the speed of light. *You think you're just going to go out there and fight her, when one of the people you think is on your side might very well stab you in the back?*

I've already sent a call out to my father. He'll send in reinforcements soon. Besides, I can't just stay in here.

Why not?

Because this is my territory. The people who live around here are my responsibility. I can't just leave them to fend for themselves.

But you expect me to? I'm supposed to stay in this cave and hide? What happened to all that stuff you said about me being able to take care of myself? What happened to the prophecy? I thought I was the one who was supposed to stop her?

You aren't close to being ready to tangle with Tiamat yet.

How do you know that? You said you've been listening to the prophecy for years, waiting for me to be seventeen. And now that I am, you want to hide me in some cave?

I didn't care about you then. The words burst from him. *Before, you were just some abstract concept who was going to go up against Tiamat and win. Now—* His hands wrapped around my upper arms, squeezed so hard he nearly cut off my circulation. *Now you're the woman I love and I can't stand the idea of your facing her or any of the other things that might be up there.*

His words pierced my heart, had tears blooming behind my eyes even as I shook my head. *You can't keep me locked away forever, Kona. The ocean's a dangerous place. You can't protect me from everything.*

That's not what I'm doing. I'm not, he insisted at the dubious look I gave him. *But if you don't believe me about anything else, believe me when I say you're not ready to face her yet.*

I—

Don't. His voice was harsh now, his eyes nearly black. *Don't ask me to send you up there. I can't, Tempest. I just can't.*

He lowered his head, kissed me with bruising force. Then pulled away. *Stay here.* It was a definite order, one that I had no desire to follow despite the fear clawing its way along my every nerve ending. But the look he gave me promised all kinds of trouble if I didn't listen to him. *I'll leave Oliwa to stand guard outside the cave and I'll be back for you as soon as I can.*

Be careful.

His wicked grin popped out, despite the seriousness of the situation. *I always am, baby. I always am.*

And then he was whipping away, swimming so fast he was little more than a blur in the cave's darkness. After he left, I sat staring at the four walls of the cave, the acuity of my mermaid vision helping me pick out little details despite the near blackness of my surroundings.

A crab scuttled by, inches from my toes, and against the wall was a bed of clams or oysters—I could never tell them apart in the light, let alone in the middle of a dank, dark cave.

I glanced toward the room's entrance, wondered if Kona had made it all the way out of the cave yet. Wondered what it was he was going to fight up there.

I wanted to follow him—had planned on it all along—but his last words echoed in my soul. The woman I love. I was the woman he loved. I didn't know how I felt about that.

Part of me was ecstatic—who wouldn't be upon finding out that the guy she was falling in love with felt the same way about her? But another part of me was terrified, and angry. How could he tell me that he loved me and then just take off toward almost certain death?

I pushed away from the wall, swam back toward the cave's entrance. I moved a lot slower than Kona, partly because my eyesight wasn't as good as his and I was afraid I'd smack into a wall, and partly because I was still making up my mind about what I was going to do.

Oh, I knew what I wanted to do—I wanted to hightail it back up to wherever Kona was and see what was going on—despite the warnings he'd given me. But he'd be furious when he saw me. Even worse, he'd be distracted, and the last thing I wanted to do was get Kona killed because he was too busy trying to protect me to look out for himself.

He loved me. Kona loved me. I hugged the words to my chest like a precious gift as I cautiously approached the first room of the cave. If he came back—*when* he came back—I was going to tell him that I felt the same. That despite everything I had fallen in love with him too.

For a moment, I thought of Mark, and my conscience screamed at me. How could I have done this, just fallen for some other guy when I was supposed to be in love with him? But the longer I was down here, the harder it was to picture his face, to remember what it felt like to be held by him.

Is it the water? I wondered. *The mermaid in me? Or just the fact that Kona dwarfs every other guy in the room?*

I swam a little closer to the cave's entrance and as soon as I did, weird little vibrations seemed to shimmer through the water. I probably wouldn't have even noticed them—or would have mistaken them for waves—but my body was different now. The mermaid side picked up on things the human half had no shot at sensing.

Holding out my hand, I let the strange water pattern run over my fingers and up my arm as I tried to figure out what it was. And then, as the vibrations reached my ear for the first time, I realized what I was doing. I was "feeling" the sound of what was going on outside the cave, above me.

The water muted noise down here—one of the many reasons I figured mermaids and selkies talked with their minds—but that didn't mean that the sound didn't travel in waves, like some kind of natural sonar. I thought back to what I'd learned in biology, during the lessons on sea animals. Mr. D'Angelo had told us a lot of animals used sonar. My mermaid ear must be able to pick it up like they could, though I still didn't know how to interpret what it was I was "hearing."

But that didn't mean I couldn't guess. A fight was going on out there, between Kona and the others and God only knew what. I shot to the cave's entrance, peered out though I knew Kona would be furious if he saw me. But the not knowing was killing me. What if he was hurt? What if he was already dead?

No! I slammed a door on the thought, refusing to believe it. Kona was smart and fast and obviously knew what he was doing when he wasn't trying to protect me from my own idiocy. Surely he could handle whatever was up there.

And yet—there was a strange feeling in the dark water near the opening of the cave. A strange consistency that made it feel thicker than usual, heavier.

Maybe I should just go check on Oliwa. We could swim out together a little ways and see if we could see anything that was going on—

A black hand reached out of the darkness, grabbed my head, and shoved me—hard—into the cave.

I wasn't braced for the attack and I flew against the back wall of the cavern, smacking against it hard enough to disorient me for a second. It was all the advantage he needed. I watched in horror as Malu swam toward me, a wicked-looking knife clutched in one of his hands and murder on his face.

What are you doing? I asked, frantically scrambling along the wall as I tried to put as much distance between us as I could. If I could get outside, get to Oliwa . . .

Another thought occurred to me as I pictured Kona's youngest brother, with his ready grin and sparkling eyes. If Malu was in here then he'd somehow gotten past Oliwa. Visions of my new friend lying injured on the ocean floor assaulted me, had me rushing toward the cave's entrance as fast as I could go.

Malu caught me and sent me spinning back against the wall for a second time.

I'm ending this thing now, before it gets completely out of control.

Seeing as how he was coming at me with the intention of killing me, I was pretty sure things were already out of control.

You don't want to do this, I said, then could have kicked myself. I sounded like every too-dumb-to-live heroine who had ever bought it in a horror movie.

Sure I do. He came a little closer.

That wasn't the response I'd been hoping for. *Why?* I demanded, even as I tried to formulate a plan. I needed to get out of there, needed to check on Oliwa, because everything inside me was screaming that the strange consistency I'd felt in the water a couple of minutes before was blood. If it was—and he was injured—I had to get him to Kona. But Malu was in front of the cave's opening. I'd have to swim right by him to reach it—which meant he'd be able to grab me at any time. And frankly, I didn't relish another spin against the cave walls. Already I could feel a bump rising on the back of my head.

Not to mention that if I actually managed to get by him, I'd end up trying to outrace him, which was patently absurd if he was anywhere near as fast as Kona. I was quick, but without my tail I was in no way able to compete with someone who'd lived his entire life underwater.

Because you're more trouble than you're worth. Tiamat has nearly died twice trying to get her hands on you. Once you're gone, she'll be safe. We all will be.

Was he for real? He was trying to protect the sea witch from *me*? What had I ever done to her besides defend myself?

I didn't have time to think about it, because Malu was getting closer. With every step he took toward me, I got a better look at him, and any hope I'd been holding out that I could reason with him—which, let's face it, wasn't a lot to begin with—died a quick, painful death. His eyes glittered with the fervor and excitement of a fanatic and his mouth was set into a grim snarl straight out of my nightmares.

No. There would be no reasoning with him and no swimming by him. Which meant my only chance was—

I took off, full speed, toward the back of the cave, zipping from one room to the next without taking the time to look where I was going. I swam by memory, by instinct, until I found myself slamming through the entrance to the seventh and final room.

I only had a few seconds—the element of surprise had bought me that but not much more—and I looked frantically for some place to conceal myself. Some place that would give me a couple of minutes' respite to try to figure out how I was supposed to get out of this.

But there was no place to hide here, other than in the jagged crevices of the wall. I ran for the biggest one I could find and pressed myself deep inside of it, bowing my back so that no part of me stuck out from behind the rocky edges.

The walls were rough, sharp, and they dug into my shoulders and back, reopening wounds that had just begun to heal. I wondered, for a second, if selkies could smell blood the way sharks could. But I wasn't planning on hiding in here for any length of time no matter what—just long enough to give myself a chance to regroup.

I ran my hands over the jagged curves of the rock, searching for a crack, an edge, any weakness that might give me a chance of prying loose a piece to use as a weapon. It wasn't great, but it was the best chance I had. Which wasn't much against a knife, but dwelling on how screwed I was wasn't going to make things any better.

And then even that thought was gone as I realized Malu was in the room with me. He hadn't found my hiding spot yet, but he knew I was here. It was only a matter of time. I had hoped to catch him off guard, had hoped it would take him a little longer to track me so that I could catch my breath and find a weapon, meager though it would be.

But that obviously wasn't going to happen. My time was up.

My heart was beating so fast that I was sure he would be able to sense it, would find me from the vibrations it alone created. With each second that passed I became more certain of discovery. With each step he took deeper into the room I tried to imagine what it would feel like to die.

My insides started to hum, to vibrate with fear until it was all I could do to stand still. I used my right hand to keep searching for a crack, for some small piece of rock I could break off to use in a fight. But the cave wall was solid and I was shaking so badly that I could barely pull at it anyway.

The humming inside me grew worse, took over me, until I felt like one huge, vibrating guitar string. I didn't know what it was, had never felt anything like it before. I wondered if it was terror—if this was what the true, absolute fear of dying felt like—and then there wasn't time for me to think. Wasn't time for me to do anything but react as Malu's eyes locked with mine.

He headed toward me, knife raised, and I threw out a hand to defend myself. But as I did, I felt something come from deep inside me, a strange pulse of energy that worked its way up from my center to my arm and then out my fingertips—heading straight at Malu.

It caught both of us unaware and he stumbled backward. I did it again and he almost fell. But the third time he was braced and ready for it and he swam right through it, like a high-speed torpedo on self-destruct.

A scream ripped through my mind as he barreled toward me, all rational thought gone as the need to survive kicked in. At the last possible second I ducked, hitting the cavern floor hard. Malu careened into the wall, but within moments had righted himself and was headed toward me again.

I crabwalked across the floor as fast as I could—I didn't have time to try to propel myself upward—my fingers desperately searching the ground for something, anything, I could use as a weapon. I was almost against the wall when I found it, a long, razor-sharp piece of shell that sliced deep into my finger.

Ignoring the pain and the blood that was making my already-slick hands slicker, I wrapped my fingers around the shard and waited.

He was almost on me, a look of murderous rage on his face as he started to bring the knife down toward my unprotected jugular. He was bent over, trying to reach me, and I took what I knew was the only opportunity I would get. I sat up abruptly, startling him, jerking my body out of the way of his knife as, screaming inside, I drove up as hard as I could with the shell fragment.

It hit his belly one second before my fist did, piercing through skin and muscles like they were little more than the water that ebbed and flowed around us. It was his turn to scream, then he fell backward, the knife clattering to the ocean floor as he stared at me in disbelief. His hands went to his stomach, where I had buried the shard as deeply as it would reach.

I scrambled for the discarded knife as he yanked at the shell, trying to pull it out. But once my hand closed over the hilt of the knife I wasn't sticking around to see what happened to him. I swam as fast as I could toward the room's entrance.

The last thing I heard before the water around me ran with blood was Malu's agonized groan. He had pulled out the shell. My rusty first-aid knowledge came back to me again and I realized he was no longer a threat. With an injury like that, he would bleed out in minutes.

As I hit the entryway to the cavern, I didn't look back. I couldn't. Instead I fled, through the cave and straight out into the unprotected ocean.

Chapter 23

As soon as I got outside, it hit home that Malu and his knife were not the worst things I would have to face that day. Oliwa lay on the ocean floor, his sightless eyes staring up at me, a deep slice across his jugular telling me all I needed to know about how he had died.

Oh my God. Kona's brother was dead and Malu had killed him. What was I supposed to do now? What *could* I do?

I glanced above me, and though I was too far down to see what was happening, sea creatures of all types were fleeing straight toward the ocean floor, trying to get away from whatever was up there.

For one long moment I wanted to flee with them. Wanted to run away and pretend that none of this had happened.

Pretend that Kona's brother wasn't dead.

Pretend that I had not just killed someone. The fact that he would have killed me if I hadn't defended myself didn't make the reality any easier to bear.

How did I get here? I wondered as I watched fish and octopuses and even sharks zoom around me. How had I gone from being a typical high school surfer to a tailless mermaid that *killed* people in the space of a few short days? I didn't want this.

I had *never* wanted this.

My stomach clenched miserably and for a second I was afraid I would throw up. I was shaking, badly, and all I really wanted to do was find a quiet place to curl up and sob. I closed my eyes, tried to get a grip, but all I could see was Oliwa with his throat slit. Malu, with the shell protruding from his stomach and his face twisted in pain.

I had killed him. I tested the words out, tried to ignore the terrible taste they left in my mouth.

I had killed someone.

I had killed someone whose name was Malu, who had dark eyes and long black hair and was little more than a boy.

I had killed him.

I did vomit then, bracing myself against the cave wall as I dry heaved again and again.

God, what was I doing? I couldn't live with this, couldn't live *like* this—always looking over my shoulder for the next danger. If this was what it meant to have power, I didn't want it.

Another influx of marine life had me straightening and looking up to where I could only assume some kind of battle was being waged. Kona would have come for me otherwise. He would have found me before Oliwa—

I shut it off, all the regret and angst that came from what had happened in the cave. I would deal with it later, when whatever danger up there had passed. If, of course, I was still alive.

Grabbing Oliwa, I pulled him into the cave, terrified that if I left him outside it, he might float away before Kona could retrieve his body. Or worse, that some of the predatory sea life swimming by might decide to snack on him.

When Oliwa's body was as secure as I could make it, I started swimming against the current, weaving my way through fish and dolphins and a group of really large squid. I shuddered when one of them brushed against me—I didn't know what it was about the creatures that disgusted me so much, but anything with tentacles really freaked me out.

Which, I realized with dawning horror, was a huge problem when I finally got close enough to register what was up there.

The Lusca, the huge vampiric human/octopus monster from the tapestry at Kona's house, was in the middle of the action. Surrounding him was a ring of much more normal-looking people—some of which appeared to be selkies, mermaids, and humans, though I knew the last was impossible as they were breathing underwater. Were they mermaids like me, without their tails? Or selkies? Or something else entirely? I didn't know, and I guess it didn't particularly matter because whatever they were, they were defending the Lusca, their sharp spears plunging into whoever dared to get too close from the small group of selkies and merpeople that had gathered to fight the monster.

Bodies of the fallen floated nearby in the water while the battle continued to rage between Tiamat's defenders and those that defended everyone else.

It was exactly like the tapestry at Kona's house only with a lot more blood—so much blood that it rivaled the deadliest action movies I had ever seen.

Horror ripped through me. People were dying, their bodies being thrown to the Lusca so that he could drain them of blood before he tossed them aside like so much trash.

Under my traumatized gaze, the Lusca ripped a selkie in half, then tossed the body to the side before reaching down for another one. Terrified for Kona and the others, I swam toward the mess, trying desperately to find them. Every instinct I had screamed that I should flee in the other direction, but I couldn't do that. Kona had never left me when I needed him—I couldn't leave him now, no matter how much I wanted to be anywhere but here.

I finally spotted Kona, fighting off two of the humanlike creatures, both of whom were armed with deadly looking spears. Kona had a sword that he'd picked up somewhere and he was using it to deflect the jabs of the spears, but how long could he hold out against two opponents who were working together like a well-oiled machine, all in the hopes of bringing him down?

I wanted to head straight for him, but the words he'd said when he'd stashed me in the cave echoed in my head. I didn't want to be a distraction to him, and with my control over my powers wonky at best, I didn't think I could be much help anyway. It was exactly as Kona had said—I was completely unready to be here.

But where was I supposed to go anyway? Heading back to the cave where Malu had attacked me and now lay dead with Oliwa was obviously out of the question, and it wasn't like there were so many other places to hide out here.

Besides, the only place I really wanted to be was home, and that was impossible. We were in the middle of the ocean and I was so turned around that I didn't have a clue which direction was Japan and which was California. The way my luck had been going, I'd end up halfway to Antarctica before I realized I was going the wrong way.

At that moment, one of Kona's opponents brought his spear forward with so much force that even I could tell it was a killing blow. *No!* I screamed, reaching for Kona, certain that the water around them would run crimson before I could get there.

But at the last second, Kona dodged to the right, and drove his sword deep into the other man's chest, then whirled around and drove the dead man's spear deep into his other opponent's neck.

Without breaking form, Kona reached back and ripped his sword out of the first guy's chest, then whirled to confront the next threat. As he did, the bodies of his fallen opponents slowly floated away.

I hovered there for a moment, my mind struggling to assimilate this new side of Kona. It was a shock to realize that the guy I'd fallen for was a warrior, capable of killing so easily. And yet, what alternative did he have? Lie down and let Tiamat's forces overrun his people?

I shoved aside my horror at how cleanly he killed, determined not to let it paralyze me right now. Later I could freak out over it, but right now I had worse things to worry about.

Kona was searching the crowd, looking for what I assumed was his next point of attack, when his eyes locked on mine. Then he was speeding across the water toward me, the light of battle still in his eyes, only this time it looked like it was directed at me.

He had almost reached me when someone grabbed me from behind. A blade came up and I froze, unable to do anything as it plunged toward my chest. And then I didn't need to do anything, because Kona was there, ripping the guy away from me and breaking his neck with his bare hands. There was no telltale crunch like in the movies, but when Kona let him fall he was obviously dead, his head hanging at an odd angle off his neck. I shuddered, despite my resolve.

What are you doing out here? Kona grabbed me and I was shocked to realize he was shaking. *I told you to wait in the cave—*

It was Malu. He was the one who sold us out.

Kona's eyes narrowed and he looked around, as if expecting Malu to jump out of the shadows. Or, I realized with a sinking stomach, to see his brother.

Oliwa's dead. I blurted it out to get it over with. *M-m-malu slit his throat and then c-c-came for me. He attacked me in the cave. I—I k-k-killed him. I'm sorry. I'm so s-s-sor—*

Don't ever apologize for defending yourself—what happened down there wasn't your fault. Rage was alive in Kona's eyes and I knew a part of him wanted to zoom down to the cave, to check if what I had said about his brother was true.

But he didn't. Instead, he shoved me behind him and started backing away from the battlefield, his sword once again at the ready.

What are you doing? Where are we going?

I'm getting you someplace safe.

But the Lusca—

He's been around for hundreds of years, Tempest. Today isn't going to change that.

But he's killing people!

We're all killing people. You don't know how sorry I am that you had to be here for this. He kept moving me, dragging me away.

No! I yelled. I was getting more upset by the second, the water starting to roil around me. *This isn't right.*

None of it's right, but I'm not letting anyone else get close to you. I lost Oliwa today. There's no way I'm losing you too. Come on! When I continued to struggle, he pulled me into his arms and took off.

At that moment, as we were speeding away from the carnage, a high-pitched laugh cut across the sea. It was like nails raking down a chalkboard and it sent chills up my spine like nothing I had ever felt before.

Who is that? It was a whisper from my mind to his.

Kona stopped in midstroke, spun us around, and I watched as one of the most beautiful women I'd ever seen swam into view. She cut through the water with the grace and glamour of an old-time movie star, her face chiseled and perfect, her long red hair flowing behind her. She had a tail, but it was different from any I had seen so far—pitch-black and long, it had numerous spikes shooting off in various directions and it curled in like a sea horse's.

Tiamat. Kona's voice was grim.

She's *the evil sea dragon?*

Yeah, well, that's not her natural form. She only looks like that after drinking mermaid blood. Without it, she looks like a cross between a fire-breathing dragon and the Lusca, except uglier. Much uglier.

Suddenly every vile word I had ever heard, and then some new ones that I had to assume were native to the selkies, whipped through Kona's head, at least until he slammed some kind of mental wall down between us.

Come on, let's go. His voice was urgent now, the fingers resting on my elbow growing more firm as panic whipped through him.

What's going on?

Nothing. I just want to get you out of here before she—

Leaving so soon, Kona? And with your pretty little mermaid too? Her voice, sharp as nails, rang through the ocean between us. *After I've gone through such trouble to provide a show for her?*

I pulled back against Kona, forcing him to stop our headlong flight. Normally it never would have worked—he was much stronger than I was—but I think he expected me to want to get away from that thing as much as he did. Which, to be perfectly honest, I did. But there was something else at play here, something I didn't understand, and every instinct I had told me to hold my ground.

What aren't you telling me? I asked, scanning the people in front of me. *What do you see that I don't?*

Don't let her get to you, Tempest. It's a trap.

What's a trap? The chills had worked their way out from my spine to cover my entire body, and alarms were shrieking in my head. Suddenly I didn't want to be there any more than Kona wanted me to be.

But it was too late. With a loud cackle, Tiamat screamed, *Bring her out!*

Her crowd of followers parted and out came one of the strange human-but-not-human creatures, leading a mermaid in chains. She was almost as beautiful as the sea witch, her long blond hair winding and curling around her body.

Kona tensed beside me and I looked at him curiously, wondered if he knew the mermaid. It was as I was looking into his eyes, dark with grief and rage, that it finally hit me. The mermaid had a bright emerald green tail.

I whipped back around and terror crashed down on me as I saw the emerald green tattoos that covered her arms.

No! Screaming as loudly as Tiamat, I tried to rush forward but Kona was blocking me.

Tempest, don't! The command was sharp, the order obvious, but I ignored him.

I'm right here, Tiamat, I said, using the universal path Kona's brothers had shown me a few hours before. I didn't know if it would work on nonselkies, but it was the only one I knew.

There she is, Tiamat cooed. *Sweet little Tempest. Come on out from behind your big, strong protector and play with me.* The last was said in a low hiss that no one could misconstrue as a friendly invitation.

She'll kill you, Tempest. Kona tried to hold on to me but I jerked away.

So what? Already rough, the ocean around us started to crash and swirl. It was responding to my emotions, to the rage that was blocking out everything else inside of me—even fear. All I could see was my mother, bound in chains. Being used as a weapon against me.

Such a brave girl. That's right, Tempest. Let me get a look at you. I've waited a long time for this moment. Tiamat swam closer, circled

275

me as a shark did its prey. I let her, even as the energy built up inside of me. Even as the power ripped through every part of me. I didn't know how to use it yet, how to harness it, but I knew it was there. I could feel it in every clench of my fist and every breath I took.

Behind me, Kona kept talking, kept trying to pull me back to him, but I slammed up my own mental block so I wouldn't be distracted by his fury—or his pleas.

Let my mother go! I sent the command spinning toward her on the back of a particularly strong current, saw her eyes go wide as she received it—and the message I had yet to put into words.

You think you can take me, little girl?

If I have to.

Tempest, no! She'll kill you. This time it wasn't Kona's voice in my head. This one was softer, sweeter, the same one that had sung me lullabies as a child.

I felt its impact like a knife to my gut.

If I don't, she'll kill you, Mom.

I've always known she would, Tempest. Why do you think I left? Better me than you.

Her words hit me like bullets, ripping into me so fast and hard that I was shocked I wasn't bleeding out. I pushed them away, tried to concentrate as Tiamat tightened the circles she was making around me until she was so close that I could reach out and touch her if I wanted to.

I have to say, your manners aren't quite what I expected, the sea witch snarled. *I came all this way to make nice and you don't seem very receptive.*

Funny how seeing my mother chained up puts me in a nonreceptive mood.

Don't taunt her, Tempest! My mother's voice was sharp now, warning. I glanced quickly at her, saw the fear for me she didn't even try to hide—as well as her resolve to die in my place. But I wasn't about to let her do that, no matter how angry I was.

You gave up the right to tell me what to do six years ago, Mom, so back off.

You don't know what you're doing.

She was right about that. But I could feel the power stacking up inside me, growing with every second that passed. Was it me doing that? Or were Kona and my mother somehow fueling the fire raging inside of me?

I have to do something!

Leave. Swim away.

I can't. I'm not like you, Mom.

I felt more than heard her indrawn breath, and I wanted to turn to her, to see what she looked like, but I didn't dare take my eyes off Tiamat a second time. Not if I wanted a chance in hell of keeping my mom, Kona, and myself alive.

I wanted to spare you from having to make a decision like the one I made, Tempest. Leaving my family was the hardest thing I've ever done.

But you did leave. And you never came back, not once. It was a child's cry, but one I couldn't hold back after all these years.

I'm sorry.

Tiamat was so close now that I could reach out and touch her if I wanted to, and I slammed a block down between my mother and myself, pushed my emotions down deep inside of me. I could deal with them later, after we'd found our way out of this mess.

I hate to interrupt such a touching scene, Tiamat said as she slithered around me.

She hadn't been able to eavesdrop on the conversation I'd had with my mother, but that didn't mean she hadn't guessed what was going on. The fury in her eyes showed how much she disliked our moments of communication.

I thought with all that rage inside of you, you'd enjoy seeing your mother this way. Tiamat made sure the words echoed around us, made sure my mother understood how angry I was at her—though I didn't know how the sea witch could possibly know what I was feeling.

Still, I refused to let Tiamat see that she'd gotten to me. *You thought wrong.*

Did I, now? Perhaps I picked the wrong . . . offering? She slid closer to Kona, trailed one long, razor-sharp talon down his chest, leaving a trail of blood in her wake. He knocked her hand away with a growl, but she only laughed. *You'll make such a good king—all that power and passion on the throne. It excites me just to think about it. That is, if I let you live.*

She's no threat to you, Tiamat. Leave her alone, Kona answered.

I'll say who's the threat, dear boy. Her eyes grew cold. *Seize him.*

Four of her guards grabbed him.

No! Kona! I reached for him.

Stay out of this! Tiamat shoved me back, hard, and a wall of water rose up between Kona and me. I tried to go through it, tried to get to him, but it might as well have been made from bricks. There was no way to break through it, though I continued to try.

I can see you come by your name honestly, Tempest. Relax, now. You'll get your chance to save him soon enough.

I was really beginning to hate that superior tone of hers. *What do you want from me?*

What do I want? Her lips pursed in fake surprise. *It's not what I want from you, it's what I want to give you.*

And what is that?

She came back over to me, ran one ice-cold hand down my shoulder, then leaned in and whispered, *Power beyond your wildest imaginings. Control over the seven seas. Eternal life. You can have it all, Tempest. I promise I'll give it to you.*

I raised one eyebrow, tried to look like I might be interested in what she was offering, when in truth I was so disgusted I could barely look at her. *You would give me all that?*

Her eyes glowed a voracious red. *I would give you that and more.*

In exchange for what?

Your loyalty. Your allegiance. Your blood. She licked her lips at the last and my stomach turned. *Imagine it, Tempest. Imagine what we could do if we combined your power with mine.*

The water had gotten so rough that her guards were having trouble keeping their positions—the waves were tossing them back and forth like so much fluff. The ones guarding my mother were being hit particularly hard and the looks they exchanged were full of alarm.

Tiamat didn't seem to notice and part of me wanted to strike right then. I couldn't stand seeing my mother and Kona at her mercy.

But I held myself back, held it together. I still didn't know how to control the roiling magic within me, so I knew I would only get one shot at this. If I blew it, we would all die before I got another chance.

I yawned, forcing a boredom into my voice that I wasn't close to feeling. *Don't you mean if I gave you my power?*

Are you laughing at me? Her teeth came together with an audible snap.

No. But I'm not interested in the lies you're trying to sell me either.

You're. Not. Interested. It wasn't a question.

Not particularly, no. It was a calculated risk—I knew that. But if I could get her angry enough, maybe her temper would give me the advantage I needed. Behind her, Kona shook his head, frantically trying to get my attention. But I ignored him. He might be the bait, but this showdown was between Tiamat and me.

Well, perhaps I'll give you some incentive. She turned to the men holding Kona. *Take him to the Lusca.*

No! The cry was ripped from my throat, and as soon as it escaped I knew I had made a huge tactical error.

From the smile on her face, Tiamat knew it too. *So it wasn't just an act. You do have feelings for the boy.*

I didn't answer, but then I didn't have to.

So let's make a deal, sweet Tempest. You come with me now, and I'll let him live. You defy me and I'll kill both him and your mother.

You'll do that anyway.

No. I'm a woman of my word.

So you'll let them both go?

I didn't say that. Cecily will pay for what she did to me, but your little boy toy . . . him, I'll let live.

My mother's and Kona's voices exploded in my head at the same time, my mother's burrowing under the block I'd slammed down between us. *Don't trust her, Tempest! Don't listen to her!*

I ignored them both, concentrated instead on gathering as much energy as I could. The ocean began to circle around us, an underwater cyclone that teemed with the rage I could no longer control.

Tiamat's guards shouted in alarm but both of us ignored them as we squared off. *Give it up, little girl. I've been planning this a long time. You can't win.*

She was going to go for Kona first, I could feel it. She wanted to torture my mother, wanted Cecily's suffering to last the way her own had—for half a millennium. But Kona, he could die now and she would have no more remorse than if she had stomped on a cockroach.

We struck at the same time, me sending every ounce of power I had directly at the sea witch, while at the same time rolling to put myself between her and Kona.

But I'd miscalculated, hugely.

Because even as Tiamat was flying backward, bleeding from her nose and ears and mouth, she was reaching for my mother, her own power blasting my mom up and into the arms of the ravenous Lusca.

No! I screamed, slamming huge waves of water into him with all the power I could muster. I started swimming, knowing even as I did that I'd never reach her in time.

Lightning sizzled inside of me, shocking me as it danced along my fingertips and over my skin. With a scream unlike anything I'd ever before uttered, I let it loose, sent it hurtling

281

across the ocean straight into the Lusca's chest—one second too late.

I watched in horror as the bolt struck home and he dropped what was left of my mother. The last thing I saw before everything went black was her torn, broken body floating silently away.

Chapter 24

When I woke up, I was back at Kona's. We were sitting on his beach, half in the water, half out, and he was cradling me in his arms. His eyes were closed and a silent line of tears were slowly making their way down his cheeks. Upset at the idea of his crying, I reached up and brushed them away with my fingertips.

His eyes flew open. "Tempest! Oh my God, you're awake!"

"How long have I been out?" I tried to sit up, to get closer to him, but something was weighing me down, making it impossible for me to move properly.

"Two days."

"Two days?" I did push myself upright then, doing my best to ignore the heaviness in my legs. "What happened?"

His eyes searched mine. "You don't remember?"

"No, I—" But I did remember; it was all coming back. Rolling over me like the nightmares of my childhood, trying to pull me back into the abyss. I fought off the darkness. "Oliwa. My mother—"

Kona shook his head. "I'm sorry, Tempest," he choked out. "I'm so sorry."

With his apology came the knowledge that Cecily was well and truly gone, and that I hadn't been strong enough to save her. "Tiamat?" I asked.

"I'm not sure what you did to her, but whatever it was, you hurt her badly. She and her minions took off right after your mother died—and they did it the old-fashioned way. She couldn't use any kind of magic to propel herself out of there."

Which explained how Kona had freed himself. If Tiamat's magic had failed, so had the bonds that held him.

I tried to take comfort in the fact that I had at least injured her, but it wasn't enough to black out the truth of what had happened. My mother was dead and I had killed her as surely as I had Malu. Oh, everyone would blame the Lusca, blame Tiamat, but it was my arrogance that had put her in the monster's hands.

I'd thought I had things under control, had thought that I was strong enough to save both her and Kona. I'd been completely, horribly wrong and my mother had paid the price.

I thought of her broken body, of the words she'd whispered to me before the showdown. She'd told me not to trust Tiamat, and what had I done to thank her but get her killed?

As I imagined all the ways I'd failed my mother—all the ways we'd failed each other—another terrible thought hit me. How was I going to tell my father and brothers that she was dead?

Would they think I'd done it because I was angry at her? That I'd chosen to try and save Kona because I couldn't get past the fury I felt at my mother's abandonment? It wasn't true—or at least I didn't think it was. I *had* tried to save her, had tried to do what I thought best. But in doing so I had made an irreversible mistake.

I thought back to the moment I had first seen the tapestry, of the stray thought that the decapitated mermaid in the Lusca's hand had the same colored tail as my mother. It seemed unforgivable now that I hadn't recognized the green tattoos across her shoulders, that I hadn't realized that the mermaid's tail was just like my mother's. If I had realized it, if I had thought it through, I never would have made the choices I had.

Suddenly, I couldn't stand to be touching the water. It was a reminder of my arrogance, a reminder of everything I'd lost because I was too stupid to understand how much my mother meant to me. I'd spent six years hating her for leaving and now I'd never get those years back. I'd never get the chance to make up for all the missed opportunities.

I pushed myself up, with some vague plan of sprinting down the beach in an effort to get away from the regrets. To get away from myself. But for some reason my legs wouldn't hold me.

I glanced down, tried to figure out what was wrong. And felt what little blood I had in my face slowly drain away.

"Okay, Tempest, don't freak out. It's not a big deal." Kona's arms tightened around me.

Not a big deal? I glared at him incredulously. NOT A BIG DEAL? I had a *tail*. A long, curvy, purple and silver tail that sparkled in the sunlight. In what world was that *not* a big deal?

"Make it go away."

"What? Me? I can't."

"What do you mean you can't?" I shoved at him, tried to

285

maneuver my way farther onto the beach in an effort to get rid of the thing. But it was a lot harder to work with than I expected, and instead of moving up the sand, all I ended up doing was flopping around like a fish out of water. Which, I suppose, in essence was exactly what I was.

"When did it come?"

"Today. After the fight you were messed up. Bleeding, unconscious—I got you home and into bed. Had a doctor look at you while my father and I went back for Oliwa's body." He paused then, took a deep breath. "But you weren't coming around. Nothing the doctor did—nothing I did—was working. So I brought you down to the water. I know it's not supposed to heal mermaids but I didn't know what else to do."

"Let me get this straight. You put me in the water and I grew a tail?" I said the last through gritted teeth.

"Almost as soon as you touched the ocean. I've never seen anything like it." He got a good look at my face and finally seemed to clue in to the fact that I wasn't happy about the change.

"Tempest, I know it's a bad time and all. But you've earned your tail. That's a good thing."

"A good thing? Are you insane?" I gaped at him, astonished. "Do you really think for one second that I want to stay here?

"Tell me one good thing that's come out of my being in this place. Malu betrayed you, Oliwa's dead, my mother's dead, Tiamat's on the warpath. Seriously, why on earth would I want to stay?"

Kona's eyes were carefully blank when he answered, "I thought *we* counted as a good thing that came out of this."

I should have stopped then, should have just kept my mouth shut. None of this was Kona's fault—I didn't blame him for anything except maybe getting me down here to begin with. But even as I told myself to shut up, to just walk—or in my case, swim—away, I couldn't keep my anger from spewing forth all over him.

"A good thing? Kona, we're nothing. We're less than nothing."

"You don't mean that."

"Don't tell me what I mean. You're a selkie. I'm a mermaid who wants to be human. We can't be together."

"Can't or won't?"

"Does it really matter?"

"It matters to me."

"Well, then, I guess it's won't. I *won't* be with you."

"Don't do this." He leaned forward, grabbed my hands and brought them to his chest. "I love you, Tempest. And I know you have feelings for me too."

"No." I bit the inside of my cheek to keep from crying. "I don't."

He closed his eyes, took a deep breath. In that moment, his features were so racked with pain that I almost relented.

Except that with every word I said to him, everything I did to push him away, something was growing inside of me. A numbness that took away the anger, took away the pain, until there was nothing left but a yawning void that was infinitely preferable to the agony I'd felt upon remembering the battle with Tiamat.

"Look, I'm sorry." Kona reached for me. "This is a bad time

287

to have this discussion. Let's get this tail thing taken care of, and then get you in the house and cleaned up. We can talk later."

Don't be nice to me! I wanted to scream the words at him, wanted to beg him to just walk away and leave me. Because with every nice gesture he made toward me, the blessed numbness threatened to wear off. And I just couldn't deal with feeling anything right now.

Still, I forced myself to be civil. It was the only way to find out how to get rid of the tail, and until I did, I would be stuck on this beach with Kona, going over and over everything that had gone wrong two days before.

I couldn't handle that; I would go stark, raving mad if I had to face it all right now.

"Okay. We'll talk later. Now how do I get rid of this ridiculous thing?" I flopped the tail to emphasize my predicament.

"To be honest, I'm not exactly sure how the whole mermaid/human–shifting thing works. But I'm guessing that it's much the same as the breathing thing. Your gills work when you need them, as do your lungs."

"Yeah, well, in case you haven't noticed, I don't exactly need this tail right now. I'm on land."

"Yeah, I did notice that. Why don't you swim out a little ways, get used to it. And then come back in."

The last thing I wanted to do was go back in the ocean, not after what had happened the last time I'd been there.

Kona must have sensed my hesitation, because he said, "Come on. I'll go with you."

"You don't have—"

"I want to."

But instead of plunging straight in like he usually did, he slipped the necklace from around his neck. Reaching inside, he murmured a few words, and I watched in astonishment as a full-blown seal's pelt came out of the tiny bag. He hadn't been lying when he'd told me that magic made it fit.

"What are you doing?" I asked, as he shook it out and then slipped it over his shoulders.

"I'm shifting."

"Why?"

"You don't think I'll really let you be the fastest thing in the water, do you?" Then with a grin that didn't quite make it to his eyes, he dived into the surf. I watched, astounded, as he surfaced about fifty yards away. Or at least I thought it was him—the Kona I knew had been replaced by one of those long, skinny seal-type creatures.

I dove in after him, then raced to catch up. Not because I wanted a closer look at him, I assured myself, but because the sooner I got into the water, the sooner I got rid of the tail. Or at least, I hoped that was how it would work.

I caught up to him in a few seconds, shocked by how fast I was now that I had a tail. But I still couldn't compete with Kona, who was twisting and flipping and racing through the water so quickly that most of the time he was little more than a blur.

The numbness wore off a little as I watched him and tears burned behind my eyelids. He was in here, doing this, not because he was in the mood to play any more than I was, but because he didn't want to leave me alone. He wanted to help me.

I felt a sob catch in my throat and knew that if I didn't get away from him I was going to lose it completely. I didn't want to

289

do that now, couldn't do it now. Not when there were still so many unanswered questions, not the least of which was the location of my mother's body.

The sob escaped then, followed by a second and then a third. Clamping my teeth together, I dove deep. Surely I couldn't cry and breathe underwater at the same time—I'd drown.

Though the pain was a deep-seated burning in my chest, one lungful of water—and the ensuing coughing fit—stopped the tears, exactly as I'd hoped.

I headed back to land, unable to take one more second of self-reflection. Instead, I concentrated on imagining myself with legs walking on the beach, thought about breathing through my lungs instead of my gills.

It must have worked, because by the time I'd made it back into the shallows, I had legs again. Thank God.

I took off up the beach before I realized that while I did have legs, I didn't have any pants on. No bathing-suit bottoms or underwear. Nothing. Except for the tank top I was wearing, I was completely naked. I wondered, vaguely, what had happened to my suit—but I hadn't been conscious when the tail had formed. This shape-shifter thing was a lot more difficult than I'd ever imagined. I made a note to pay better attention the next time it happened.

Glancing frantically around the beach, I saw a couple of towels piled on the sand. I grabbed one and wrapped it around myself just as Kona emerged from the ocean clutching his pelt in front of him. Obviously, he had the same problem I did.

I tossed him the extra towel and then booked it toward the house. I didn't want to talk to him anymore, didn't want to talk to anyone right now. Not when my emotions had turned to poison within me, ready to spew out and cover anyone who got in my path.

At first, I thought he was going to follow me, but about halfway up the beach he must have changed his mind. Right before I got to the house I turned around and found him standing on the beach staring after me.

I went into the house and closed the door firmly behind me.

⟨∾⟩

Twenty-four hours later, I stood about two miles down the beach, staring up at my mother's funeral pyre. There had been numerous funerals during the two days I'd been unconscious, farewell ceremonies for the selkies who had died at the hands of the Lusca and Tiamat's forces.

There had also been a huge memorial for Oliwa, the fallen prince. I was sorry to have missed that, since he had died defending me.

There were funerals for the merpeople too, but those had happened back in my mother's territory. The only reason Cecily was being honored here, Kona had explained, was as a tribute to me. Merpeople and other sea creatures had come from all over to pay their respects to her, the greatest priestess her people had ever known.

By the time I stood on the beach, watching what was left of my mother burn, the numbness that had started coalescing inside of me the day before had taken over my entire body. There was no part of me untouched by the bitter cold of it and I had never been more grateful.

...ring the ceremony, people had been staring at me. ...a, his family, those who had come to say good-bye to my mother. They'd all been watching, waiting for I don't know what. Maybe they wanted to see if I could hold it together, maybe they wanted to see me break down. Either way, I'd never been one to put on a show unless there was a surfboard involved, and I certainly wasn't going to start now, in front of these people whom I barely knew.

Kona had been a rock through the whole ordeal, despite the ugly things I'd said to him the day before. He'd stayed by my side, had fielded questions and condolences and basically kept people away from me. He'd wanted to come with me down the beach too, but I hadn't let him. For me, saying good-bye to my mother was an intensely personal thing, though I had no idea how to do it.

I'm not sure how long I stood there staring up at her, a bouquet of fuchsia stargazers for her in my hand. Kona had given it to me earlier—another thing he'd thought of that had completely slipped my mind.

She'd been wrapped in an emerald green sheet of the finest silk so no one could see the destruction the Lusca had done to her. But then, I didn't have to see it again to remember. Every time I closed my eyes it was there in gory detail. As she burned, the last of the sheet fluttered in the early afternoon breeze.

I was exhausted, my mind and body drained from everything I'd endured since leaving home. Even so, I'd lain in bed most of the night staring at the ceiling, afraid to close my eyes. Afraid to so much as blink. I'd eventually dozed off sometime before sunrise, but my dreams had been terrible things, odd glimpses of the moments before my mother's death combined with images of Oliwa and those few seconds after I had plunged the shell into Malu.

As I laid the bouquet of stargazers next to the other flowers decorating the pyre, I wondered if Malu had a family. Were they somewhere right now doing this very same thing over *his* funeral pyre?

I hoped they were. Malu had died alone. No matter what he'd done, or what he'd planned on doing, nobody deserved that. I hoped he had a family that mourned him as I mourned my mother. As Kona and his family mourned his brother.

I figured I was supposed to say something profound to her as I stood here, to tell her all the things I hadn't been able to say to her when she was alive. But I didn't. Not because there weren't things I wanted to say, not because I didn't know how to say them, but because I didn't believe she was up there. Her body, or what was left of it, was there, but the mother I knew—the one I wanted to talk to—was already too far gone from this place to hear me.

So I didn't say anything at all. Instead I murmured a few small prayers left over from my childhood and then turned away. I didn't want to be there when the fire finally went out. Then I simply turned and walked back in the direction of Kona's house. I wanted to get out of this strange black dress and the heels that gathered sand. Wanted to get away from the prying eyes. Wanted peace.

But, in the end, I got none of those things—at least not in the time frame I was hoping for. I was about a half mile down the beach when I heard Kona calling my name.

I almost ignored him, almost kept walking, but something

293

made me turn around and face him. Maybe it was the idea that now was as good a time as any to have it out between us—when I was so numb I couldn't care about anything.

Only, he hadn't called me to talk, at least not to him. Clutching onto his arm was an old woman in an emerald green suit the same color as my mother's tattoos and tail. I wondered, vaguely, if it was a tribute to her, and then even that thought flew out of my head as Kona introduced us.

"Tempest, this is Queen Hailana. Your mother was her most trusted confidante for over three hundred years."

What exactly am I supposed to say to that? I wondered. It wasn't like a curtsy and a how-do-you-do could compete.

The queen must have figured that I was completely out of my depth, because she reached one frail, trembling hand to mine and squeezed. "I adored Cecily. She was a daughter to me, a sister, a high-ranking member of my court, and the best friend I ever had."

How nice for you to have seen that many sides of my mother, I thought bitterly. Cecily had actually given birth to me, yet she hadn't bothered to show me much more than the basics. And this woman, this queen, knew almost everything there was to know about her. Did she really expect me to be pleased about that?

In the end, she didn't wait for me to comment. Instead, she said simply, "I have some things for you. They belonged to your mother." Reaching into her bag, she pulled out a long, flat box made of mother-of-pearl. It had an odd clasp at the front and was inlaid with gold leaf on both sides.

She tried to hand it to me, maybe eager to be rid of its weight.

But I recoiled the second it got close to me and the queen dropped it. Kona saved it by plucking it out of midair before it hit the ground.

They both stared at me, the queen with compassion and Kona with an emotion I couldn't even begin to contemplate. If I did, I might never leave, and I had to get away from this whole sad, sorry mess. I had to get away from me, from the Tempest I was when I was down here.

"Don't you want it, child?" the queen asked. "There are only a few things in it."

"Of course I do," I lied. "It just startled me. I have one almost identical to it back at home." At least that much was the truth.

"Ahh, home. You mean San Diego?"

"Yes."

Despite her age, the queen's eyes were clear and shrewd when they looked at me. "Do you miss it?"

"Miss" was too mild a word for what I felt. I longed for it, longed for the way things had been only two short weeks before.

"You don't have to answer that. I see that you miss it very much." Her smile was sad when she continued. "Your father has done a wonderful job with you, Tempest. Please give him my regards when you see him again and tell him how dreadfully sorry I am that things ended up the way they have."

"You know my father?" I blurted out the words before I remembered that I wasn't supposed to care about her. Wasn't supposed to care about anything.

"I met him, once, at your parents' wedding. He was very charming and very handsome."

That was my dad all right. "It was nice meeting you," I told her. "Thank you for bringing me my mother's things." I turned away.

"Tempest." There was an urgency to her voice that I couldn't ignore.

"Yes?"

"Inside the box is a letter. From your mother. If you don't take anything else from there, please take that. She made me promise to get it to you if anything ever happened to her."

That's when I knew I had to escape, knew that I wouldn't be able to wait until morning. And there was no way I was taking that beautiful box—and its destructive contents—with me. I had enough guilt to last a lifetime. I didn't need any more.

PART FIVE

Kick-Out

Roll on, deep and dark blue ocean, roll . . .
Man marks the earth with ruin,
but his control stops with the shore.
LORD BYRON

Chapter 25

"So you have to go?" Kona's face was paler than I had ever seen it, his mouth set in a grim line that reminded me I wasn't the only one who had lost someone in the battle with Tiamat.

"I can't stay here."

"Why not?"

"You know why not. Everything's strange, foreign. I don't fit in."

"You've been here less than a week. Half that time you were unconscious and the other half you were battling sea monsters. I don't think you can really use this time as an example of the norm."

"Come on, Kona. This life isn't for me. I don't want to be mermaid. I never did."

"Yeah, but do you really believe now is the time for you to be making that kind of decision? You've been through a lot. Can't you just think on it for a few days?"

Why wouldn't he just go away? Before all the emotions I'd been holding back came crashing to the surface and I lost it completely. He had to know how hard this was for me, saying good-bye to him when so much of my heart was tied up in his. Already I could feel the ice I'd wrapped around myself starting to melt, the numbness beginning to wear off.

I didn't want that, couldn't stand it. I didn't want to feel right now—not what it felt like to be a murderer. Not what it felt like to know I would never see my mother again. And definitely not what it felt like to walk away from Kona.

I closed my eyes, worked on shoring up my defenses. If I didn't look at him I couldn't see the hurt in his eyes, the look that pleaded with me to stay with him. I wouldn't be able to think about the small part of me that wanted nothing more than to do just that.

I won't give in. I won't give in. I said the words firmly to myself, again and again, in an effort to keep the tears at bay. *I won't give in.* If I did, if I let myself break down in front of Kona, if I let him comfort me, I wasn't sure I'd ever be able to work up the strength to leave him.

He walked me down to the beach, his hand warm and soothing against the frigid skin of my bare back. "Here, take this," he said when we were right at the edge of the water.

For the first time I realized he was carrying a small, waterproof backpack over one shoulder. "What's in it?"

He grinned and for a second he looked like himself again, like the sexy, mysterious, happy guy who had ridden a wave all the way in to me. "A change of clothes—if that tail of yours comes back, your suit will rip and you'll end up climbing out of the ocean in nothing but your bikini top."

"That would be a bad thing." I smiled at the image, then immediately felt guilty. How could I be smiling when my mother

300

was dead? When Oliwa and Malu and so many others were gone as well?

"It would be a very bad thing, particularly if Mark or any of the other guys are out surfing." It was the first time he'd brought up Mark's name in days, and he nearly choked on it.

"I'm not going back because of him," I offered, not sure why I needed to say it when I was so determined that things would end with Kona here.

"I know." He shoved a hand through his hair and for one second looked much more like a vulnerable boy than the tough, strong guy I knew him to be. "Stay. Tempest. For me. For us. Please stay."

I shook my head, backed away even as the need to do exactly what he said rose inside me. But I couldn't. I had responsibilities back home—my family, school, Mark. I had a life back home.

Why then was it so hard to picture that life?

"It would be a disaster, Kona."

"You don't know that."

"I do. I can't spend my life pretending to be something I'm not."

He shook his head and when he looked at me this time, I swore those silver eyes of his could see straight through the brave face I was putting on to the terrified girl who lurked just under the surface. "Funny. That seems to be exactly what you're going to do."

I stiffened, started to argue, but he laid a soft finger across my lips. "I'm sorry. That was uncalled for. You're right—you need to be where you feel most comfortable. I just wish that was here with me."

So did I. Dear God, so did I. The thought came to me too late, just as he lowered his mouth to mine. And then I couldn't think of anything as my head started that familiar whirl it did whenever he kissed me. Only this time it was so much worse, because I realized that this really was the very last time he would ever hold me.

Thunder clapped across the sky, but I held it in check. This wasn't the time for one of my temper tantrums. If this was the last moment I'd ever have with Kona, then I needed it to be about more than just dodging lightning.

Because he was so much more.

This time it was *my* hands that came up, my hands that cupped his face and held him to me as his lips moved over mine. He smelled so good, like cinnamon and the sea. Like love. I pressed myself against him, wanting to savor every sensation of this kiss. Not wanting to forget one single detail.

He inhaled sharply and tensed against me, then wrapped his arms around my back and pulled me even closer to him. So close that I could feel the tremors racking his body. So close that I could bathe in the heat of him.

It was a mistake—even as I did it, I knew that I was making a huge blunder. Because the numbness started wearing off the second he touched me, the cold dissipating under the onslaught of his warmth.

It soaked inside of me then, everything that was Kona and the two of us together. It lit me up from the inside, until there was nothing but the two of us, this moment and this kiss.

I wanted to devour him, to take everything I could get as my lips moved ravenously over his. I wanted to lose myself in his arms, to forget everything that was driving us apart and everything that might keep us together. If I could just get beyond the tenderness to the need, then maybe . . .

But he wouldn't let me. Like me, he knew this was our last kiss. Unlike me, he wasn't willing to waste it in the flash and dazzle of one quick moment of passion. Instead, he gave me the one thing guaranteed to choke me up, the one thing I didn't want but desperately needed. Tenderness.

His mouth moved gently over mine, soft and sweet and oh so good. It was different from his other kisses, less exploration, more giving. And then it was my turn to tremble as his tongue stroked slowly over my own.

I wish I could explain what it felt like, those moments with Kona as the moon shone brightly overhead and the ocean played tag with our feet. My heart was beating so fast that there was no longer any space between my heartbeats. My breathing was ragged, a mixture between the pain of leaving and the pleasure of this moment. And my soul, my soul was screaming out for him, for my mother, for the innocence I'd lost when I stabbed Malu and watched his lifeblood leak through the water. I'd woken up this morning convinced I was covered in his blood.

It was that thought that got me moving, that had me ripping myself away from Kona and stumbling a few feet down the beach. The world was spinning around me and I didn't know if it was because of the kiss or everything that had come before it.

In the end, it didn't matter anyway.

"It won't bring her back, you know."

"What?" I asked hoarsely, my eyes shooting up to meet Kona's for what might very well be the last time.

"Running away. Giving all this up. It won't bring your mother back."

"I know that!"

"Do you? Really?" The understanding was gone from his face, the patience and the sorrow buried under a layer of anger that made it so much easier to step into the water. So much easier to leave. Maybe I should thank him for that.

"Of course I do. I'm not a moron. Humans don't come back from the dead." And neither did mermaids, no matter how badly you wished that they could.

Bile burned in my throat, made swallowing a nightmare as I waded deeper, preparing to dive under the ocean. Preparing to lose myself in the clear, blue waves.

At the last minute I turned around, wanting one final look at Kona. And there he was, his strong, muscular body silhouetted against the darkness of the night sky. But he was blurry and I had a moment's panic that my mermaid's vision was deteriorating, that I was already turning human despite the long journey in front of me. Then I blinked and he came into focus—it wasn't my humanity, after all, that had made him so fuzzy.

Or maybe it was. I wiped the tears off my cheek. Maybe it was exactly that.

Taking a deep breath, I waved good-bye and could have sworn I felt his fingers brush against my cheek, though he was yards away. And then I dove, straight under the water and into oblivion.

The ocean welcomed me with open arms.

〜

I came up to the surface nearly forty hours later, weak, starving, exhausted by the swim. I'd tried to follow the map Kona's butler had drawn for me, but I'd gotten lost too many times to count and it had made for an even longer swim than I'd had when I'd plunged into the ocean after Kona.

It was dark here, the middle of the night judging by the emptiness of the beach and the stars twinkling in the sky, and I wondered how long I'd been gone. In Kona's world it had been a week—did that mean it had been two here? Three?

What had my father told my brothers about my absence? What had he told my friends? Then I decided it didn't matter. Nothing mattered, not anymore.

Though my gills were still functioning and I was about a mile out, I struck out for home above the water—using the freestyle stroke and breathing I had learned so many years before. My tail, which had emerged minutes after leaving Kona and had torn my swimsuit in half, was more hindrance than help as I kept wanting to kick my feet individually, and for a moment I thought about diving back under the sea and zipping this last, short distance to shore.

In the end, I didn't, though. Because it felt right to be doing it this way, to be slowly regaining my humanity with each turn of my head. With each breath I pulled into my lungs.

It took a lot longer that way, but now that I was so close to home I was in no hurry. Going home meant facing my father, explaining where I'd been. Explaining how I'd watched my mother get ripped apart in front of me and done nothing to stop it. It was a conversation I wasn't relishing, but one I knew I had to have.

By the time I got to shore, I was completely human again. My gills had stopped working, my tail had disappeared, and I was so tired I could barely make it up the sand. I forced myself to do it, though, ignoring the pain—physical and emotional—that grew with each step I took out of the ocean.

Finally, I made it far enough to avoid the water's pull, and I reached into the bag of clothes Kona had given me. I yanked out the first thing I touched, a tropical sarong in every shade of purple imaginable. I had never seen it before, and as I wrapped it around my waist like a skirt, I wondered absently if it was a gift from Kona. I decided it didn't matter as I started the short but endless journey across the narrow street to the house I had grown up in.

As I walked, I looked around this beach I knew more intimately than I did my own face. A little ways down the sand, on my left, was a rock formation the guys liked to climb and jump off of, despite the fact that it was over six feet off the ground. On the right there was only crisp, clean beach, little hills and valleys that made a stroll on the sand almost as interesting as catching waves. Almost.

My house was the same too. I stopped in front of it, wondered how it could be that nothing had changed here when I felt so incredibly different inside. When the way I felt about this place, my home, seemed so incredibly different.

That's when I saw it, the small lamp burning in the living room window. It was the same light my father had kept lit for years after my mother had left, his way of telling her she always had a place here, with us. Now it burned for me.

I was trembling when I retrieved the spare key from the flowerpot where my dad hid it.

Trembling when I let myself into the house.

Trembling as I crept across the floor to the stairs.

I was starving from the long hours of swimming, knew I should eat something before I went to bed. But I had no appetite, no energy for food. I felt like I could sleep, like Rip Van Winkle, for twenty years.

I was halfway up the stairs when the light clicked on, its sudden brilliance blinding me for a few long seconds. And then I saw him—my father standing at the top of the stairs in nothing but a pair of old sweats. His hair was tousled, his face drawn and tired looking. But the smile on his face was as familiar—and welcoming—as ever.

"Daddy." It was a cry from deep inside myself and then I was hurtling up the stairs at him. Throwing myself into his arms and absorbing the love he'd always given me unconditionally. It wasn't until his arms tightened around me that I realized I was crying. And it was just like I feared.

Now that I had started, I wasn't sure I would ever be able to stop.

Chapter 26

I woke sometime the next day to bright sunlight pouring into my room and my youngest brother's arms around me. "Tempest, you're home!" He planted a wet, sloppy kiss on my cheek. "I missed you."

"Oh, Moku, I missed you too." I wrapped my arms around him, pulled him onto the bed with me, and tickled him until he shrieked with laughter.

"Dad told us to check on you, to see if you were ready to get up or if you wanted to sleep more." This came from Rio, who was slouched against my wall, hands in his pockets. He seemed as irritable and unfriendly as ever, except for the look in his eyes. It was a tentative kind of joy, a disbelief, like that of a kid on Christmas morning when he's confronted with the toy he wants more than any other.

"Well? Are you going to stand there all day trying to look cool or are you going to get over here?" I demanded.

At first, he didn't answer and I wondered if I'd misjudged him, wondered if he was as angry at me for leaving as I was at myself. Then he let out a whoop and ran, full powered, at my bed. He launched himself on top of me and the three of us wrestled and tickled each other until my father appeared in the doorway.

"Okay, okay, break it up, guys. Tempest needs to eat something." He was carrying a tray and on it was a huge In-N-Out Double-Double burger, an order of fries, and a large cup that I knew contained a chocolate milk shake.

My stomach growled and for the first time in days, I thought I might actually be able to keep something down. I reached for it, spent a minute inhaling the scent of the greatest hamburger on earth, before I dug in.

After a couple of bites, I looked at my father with a smile. "How did you know this was exactly what I wanted?"

"Because whenever I'm gone for a while, it's exactly what I crave too."

We sat like that for a long time, my brothers on my bed sneaking fries and my father sitting in the comfortable armchair a few feet away. The boys filled me in on what they'd been doing in the two and a half weeks I'd been gone, talking about classes and the new nanny my father had hired, though Rio was convinced he was too old for a babysitter.

It took me a couple of minutes to absorb the news that someone else had been taking care of my family while I was gone, that things really weren't exactly the way I'd left them. But then, why should they be? I wasn't the same either.

Eventually the boys tired of telling me about their lives and started asking questions about what I'd been doing.

"What was it like down there?"

"Did you see any sharks?"

"How far away did you go?"

"Did you see the ocean floor?"

"Did you bring us presents?"

I answered all the questions, including the fact that I had forgotten to bring gifts. Moku looked so disappointed that I promised him I would take him out shopping later that day and buy him whatever he wanted. As he whooped in delight, I berated myself—how could I have been so wrapped up in my own traumas that I'd forgotten to scoop up a couple of shells for Moku? He didn't ask for much, wasn't hard to please, and it would have taken such little effort on my part. It was just one more thing that I hadn't managed to get right.

And then Rio asked the question I'd been waiting for, the one I'd been dreading since I'd fallen, hysterical, into my father's arms the night before.

"Did you see Mom?"

My dad didn't move, but I could sense the subtle tension in him, the need to know everything he could about the woman he loved. And I knew I couldn't put it off any longer, knew I had to tell him. But when I looked at my brothers' bright, happy eyes, I couldn't force the words past my throat. I just couldn't.

My father must have figured out that something was wrong, because he quickly herded my brothers from the room with promises that their own lunch—complete with milk shakes—was on the kitchen counter downstairs.

Moku ran out right away, happy as a bug. But then he didn't remember Mom at all. It took a little longer to get Rio out of the room and the look he shot me as he left promised that he would be asking more questions again soon.

My dad waited until he heard my brothers' footsteps on the stairs before turning to me and saying, "Tell me." His hands were clenched into fists and I could tell he was bracing himself for the worst.

I thought about trying to break the news to him easily, but the truth was there was no easy way to say it. And besides, it seemed more merciful to just get it out there.

"She's dead, Dad. Mom's dead."

He jerked as if the words were bullets slamming into him and his eyes closed, like he couldn't even stand to look at me. Not that I blamed him—I couldn't look at myself.

We sat that way for a long time, both of us lost in our own little worlds. I wondered if he was thinking of what things had been like before she'd run off, of what it had been like to love— and be loved—by her. I couldn't remember those times anymore, couldn't remember anything but what it had felt like to watch that thing rip my mother apart like she was nothing.

Just when I was sure that my father wasn't going to say anything—that he wasn't ever going to talk to me again—he opened his eyes. There was a sheen of tears covering them, turning them darker, but they were calm, resolute. Accepting.

"After a few years of not hearing from her, I started wondering if something had happened to her. If that was why she'd never returned." He ran a hand over the back of his neck, shook his head. "I guess I was right."

It would have been so easy to let him go on believing that, to let him think she had died long ago and that was why she'd never returned to him. But that didn't seem fair, especially since it would hide my own responsibility for the mess.

"It wasn't like that, Dad."

He didn't answer and I realized he hadn't heard me. He was lost in thought, far gone from my bedroom with its violet walls and glow-in-the-dark stars.

"Dad." I called his name again, waited until his slightly dazed eyes focused on me.

"What, Tempest?"

I killed her. I killed Mom. The words were right there on the tip of my tongue and I wanted to say them. I really did. But he looked almost peaceful, as if all the years of waiting for Mom to come back weren't so hard to bear. And I realized that maybe that was exactly how he did feel. Maybe it was easier for him to believe that she hadn't left him voluntarily, that she would have eventually come back to him if she hadn't died.

I knew better, but what had that gotten me? Nothing, except enough anger and guilt to fill a football stadium. Maybe what my father didn't know wouldn't hurt him.

"Nothing. I just wanted to say thank you for lunch. It's good to be back."

"It's good to have you back. I missed you."

"I missed you too."

"So, do you feel up to getting dressed?" His smile was warm when he looked at me, his eyes focused. He was back from whatever strange side trip he'd gone on. "We can get the boys ready, go to the park. Catch a movie. I'll even spring for pizza afterward."

"Right. Pizza." I forced a smile. "I think I'd like that."

"Good." He leaned over, dropped a quick kiss on the top of my head. "I'll meet you downstairs in twenty minutes."

"Thirty minutes." It was easy to fall into the rhythm of the old game.

"Twenty-five minutes—and that's my final offer."

"I'll take it."

It was a good day. Better, certainly, than I deserved.

I spent the early afternoon chasing Moku and Rio in the park—it was nearly empty because everyone else was in school, but Dad had let the boys stay home to celebrate my return. After I'd tired them out, I had taken to the swings, pumping my legs as hard and as fast as I could, looking for something I couldn't quite put my finger on.

I hadn't found it, and it wasn't until I was sitting in the movie theater, a big tub of buttered popcorn balanced on the armrest between Rio's chair and my own, that it hit me. I'd been trying to fly, trying to recapture those blissful moments when I was wrapped in Kona's arms, speeding through the ocean. Before all hell had broken loose.

After that, the movie lost its flavor. I was too busy trying to fight off the memories of Kona and my mother, of Malu and Oliwa. Even so, there was something comforting about sitting in the dark with my family, Moku's little hand resting so innocently in mine. Of all the things I'd missed in the time that I'd been gone, I had definitely missed my youngest brother the most.

When the movie was finished, both my brothers came out of it pretending to be robots like the kind we'd seen in the theater—of course Rio was a lot more subtle about it because we were in public, and at thirteen, he was far too cool to indulge in such "childish behavior." Or so he said, right before he "shot" Moku between the eyes.

Watching them made me smile—something I hadn't been sure I'd ever be able to do again just twenty-four hours before—and by the time the four of us made it home, I'd found myself drafted to play the bad robot, bent on mayhem and destruction.

I barely made it out of the car before I was riddled with holes from Rio's and Moku's pretend guns. After roaring in a bad imitation of the robot in the movie I chased them through the house, my own cannon blaster blazing. Before too long, my dad joined in and the war that followed was the most fun I'd had in a long time. The four of us ran around the house like crazy people, firing pretend blasters at each other and scoring points for every hit.

By the time the game ended, my dad and I were down by a huge margin, and Rio and Moku were the self-professed champions of the universe. Afterward, I settled on the couch with champion number two and his favorite book, *Fright Night*, but before I was three pages in, Moku had drifted off to sleep.

I was a little drowsy myself, so instead of carrying him to his room like I normally would have, I wrapped my arms around him and snuggled into the couch. It felt good just to hold him, to know that he was safe and I was safe, even though it felt like my entire world had fallen down around me in the last few days.

Still, I couldn't help going over and over my confrontation with Tiamat, couldn't help trying to figure out how it could have gone differently. Logically, I knew it was over but I couldn't let it go. I wasn't sure I'd ever be able to.

Which was why, when my dad came through, brandishing his wallet and the car keys, I volunteered to run to Frazoni's and get the pizza. Anything was better than sitting around the house, staring at the ocean.

"Are you sure?" my dad asked. "You look tired. I'll be happy to go get it."

"I'm fine," I said. "Honest. It's just been a long few days."

"I can imagine." He slung an arm around my shoulder and peeled three twenties out of his wallet. "On the way home, stop at that bakery you like and pick up whatever you want. We should celebrate."

Celebrate what? The fact that I had gotten two people killed and had actually killed a third? Or the fact that I had hurt Kona when all I ever wanted to do was love him? Or maybe we should celebrate the fact that during my brief stint as a mermaid I was, hands down, the worst one ever?

I wondered what my father would say if I busted out with that. I'm pretty sure I would have lost him at the beginning, right around the revelation that I had killed someone. Not that I could blame him—that's when I pretty much lost my mind too.

There was so much I wanted to say to him, so many things I wanted to get his opinion on. But for the first time in my life, I found that there was a gap between us, one I had no idea how to bridge.

So instead of pouring out my problems to him, I took the money and asked, "What do you want me to get?"

"I already ordered the pizzas—they should be ready in twenty minutes. As for dessert, I don't care. You choose—preferably something fattening."

I looked at my father in mock disbelief. "I think that's the first time I've ever heard you say that."

"Not for me. For you."

I snorted. "So far today you've stuffed me with In-N-Out, popcorn, and now pizza. I'm not sure how much food you want me to eat."

I expected him to make a joke, but he was serious when he said, "Have you looked in a mirror lately?"

I shook my head. After what had happened, I couldn't look myself in the eye.

"You were gone over two weeks and I'm pretty sure you lost ten pounds that you already couldn't afford to lose. You're skin and bones."

"All that swimming," I joked. "It burns a lot of calories."

"Yeah, well, now it's time to get them back." He paused, then asked a question that had obviously been bothering him for a while. "How far did you go, Tempest?"

"I don't know. Maybe a few thousand miles."

That's when my cooler-than-cool, find-your-niche-in-the-world dad paled visibly. "You traveled a few thousand miles? Through the ocean? On your own?"

"It wasn't as bad as it sounds."

"I hope not, because it sounds pretty damn awful."

I nearly laughed. If it only sounded pretty awful, I must have done a better job downplaying it than I thought.

It hadn't all been awful, my conscience reminded me.

Maybe not, but the last days I was there pretty much overshadowed anything else that had happened.

Tired of talking about it, even more tired of thinking about it, I snatched the money and the keys from my dad's hand and then headed for the door. "I'll bring you something chocolate," I called over my shoulder.

"Bring yourself something chocolate. And Tempest, if you think we're done with this conversation, you would be mistaken."

With those ominous words ringing in my ears, I headed for my dad's car. Usually, I drove my own but the keys I'd grabbed had been for his Corvette and there was no way I was going back in there now, not while he was wearing his very rare, very effective on-the-warpath look, as Rio liked to call it. The fact that he didn't chase after me, demanding that I give the keys back, proved that he had missed me even more than he'd let on.

After driving, very carefully, down Prospect, I snagged the last spot in back of Frazoni's and headed inside. I was a little early—the pizzas probably wouldn't be done for another ten minutes, but I figured I could while away the time playing one of the old-school arcade games that lined the back wall. When I came here with Mark, he usually monopolized all the good ones.

But as I was approaching the original Pac-Man game in the corner, I froze as I realized that Bach was playing it. Tony and Logan were standing behind him, paper cups in one hand and slices of pizza in the other.

Part of me wanted to back away, to pretend that I hadn't seen them. *I wasn't ready for this*, something screamed inside of me. I wasn't ready to be the Tempest they remembered. In their minds only a couple of weeks had passed since they'd seen me, but for me it felt like an entire lifetime. Maybe two.

I had just taken the first step to retreat when Logan glanced up. His eyes met mine and he started to smile, casually, until he realized who he was looking at. Then he let out a gigantic shout, emptied his hands onto the table behind him, and picked me up in a gigantic bear hug.

"There you are, Tempe! About time you showed up around here, girl!"

Despite the fact that I'd tried to avoid seeing him, once Logan's arms were around me, I hung on tight. He felt good and familiar and right, so right. After how wrong everything had been the last few days, a hug from him was exactly what I needed.

"Hey, my turn." Bach nudged him out of the way and took his time whirling me around.

"I feel honored. You gave up a winning game of Pac-Man for this hug."

He shrugged. "Yeah, well. I missed you. We all did."

"Right." Tony slung a companionable arm over my shoulders and tugged on my ponytail. "You've been gone forever."

"It's been boring without you," Logan said, picking his pizza back up and taking a huge bite. "I mean, Mark's been moping around like an idiot, and without the two of you, who's going to give me any competition for the waves?"

Bach flipped him off. "Yeah, right, man. You're a legend in your own mind."

"Exactly," Tony agreed, deadpan. "He's the surfing stud of La Jolla."

We all laughed, but within seconds the sound dried up in my throat. A quick glance over Logan's shoulder revealed that Mark was halfway to the table. He hadn't seen me yet—I was pretty much covered by the guys—but that would change any

318

minute now. And I didn't have a clue how I was supposed to act around him.

Bach spotted him at about the same time I did, but instead of shrinking back like me, he shouted across the restaurant, "Hey, man, get over here! Your girl's back."

Mark's reaction was a lot more subdued than the other guys. I wasn't sure what I'd been expecting, but the quiet hug and searching look weren't it.

"You okay?" he asked, running a hand down my cheek.

"Yeah." I forced a smile. "I'm fine. Why?"

"I tried to call you a few times, you never picked up."

"Oh, right. Things were just really crazy." Not to mention the fact that I was a few thousand feet out of range. I was pretty sure cell phones didn't work at the bottom of the Pacific.

"Crazy. Right." He nodded, but he didn't look happy. Why hadn't I thought of an excuse? I frantically searched my mind for something to say. Sooner or later someone was going to ask where I'd been and it wasn't like I could tell them the truth.

"How's your mom?" asked Bach.

"What?" I whirled on him. "How did you—"

"Your dad told us, when we stopped by the day after your party. Said your mom was sick and you went to take care of her for a few weeks." Logan nodded. "That was really cool of you, Tempest."

"Oh." I smiled sickly. "Thanks."

"So, how is she?" Tony asked, reaching past me for another piece of pizza.

"She died four days ago." The words were out before I knew I was going to say them. But I didn't want to call them back—it was a relief to finally say them out loud. A relief for someone to know what had happened, even if I couldn't tell them the whole story.

"Oh, shit." Logan stared at me in horror. "Tempe, that sucks."

"Yeah, pretty much." I looked away, completely unprepared to deal with the sympathy on their faces. They must have gotten the message that I didn't want to talk about it, because after a few bumbling but sweet apologies, they turned the discussion to—what else—surfing. But they were a lot more subdued than they had been a few minutes before.

The guy at the counter chose that moment to call out, "Two pizzas for Maguire," and I started to make my excuses.

But before I could say more than "That's me," Mark had grabbed me around the waist and pulled me down onto his lap. He rested his forehead against mine and we were so close that after a few seconds his eyes blended into one large one in the center of his forehead. I know mine must have done the same. "I'm so sorry, babe."

"It's not your fault." But I didn't look away. I couldn't. I'd thought my feelings for Kona would supersede any emotions I had for Mark, but they didn't. It felt good to be held by him again. Different, but still good.

"I do wish you'd told me. I would have come to the funeral."

I shrugged. "It was pretty far away."

"Your dad said you were in Hawaii. That's not that far." He pulled away slightly and cupped my face in his hands. "You okay?" he whispered, his breath warm against my face.

"Yeah. I mean, as okay as I can be."

"You want to talk about it?"

"Not really."

He stood up with a nod. "Okay, then. Go get the pizzas. I'll ride home with you."

"You don't have to do that—"

"Tempest. You're my girl. I haven't seen you in two weeks and your mother just died. I think a night out with the guys can wait."

"Yeah, absolutely," seconded Bach. "Go take care of her, man."

"I plan to."

And just that easily, I had my old life back.

Chapter 27

Only it wasn't that easy, not even close. I went through the motions, but nothing felt the same as it had before I'd left.

When I was with Mark, I thought about Kona.

When I was with my friends, I thought about Mark.

When I was with my father, I thought about my mom.

And when I was surfing—which didn't happen nearly as often as it used to—I thought about those few days of swimming underwater. Of being mermaid.

I'd once heard the expression "You can't go home again," and I'd always found it a little odd. I mean, what was the definition of home if it wasn't a place you could return to when you were done being someplace else?

Now I realize that I should have paid closer attention—it wasn't like I hadn't seen the principle in action, up close and personal. My mother had walked away one morning and never come back and I'd spent six long years blaming her for it. Now, here I was. I *had* come back—I'd never even planned on leaving at all—and still nothing was the same.

Then again, maybe *everything* was the same. Maybe it was just me who'd changed. All I knew was that when I got up every morning and went to school, I felt like I was living somebody else's life.

But those days under the sea—they weren't my life either. I'd felt at least as uneasy there as I did here. In fact, the only time I'd ever felt really comfortable was when I was with Kona. But even if I went back—even if I turned mermaid—I couldn't just be with him all the time. I had to find my own way. I couldn't spend the rest of my days expecting him to take care of me. That would drive me nuts.

And yet, sometimes I caught myself staring out at the ocean, wanting to swim as far out as I could and let it take me. Let it pull me back to the life I'd had for such a short time. I was angry, disappointed, horrified by what had happened at the bottom of the ocean, but still a part of me couldn't let it go. I yearned for the water, yearned for the life I could have had.

Everything came to a head for me after class one day. Normally, I might have gone surfing with the guys, but the wind was too high to make the water anything but bad. So Mark had invited us back to his place to hang.

I'd almost canceled, but I'd been doing that a lot lately—to him and to the rest of my friends. Bri and Mickey kept coming around, almost every day, wanting to hang out. I usually brushed them off—not because I had anything better to do, but because I'd rather sit in my room and look at the Pacific than try to come up with something to say to them.

I'd imagine how things could have been different, how my last image of my mother might not have been seeing her ripped apart by the Lusca if I had just been a little less angry, a little more careful.

But the worst part of sitting there thinking about her wasn't even picturing her death—and my complicity in it. It was finding that, after everything, I was still selfish enough to be mad at her. Even after knowing everything that she'd gone through, even after finding out that she had had almost complete control of her clan for the last six years, I was still furious that she had left Rio, Moku, and me without her guidance.

My dad was a great father but what did he know about being mermaid? And while I'd come to grips with her leaving me, I couldn't help resenting the fact that she'd abandoned my brothers as well. I thought turning into a mermaid was bad, but when I'd been down there I'd realized that there was something even worse—at least if you were raised to be human. And that was becoming a mer*man*.

The selkies and other half-human creatures chased after the mermaids because they were sexy and powerful, but I'd seen the look of disgust on Kona's face when he'd spoken of mermen. The mermaid clans were the only female-dominated society under the sea and the mermen took a lot of heat for that.

What did that mean for Rio and Moku? We all knew they would be faced with the decision of whether or not to remain human on their seventeenth birthdays as well, but Mom's letters to them had made it seem like their choice was somehow less important, less life altering, though I didn't know why.

I hoped she was right, hoped they weren't destined to go through the same pain and confusion I was going through. That they weren't destined to make the same mistakes I'd made.

But it was still just one of the many reasons why I was angry at my mother, still angry at Cecily the great mer priestess. Of course, the fact that I was furious with her only made me feel more guilty. It was a vicious circle, one that was slowly eating me alive.

Which is why, when Mark texted me during the last period of the day, I decided to take him up on the invitation. Anything was better than sitting in my room and trying to decide who I hated the most: myself, my mother, or Tiamat.

I'd gotten stuck helping Rio with his homework—today was the new nanny's day off—so I was the last one to get to Mark's. As I stood on the front steps, waiting for him to answer, I could hear the music and laughter coming from inside.

Mark opened the door with a grin and a warm hug that made me smile. But when he bent down and tried to kiss me, I instinctively pulled away. He didn't say anything, but I could tell he was upset, and I couldn't blame him. It had been almost four weeks since I'd gotten home and the most I'd let us do was a quick peck on the lips.

And the worst part was he'd been really patient, trying to give me time to grieve for my mother and everything. But the sad fact was, my mother wasn't the only one I was grieving for.

I missed Kona, missed the way his lips felt against mine. Missed the way it felt to be in his arms. And most of all, I missed the way he looked at me, like I was the most important thing in the world to him.

I had spent the last few weeks alternating between breaking up with Mark and telling myself not to be hasty. Once, not that long ago, I'd been completely in love with him.

And the truth was, I loved him still—it was hard not to. He was smart and funny and sexy, and he took such great care of me—when I let him. Why shouldn't I try to continue my relationship with him? I'd made up my mind, four weeks ago, that I was never going to see Kona again. So what was I supposed to do, sit around and pine for him for the rest of my life?

"Hey, earth to Tempest. You want something to drink?" Mark asked, gesturing to the mini fridge under the bar.

"Sure. I'll take a Diet Coke, if you've got it."

He grabbed my soda and a beer for himself, then settled down on the sofa beside me.

Someone had put *Crazy Days* on Mark's huge flat-screen TV, but no one was paying much attention to the wipeouts on the DVD. Instead, they were trading stories of the worst ones they'd ever had and laughing like hyenas. Though he kept his arm around me, it only took Mark a minute or so to get into the action.

I listened for a little while, but it got boring fast. I mean, seriously. How many times can you hear about a wave shrinking a guy's nuts before it's one time too many?

Shrugging out from under Mark's loose hold, I wandered onto his balcony. It only took a minute before Bri and Mickey joined me.

"Thank God!" Mickey said with an exaggerated eye roll. "If I had to hear about one more of their private parts I was going to hurl."

"Even Scooter's?" Bri teased with a grin.

"Especially his. I am so over that, girl."

"I told you he was a bad bet," I said.

"Yeah, well, there's bad bets, Tempest, and then there's him.

That guy is a walking relationship repellent. I swear, I walked in one day and he said, 'You're so sexy.'"

"What's wrong with that?" asked Bri, confused. "I wish Bach would tell me I was sexy every once in a while."

"He was talking to his *board*!" Mickey and I answered at the same time.

"Okay, that *is* bad."

"Really bad," I agreed.

"Yeah, well, we can't all have fine boyfriend material like you've got sitting over there, Tempest."

I nodded, though I really wasn't paying attention. We'd had this discussion so many times I could carry on my part of it in my sleep.

But when it came time for me to say my patented "Yeah, Mark's great," both of my friends looked at me like I had grown another head.

"Are you even listening to us?" Bri demanded.

"I just told you I saw some skank putting the moves on your guy and that he wasn't resisting, and all you can say is he's great?" Mickey stared at me in disbelief.

"What?" I stared back in confusion. "Mark's *seeing* another girl?"

"Not seeing her exactly."

"Not yet, anyway." Mickey twirled one of her long curls around her finger.

"Okay, look, go back to the beginning and tell me everything."

Ten minutes later I was convinced Mark wasn't as patient as I'd thought he was. Oh, he hadn't done anything—at least according to the information Mickey and Bri had—but even they admitted they didn't hear everything, on account of their relationship with me. But if my friends were to be believed, a certain cheerleader had spent a lot of time looking at Mark lately and he'd been looking back.

I didn't know how I felt about that. I mean, it wasn't like I had any room to judge after what I'd been doing with Kona a few weeks before. My friends, however, had no such reservations. Bri wanted me to have a heart-to-heart with Mark, and Mickey just wanted me to brain him with something. As for me, I didn't know what to do. Of everything I was feeling, the most overwhelming emotion was relief. As if I had one last loose end to tie up.

I stayed outside long after Mickey and Bri went in, complaining about the cold. Though I was freezing and the wind felt like a whip against my too-sensitive skin, I wasn't ready to face Mark yet. I didn't know what I wanted to say to him, didn't know how I could tell him—after all this time—that I understood what he was going through.

He was a good guy and he had stuck by me, but I couldn't expect him to hang around forever. I wasn't even sure I wanted him to, not when I didn't have a clue how I felt about him anymore.

It was almost dark and the others had started heading home to do homework when Mark finally joined me outside. His hands were in his pockets and his eyes were more troubled than I had ever seen them.

He shuffled his feet for a few seconds, looked at everything but me. And then said, "Tempest," in that voice of his that meant we needed to talk.

And suddenly it was easy, so much easier than I'd expected it to be. "It's okay, Mark."

"What's okay?" He looked at me warily, as if he thought I was trying to trick him.

"Chelsea. She's cute and seems really nice. If you like her, I think you should ask her out."

"Ask her out? Where's that coming from?"

"Come on, Mark. We've been friends for a long time, longer than we've been going out anyway, even off and on. Let's not ruin that by holding on to this thing too long."

He seemed confused, as if he'd expected this to be a lot harder. And maybe he had—our first two break-ups certainly hadn't been this calm, on either side. Maybe that was because we'd been unfinished then. I didn't know, any more than I knew if we were really finished now.

All I knew was that after all this time, after everything that had happened to me in the last couple of weeks, I wanted Mark to be happy. If Chelsea could make him happy, then I certainly wasn't going to do anything to mess that up.

"Are you sure? I mean, I know you've been going through a rough time and I didn't want to hurt you."

"You didn't hurt me, Mark. Honestly."

He reached for me, dragged me closer so he could see my face in the porch light. "You swear, Tempest? Because I haven't done anything—"

"Shhh." I laid my fingers on his lips. "I swear, Mark. I'm fine."

He reached out a finger, traced it down my cheek. "You really are the most beautiful girl."

"You'd better be careful or I'm going to think you hit your head."

"That's one of the things I always liked about you—you never see yourself the way the rest of us do."

329

I laughed. "Yeah, well, don't get used to it. Cheerleaders are a whole different breed from surfers." And then I was standing on tiptoe, brushing my lips softly across his. He kissed me back, his lips warm and firm, and for just a minute there was that old spark, the one that had kept bringing us back together no matter how many times we'd broken up.

And then it was just us, two friends, moving on.

"Good-bye, Mark." I squeezed his hand.

"Good-bye, Tempest."

I let myself out into the rapidly darkening night. The stars had just begun to peek through the purple sky and I watched, starstruck, as one shot across the heavens.

I wished on it, like my mother had taught me to when I was little more than a toddler, and then walked slowly home.

Chapter 28

When I got home, my father was sitting in the family room, reading a book while Moku and Rio watched *Batman* for the three thousandth time.

"Did you have fun?" he asked, watching my face closely.

"I did, actually." I headed up the stairs. "I'm going to go start on my homework now."

"There's dinner in the kitchen. I left a plate for you."

I started to tell him that I wasn't hungry, that I'd get it later, but the look in his eye warned me not to push it too far. He'd been trying to give me more space than usual since I'd gotten home, but there were limits to that. And starving myself was definitely outside of those limits.

As I waited for my chicken and broccoli to heat up, I couldn't help thinking about how funny life was. Six weeks ago, I'd had a mother I hated, a boyfriend I loved, and a life I was almost comfortable with. Now, I had no mom—to hate or otherwise—no guy, and a life that was anything but comfortable. And yet, for the first time in a very long time, I was close to being at peace.

Who would have thought breaking up with my boyfriend could change my perspective so completely?

Since I was in the kitchen, I took the back staircase up to my room. But once there, I couldn't settle. I kept looking out at the sky, at the ocean, and thinking about my mother. Thinking about Kona.

What was he doing now? Had he seen the shooting star? Had he wished on it like I had? Or was he too busy keeping up with all his princely duties to notice?

I opened my chem book, tried to get started. But the last thing I was interested in was the periodic table. Tossing it away, I tried English and then precalc. Nothing stuck. I was too restless, too twitchy, to concentrate on anything.

I prowled my room looking for something, anything, to do, but I couldn't take my eyes off the ocean. It was wild tonight, the wind whipping the surf into a frenzy. It was beautiful and I wanted to be out there, wanted to dive deep and swim until I was too tired to go any longer.

But that was impossible. That wasn't my life, wasn't what I wanted for myself. And yet I couldn't help wondering if I'd felt so peaceful earlier because I'd cut one more tie to my human life.

My eyes fell on the backpack Kona had given me so many weeks ago. I hadn't touched it after I got home, hadn't done anything but fumble in it that one time on the beach, when I'd pulled out the sarong.

Suddenly I had to know what was in there. I picked it up and my fingers were working the zipper before I'd even made it to the bed. I dumped the contents on my paint-splattered purple comforter and slowly started sifting through them.

At first I was disappointed. There was a pair of cute flip-flops with seashells on them, a violet tank top that matched the sarong, and my mother's box. Nothing personal. Nothing that might have carried a message from Kona to me.

Not that I should really expect one—I'd dumped him and I hadn't been nearly as nice about it as I had been with Mark. Why should he want to have anything to do with me after that?

But as I lifted up the T-shirt and shook it, something round and shiny fell out of it and bounced onto the carpet.

I scrambled off the bed and started searching my less-than-pristine floor. I tossed aside my dirty clothes, the book I had been reading the day before, and a bunch of pillows before I found it, nestled against one of my canvases.

I picked up Kona's gift gingerly, shocked by how much it glowed in the dim bedroom light. My first good look at it told me it was an amethyst as big as a baby's fist. It was a deep, rich purple—so dark that it was almost black—and cut so that all of its many, many facets reflected light.

I held it under my lamp, then gasped as it seemed to catch fire. Kona had sent me a sunburst, a moonbeam, a shooting star to light up the darkest nights of my life. I clutched it to my chest and tried not to cry—for everything I had already given up and everything I would give up in the future.

I sat there, curled up on my bed, for a long time, clutching the stone to my chest and watching as night quietly settled over the ocean. And then figured, since I'd already come that far, that I might as well go all the way.

I reached for my mother's box and flipped the clasp open. I was nervous, my hands trembling just a little bit, but I refused to give in to the nerves. It was just a box, I reminded myself. Just a box, and whatever was inside of it didn't have the power to hurt me. I wouldn't let it.

I lifted the lid and on top, just as the queen had said, was a letter in my mother's handwriting, addressed to me. I pulled it out, laid it on the bed without reading it. There would be time enough for that later.

There wasn't much else in the box, just my mother's engagement and wedding rings, a drawing of the ocean I had made her when I was seven or eight, and a picture of the five of us. In it, my mother was seated with Moku on her lap and Rio and I on either side of her. My father stood behind us, his hand on her shoulder and a huge smile on his face.

I studied the picture for the longest time. I had never seen it before and was shocked at how happy we all looked. At how much of a family we seemed. I turned it over, was shaken by the date on the back. It seemed impossible to imagine that in less than a year from when the photo had been taken, my mother would be gone.

I wanted to resent her, wanted to keep up the rage that burned within me, but looking at her in the picture—so young, so vibrant, so obviously in love with her husband and children—it was hard for me to stay angry. I didn't know why she'd chosen to leave all those years ago; I'd probably never know. But wasting my life hating her, not wanting to be like her, wasn't doing me any good.

I slid the photo back into the box, along with the rings and my drawing, then closed the lid and put it on my dresser next to its twin, the one I'd had for as long as I could remember.

The letter I kept.

I was scared to open it, terrified to read my mother's last words to me. Would they be enough to satisfy the questions in my soul, or would they do nothing but give me more? I didn't want to spend the rest of my life without answers, looking over my shoulder and trying to figure out what should have been.

I debated whether or not I wanted to open the letter for a long time, until finally I grabbed my hoodie and pulled it on. I shoved the envelope and Kona's stone into my pocket and took the stairs two at a time.

"Where are you going?" my dad asked. He had given up on the couch, was now sitting at the dining room table on his laptop while my brothers played video games in the other room.

"Down to the beach for a while."

"It's night, Tempest. And cold out. Don't you think you should stay in?"

I knew what he was asking, knew there was so much more to the questions than the words he said. I wanted to reassure him that there was nothing to worry about, but I didn't know if that was true. If my time underwater had taught me anything, it was that there were no guarantees. And something inside me was pushing at me, telling me to hurry. Already my body was awakening, yearning for the sweet kiss of the water against my too-cold skin.

I stopped beside him, kissed him on the cheek. "I love you, Daddy."

"I love you too." He squeezed my hand, then turned back to the computer. "Don't stay out there too long. I don't know how safe it is."

I wanted to laugh. After what I had faced down, there wasn't much that I was afraid of anymore.

Then I was letting myself out the door and running to the beach, my hair and my worries trailing behind me like forgotten lore.

Once I hit the sand, I yanked the letter out of my pocket and positioned myself so that I was under the big yellow streetlight that was as much a beacon as it was a lamp. The paper was older than I thought and a million times more fragile, so I was careful as I began to read.

My darling Tempest,

I wish that I had an excuse. Wish that I could point to a definitive reason and tell you this was why. I know that even after all these years, this is what you are looking for. Something to tell you why it happened. Something that you can blame.

But you see, you had it right all along. Blame me. No one forced me into that sea six years ago and no one forced me to stay. It was a choice just as what you do now is a choice.

I sit here writing this, and I have to admit that I am curious. How did things work out? If you have this letter, it means you've come into the ocean to get it and that makes me doubly curious—as your mother and as the woman who has battled Tiamat for far too long.

I'll be honest. Mermaids are supposed to live close to one thousand years and I am little more than six hundred. But I am tired, Tempest, so tired of the life that I have chosen. I miss the comforts of home, miss you and your father and the boys. How is Moku? How strange to know that my baby is eight and you—you are seventeen.

Which means I should have some advice for you—for you and Rio and Moku. But I don't, because there is nothing I can tell you that you'll believe. Nothing that I can say that you won't need to find out on your own. Except choose wisely. Please, Tempest, choose more wisely than I ever did.

Saving your family, saving your clan, saving the world, is an addiction. But at the end, when you are old and tired, it is not enough. Nothing is enough that doesn't come with peace of mind. Nothing is enough that doesn't come with love. That is the lesson I have learned and I have learned it too late.

That being said, I have a favor to ask of you. I have no right to ask it, but I find that I must. My queen is ancient, my clan more so, but in a very precarious state. Despite our longevity we are on the brink of disaster— too many have had to put themselves above the clan.

Hailana needs you. My clan needs you.

I won't beg, won't take up any more of your time, except to say that you are more than I ever dreamed and yet still less than you could be. Thank you, Tempest, for loving me when understanding was too hard. Thank you for understanding when loving me is impossible.

Choose wisely.

I love you,
Mom

My hands clenched into fists and before I knew what I was doing, I had crumpled the letter into nothingness. Opening my fingers slowly, I watched as the wind caught the small fragments. Watched as they danced away on a current so sweet and pure that for a moment they looked like butterfly wings beating against the night air.

I watched the tiny pieces until they were out of sight and thought about choices. Thought about love. And when I turned, he was there, as I somehow knew he would be.

"Kona."

He smiled. "Tempest. What are you doing here?"

"I think that's my line, isn't it?"

"No. I'm pretty sure it's mine." He watched me with those smoky eyes I had come to love so much. "I'm here a lot more often than you are, at least at night."

"You are?"

"I am." He reached for me, turned me gently around until I was facing away from the water and toward my house. "You see, if I sit here long enough and look hard enough, I can just make you out through one of those windows." He pointed to the family room and then to my bedroom.

"You've been watching me?" My breath caught in my throat, making it almost impossible to get the words out.

He mistook my tone for anger and stepped away. "I'm sorry. I knew it was wrong, but it was the only chance I had to see you. You never came down to meet me."

I thought of all those nights, like tonight, when I had felt restless. When I had wanted nothing more than to walk along the ocean and let the waves tickle my toes. When I had wanted him with an intensity so painful it had all but crushed me.

I had ignored the longing for weeks now, had crushed it out beneath the weight of my anger and my guilt. I'd almost done the same thing tonight.

If I had, would that have been it? I wondered, horrified. Would I have missed this chance?

Kona stepped closer, close enough that I could feel his body heat and his breath as it mingled with my own. "No. You wouldn't have missed anything." He reached for my hands, brought them to his lips, and brushed feather-light kisses against each one of my fingertips.

"I'm not going anywhere, Tempest. I'll stand out here as long as I have to. As many nights or weeks or months as it takes."

"And years?" My voice was rusty, my throat thick with tears. "Will you wait years for me, Kona? If you have to?"

"I'll wait forever." He swallowed and his hands tightened on mine. "But please don't, Tempest. Please don't make me wait that long. I'm useless without you."

I didn't answer him for long moments, just stood back and looked at him. I was starved for the sight of him, for the feel of his body under my fingers and the soft brush of his mind against my own.

The joy of being with him again swelled like a balloon inside of me, until it filled up all the holes and crevices that had stood empty since I'd left him.

I smoothed my hands up his chest, wanting to touch all of him at once. Wanting to crawl so deep inside of him that he could never get me out.

And then I was in his arms, my mouth pressed against his.

It was a sunburst. A rainbow. A million brilliant colors coalescing into one and then exploding outward.

I love you, Tempest. I love you. He didn't say the words out loud, but then he didn't need to. I could hear them in my heart, could feel them in my soul.

I love you too, Kona. I really do.

I pulled away then, and though he made a sound of protest deep in his throat, Kona let me go. And that made all the difference. Was this what my mother had felt like all those years ago, when she had walked out of the ocean and straight into my father's arms? Like his love filled her to bursting even as his understanding gave her the confidence to take a huge leap of faith?

I thought of her letter, of her warning to choose more wisely than she had. And then I looked at Kona and the ocean and knew I had done just that. They were my present and my future and nothing I had known before or since could ever compare with the way I felt when I was with Kona, really with him, as a mermaid. As I was meant to be.

"Take me home, Kona." I said the words out loud, wanting there to be no misunderstandings.

"Are you sure?"

I turned and looked at my house one last time, saw that Kona was right. If I looked hard enough I could just make out my father and Moku and Rio standing at the family room window, looking down at us. Moku's hand was pressed against the glass.

I extended my own hand and for a second I swore I could feel the cool smoothness of the window beneath my palm. I smiled and my family smiled back, nodding as if they understood my unasked question.

It was enough, though my heart broke just a little at the sight of them.

I turned to Kona, grabbed his hand. "I'm more than sure."

And then we were running toward the surf as fast as our human bodies could carry us. As I dove beneath the surface, relishing the feel of the water in my hair, I realized that I had been right all along.

You really could go home again. You just had to want it bad enough.

ACKNOWLEDGMENTS

This book is the book of my heart and as such is very special to me. That it couldn't have been written without the help of a bunch of wonderful people makes it even sweeter. I am so grateful for all of your love and support.

Emily Sylvan Kim—an incredible woman and the most amazing agent on the planet—who is responsible for this book's very existence. What do I think about mermaids? A whole lot, obviously.

Stacy Cantor Abrams, for taking a chance on Tempest—and me—and giving us a wonderful home. I so appreciate everything you've done for me and this book and can't imagine what the journey would have been like without you.

Everyone at Walker Books who chose to take on Tempest and gave me the opportunity to finish the book I was dying to write.

Shellee Roberts, Emily McKay, and Ivy Adams—because it's been a crazy, mixed-up ride so far and I can't wait to see what the future holds.

Sherry Thomas, for all the hours of fun and gossip and chocolate cake.

My mom, for knowing I was born to write YA long before I ever did.

And my guys, who put up with mismatched socks, way too much Chinese takeout and frozen pizza, and me at my most excited—and most frantic—as this book slowly took shape. I love you and wouldn't want to do any of this without you.

Fill your Need
with another spine-tingling series

 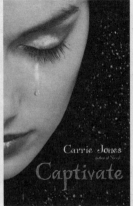 

Catch pixiphobia, the fear of pixies, at

www.needpixies.com

✳ Watch the book trailers

✳ Read chilling excerpts

✳ Download wallpapers, widgets and more